D1434560

STROUD
SHORT
STORIES

VOLUME 2
2015–2018

Edited by John Holland

Published by Stroud Short Stories

995043892 6

Copyright Information

STROUD SHORT STORIES VOLUME 2 2015-2018
Edited by John Holland

© 2018 Each story is the copyright of its author
Published by Stroud Short Stories
Foxmoor Lane, Ebley, Stroud, Gloucestershire, GL5 4PN, England

Cover design by James Holland

ISBN (paperback) 978-1-9164118-0-7
ISBN (ebook) 978-1-9164118-1-4

John Holland

Introduction

Welcome to the second volume of short stories featured at Stroud Short Stories (SSS) events. I heartily recommend this anthology to anyone who enjoys the short fiction form. All these stories are an excellent read and many, in my view, are quite brilliant. As both organiser of these events and editor of this volume, you might expect me to say that, but just read a few stories and you'll be hooked.

These stories were read by their authors at the six SSS events at the SVA (Stroud Valleys Artspace) from November 2015 to May 2018. The authors - newcomers, skilled amateurs, professional writers - are from the counties of Gloucestershire or South Gloucestershire. All their stories went through a 'blind' selection process, in which I and a fellow judge reduced the hundred or so submissions each time to the ten which were read at the event. All the events sold out in advance, so the authors read their tales on the night to an audience of around 70 people. If you were there, you can now re-visit your favourite stories. And if you weren't, you can immerse yourself in what you missed.

It's the aim of SSS to showcase and promote local writers in order to provide an enjoyable, varied and inspirational evening's entertainment. SSS is completely non-profit making. No one involved in the organisation receives a financial return for their efforts. To encourage writers to 'enter' there is no charge to submit stories. And equally no winner is chosen. Nor are there any prizes. Sometimes there is a theme to the evening (eg 'The Eerie Evening' and 'All You Need is Love' events), but usually there is no restriction on contents or style. Events are often named after the story with the most exciting title, which may or may not be the 'best' story.

The stories presented here are in the chronological order in which the events were held and in the running order of readings on the night. The latest event represented in this volume, On Pulling Newts from Ponds & Other Stories, held in May 2018, was our 16th and featured the 100th author to read at SSS since its inception in 2011. Many more will follow.

In October 2016 SSS celebrated its fifth anniversary with a sell-out *Greatest Hits* event at Cheltenham Literature Festival. Of the seven stories I chose as my favourites from 2011 to 2016, four were published in our first anthology, but three appear in this volume - *A Good Old-fashioned Copper* by Andrew Stevenson, *Silver Harvest* by Ali Bacon and *A Small Change* by Melanie Golding.

Congratulations to all 45 authors whose 57 stories are published here for your enjoyment. Huge thanks to them for submitting their wonderful stories to our event in the first place, and for allowing me to publish them in this volume. Do check out the **Author Biographies** section at the end of this volume. You can also watch some of the authors read their stories on our **YouTube channel:**

www.stroudshortstories.blogspot.com/p/youtube-channel-videos.html

I am incredibly grateful to Debbie Young for formatting this anthology (I could never have done it myself!); to my co-judges for these events Debbie Young (again), Ali Bacon and Nimue Brown; to the SSS administrator and lately my better-half, Christiane Holland; to Jo Leahy and Neil Walker for the use of the SVA; to Bill Jones for founding SSS back in 2011 and continuing to show his support; to James Holland for the anthology cover design; to James (again) and Tom Brown for the events poster designs; to Ed Holland for both the music at our events and for reading two of these stories when the authors were unable to do so; to David Penny for the videos; to Tim Byford and Angela Fitch for photography and to everyone who has come along to one or more of our events. Lots more people have supported SSS in lots of ways and I am grateful to all of you.

It's a huge honour and an enormous pleasure to be the Stroud Short Stories organiser.

Do feel free to get in touch with me.
Email: stroudshortstories@gmail.com
Website/blog: www.stroudshortstories.blogspot.com
Twitter: @StroudStories

John Holland

Personal writing website: www.johnhollandwrites.com

Twitter: @JohnHol88897218

CONTENTS

Eerie Evening
November 2015

Kirsty Hartsiotis

The Woman's Wraith

Martha Legg pulled her shawl tight around her shoulders as she left her parents' cottage and walked quickly away from Kempsford's village green. The thatched cottages away from the road were wreathed in mist, and the sky above was the deep blue of very early morning. The only person about at this hour, she envied those able to lie in a little longer in the autumn. She still had to go to the fields. Money was money. Every penny earned made her engagement to Ned Coule a little more likely.

She walked down to the swing bridge and exchanged a weary smile with the bridge keeper as she crossed over the canal to walk along the towpath. Soon she was out of the village and into the fields. It was brighter now, grey light filling the sky, but a white mist still clung to the still waters of the canal. Martha shivered as the moisture seeped through her woollen shawl. The newly risen sun was struggling to break through the mist here on the canal, but straight ahead it was shining on the brickwork of Oatlands Bridge, turning it a vivid red, the brightest colour in the flat autumn landscape of brown fields and almost bare trees. Walking in a tunnel of whiteness, Martha had a sudden feeling of being trapped. The sun shining into the mist made it bright, almost blinding.

She walked on with quick steps. If the sun was coming out, maybe the day wouldn't be too bad after all. She looked up again to the bridge, and frowned. Below the arch on the near side the mist was very thick – and it was flowing and shifting about. She scrubbed at her eyes. When she looked again the mist was coalescing. A misty form was rising up from the water, a form that was almost human. It hung there by the towpath, just short of being under the bridge.

It seemed to be waiting.

3

Martha's breath caught in her throat as she swallowed the impulse to scream. She rubbed her eyes again, but the thing was still there, still and silent. She took a step back without meaning to, and, heart pounding, felt a rush of need to turn tail and run back to the village. But what would she say? A foolish tale about a bugaboo by the bridge would lose her this hard-won job. It was surely just a trick of the light.

She took a deep breath and walked on, but, although the mist was clearing off the water, the figure didn't go away. It just hung there, its misty form shifting as if a breeze had caught it, yet the air was completely still. She really didn't want to walk past it, but she had no choice if she wanted to get to work. She dropped her gaze to her feet and held her breath as she walked on towards the bridge. She could still see the figure's hazy legs drifting over the water by the towpath. Her resolve began to weaken.

Keep your eyes on the path! By the time she reached the bridge all she could see was the muddy track in front of her. If she couldn't see it, then perhaps it wasn't there. A child's logic, but all she had to cling to. Going under the arch, she reached out to touch the cold but reassuringly solid bricks. She had to keep walking on. But she couldn't quite stop herself glancing slightly to the right, to check she was past the figure. Her breath caught again and she almost fell. Right beside her, as if it was pacing her, were the thing's misty legs. With the next step she glanced again and the figure was again beside her. Without making a conscious decision, she began to run. She was out from the bridge in a flash, legs pounding, and on into the morning light. But she couldn't run for ever. She slowed, chest heaving, and her head traitorously turned to the right again. For a moment she thought she'd outrun it. Then the misty legs drifted into view beside her once more.

Ahead was the entrance to the field where she worked. She heaved a great breath and ran again. If this was a thing of the water, surely it couldn't follow her across the land. She turned from the towpath and stepped into the muddy field. A quick backward glance. It was there. Right behind her. An eyeless thing of white swirling mist, only inches from her face. A ragged scream tore from her throat. The air expelled from her mouth shifted the misty form, but soon it recoalesced. She turned away, gasping. There was no escape. She understood that now. All she could do was endure. She went about her work, pulling up swedes, giving them a quick scrub down, chucking them into piles to be collected later.

The ghostly figure was constantly by her side.

Pulling swedes is heavy, backbreaking work, but usually she enjoyed the solitude it brought, away from her parents' house and the clamour of her younger siblings. Today she'd have given anything to hear their voices. All day long she saw not a soul. No voice rose in greeting from the path. No heavy clop of horse's hooves. No swoosh of a boat passing by. Only the silent figure of mist kept her company.

As the day passed she sank into a weary lassitude. A dull pain lodged itself in her chest. Her limbs felt like lead as she hauled the swedes. She didn't dare think, but a small part of her mind panicked every time she caught a glimpse of the misty form.

At last the lengthening shadows told her it was time to go home. It was no surprise that the figure followed her to the towpath and paced her as she trudged back towards the bridge. In the gathering gloom she imagined it following her all the way home and hovering above her in her bed that night. Now she was at the bridge, dark and forbidding in the failing light. She stepped into its shadow and walked quickly through, looking nowhere but straight down at the ground in front of her.

She went quite a few steps beyond the bridge before she had the nerve to glance to her left. She saw only the dark water of the canal. The thing was gone from beside her. She didn't dare look back. She jumped when the village church began to ring the bells for seven o'clock. She looked towards the village, blinking in the fading light. Such a distance she had yet to walk! Still she didn't look behind her, but she could feel a prickling on the back of her neck.

It was a slow slog home, never looking back. She didn't answer the bridge keeper's smile as she crossed back into the village. When she got home her mother was dishing up the tea, but Martha couldn't eat. As soon as the things were cleared away she took to her bed.

The next day she wouldn't get out of it; just lay there, staring at the wall. Her mother sent for the doctor, then for young Ned Coule, but neither could rouse her. After a week her mother had to call the vicar. While he sat beside her, Martha whispered out her tale, "I do warrant, reverend, as that bugaboo were my own spirit, like, a-calling me away."

It seemed that was true, as that very same day she died.

Oatlands Bridge is an even lonelier place today. The canal is long gone, and the bridge overgrown and desolate, marooned in a field down a private path. There's no water there now from which a form might rise like the one Martha saw, but on misty days perhaps it's best to stay away.

'The Woman's Wraith' was first published in Gloucestershire Ghost Tales' by The History Press in 2015.

Tony Stowell

The Spirit Is Willing

Thank you for coming.

I think we all know why we are here, and I hope I can count on you for support in the proposition I am now in a position to put to you.

Only another ghost can realise just how infuriating it is to be invisible. We can wait for days in a corridor and wave our arms intimidatingly, but Living people simply ignore us. We can move behind a man reading a book and breathe down his neck, and he merely checks the window or shuts the door. We might just as well not exist.

As you all know, there are a very few smart-arse ghosts who have discovered how to make themselves visible to the Live world, and they have a great time, or so they say. But for the overwhelming majority of us, any amount of Spectral Needs training doesn't begin to help us materialise in any significant way.

It is the same with sounds. Very few of us can manage an audible groan, certainly not a hoarse or rasping whisper; and this, combined with invisibility, makes it almost impossible to conduct any responsible haunting.

However, I have definitely rejected the temptation to become a poltergeist. To begin with, it takes a very long period of training, and is really only open to ex-psychopaths, former rock-stars and Millwall supporters. In any case, they are regarded as the hooligan element of our ghost world, and I don't particularly want to be associated with them.

Unfortunately, this leaves many of us with a deeply unsatisfactory existence. I feel unrecognised and therefore unfulfilled, without any purpose   So there you have it. I have outlined the problems of boredom and lack of recognition on our part, and of general ignorance in the Living world. The question now arises, what can be done about it?

There are two main problems: one of perception and one of practicality.

The first is that I have no wish to upset the world population or attempt to scare them out of their wits. I simply want to talk to them; and as most of the Live world think ghosts are there only to throw things about or frighten them to death, it is important to use a modicum of tact.

The second problem is how to achieve a breakthrough in Manifestation Technology. So far, this line of development has barely come out of the Middle Ages, and is ripe for exploitation. Almost nobody in the Living world claims to have seen a ghost or to have had have had any meaningful converse with us. An attempted contact usually results in a stifled scream on their part, with possible loss of consciousness, followed later by a garbled and incoherent recollection of what actually happened. People only have to find themselves in a dark, unfamiliar place and their imagination does the rest. They will see what they expect to see. One of us might actually be there and try to stir things up a bit, just for fun; but the point is, that nothing very meaningful ever comes of such encounters. It has always been like this; few of the Living have ever been able to communicate with us or understand more than an occasional almost inaudible word. Very few can be like Hamlet, and even he had to read between the lines. It is time that we applied modern techniques to obtain more constructive dialogue, and exploit the huge market which I am sure exists.

I am proud to announce that I, after prolonged researches, am in a position to propose a plan where these problems may be solved in an acceptable, one-step development.

It is well known that otherwise inaudible sound can be recorded and then processed so that it can be replayed within the range of human hearing; examples of this have been demonstrated in the singing of whales, the squeaking of bats, and the voice of Charlotte Church. Well, I am in the process of designing equipment which will do the same for ghosts. Any spirit will be able to speak into it, and instantly the sound will be processed and transposed to the audio range of the Living. It will only be necessary to have a one-way system, as ghosts can hear living speech without any assistance - so much so that we sometimes wish we could hear less of it, especially about the time of the Eurovision Song Contest or any Jonathan Ross programme. My invention is a simple device, a small box housing a special filter/amplifier, and I have given it a working name of 'Tele-phantom' until it receives a proper marketing treatment.

The vision thing is slightly different, but space research has had a spin-off which is there to be exploited. Like sound, where only certain frequencies can be heard by the Living ear, so only certain wavelengths of light can be detected by the Living eye. The remedy is clear. A lens can be specially treated to filter the light coming into the Living eye allowing only those rays emanating from the spirit world to be seen. All the usual clutter of *News Twenty Four* or *Celebrity Love Island* can be eliminated. Since our Unliving world does not have access to an off switch, these prototype devices have already become popular amongst my friends and colleagues.

In case you are thinking that this is all very fine in theory, but impossible in practice, then I have to tell you that the technology already exists. You will almost all have seen 'ghosting' on television sets, and strange 'ghostly' figures on developed film from cameras. You probably put these things down to freak weather or strange light conditions, but you would be wrong.

It was me, experimenting.

And I can now reveal that I am in a position to put the design for my special filters out for contract. It has classic simplicity, and consists of a couple of specially treated lenses, worn like glasses, which I refer to as 'Spectre-clear'.

This is how the system will work. Anyone in the Living world who wants to communicate with us can do so merely by purchasing the new Tele-phantom and Spectre-clear technology. They will have access to life-long speaking time with as many of us as they like; and return calls will be entirely free. On the more advanced models, we might introduce an LED display window in the Spectre-clears for split conversations or even conferencing. Also in the design stage is an optional Parental Control device, known as a

9

Paxman Button, for censoring sights and sounds considered too frightening for children. The possibilities for future development are endless.

The great advantage of this programme is that only those people who are interested will wish to make use of my state-of-the-art technology, rather like their mobile phones. The devices may possibly be abused by the Living - for instance, if they seek to monopolise the frequencies with futile questions to some of their departed relatives on mundane matters such as which car to buy or what the weather is going to be like on Tuesday or which horse will win the Derby - but we shall be in a position to prevent this by simply not responding. Too much familiarity would breed contempt, and I am sure that the Unliving world would wish to retain a certain degree of mystery and distance.

I have great hopes for my new technology. It will open up an exciting world for entrepreneurial spirits like me by relieving the crushing boredom of a purposeless existence. At the same time, those in the Living world who do wish to communicate with us - for instance, with ancestral voices prophesying war, and such - could do so in a rational and user-friendly way.

Those who do not wish to acknowledge our presence can happily continue to imagine that we do not exist. It is a win-win situation.

There is only one problem. At the moment I do not have the ability to mass-produce the advanced, but comparatively simple, devices which are the culmination of my research. The concept and the technology are both in place, and all I need now is a partner to secure the manufacturing rights. If it is to be properly marketed, it will have to be done soon - well before the autumn, so the Living can have a chance to accustom themselves to the system and prepare for the shortening days and darkening nights that are the natural prerequisites for serious Manifestation - and a commercial launch in time for the Christmas market.

So, you have the business plan before you, and I can see that you are all as excited about the project as I am. I have just one request. Can anyone suggest how I might urgently communicate with Bill Gates?

Stephen Connolly

A Winter Wedding

The snow is gone. When I open my eyes, the snow is gone and all I can see is grass, beautiful green grass everywhere I look. Blackbirds sing, spectators murmur in the grandstand and beyond lies the city, hazy and beautiful.

*

We should have stayed with the ship. She might yet be freed from the ice. Help might still find us, a ship from home even. We have been gone so many years, surely they have missed us? "One more ridge," the lieutenant calls, with as much encouragement as he can muster. "Just one more ridge." We have been dragging the boats across the ice for weeks now, an act of madness. It has ruined the health of all of us. We shall be scattered and lost and nobody will ever learn our fate. We should have stayed with the ship.

*

I laugh to see the city, its towers and buildings so familiar, the sun so warm. It is so good to be home. My friend the bear pants in the heat, his fur white gleaming in the sun. "You'll like it here," I tell him, patting his mighty shoulder. A flock of sheep grazes the wicket but nobody minds. The players chat, they throw a ball between each other, red as a Cox's Pippin. I wait at mid-on, patting my pockets, but my friend the bear has the ring. He holds it aloft, immense and studded with diamonds of light, so large it encircles the sun.

Your father escorts you onto the wicket as the spectators applaud. I know it's you, despite the veil, despite the Dandelion blossom in my face, in my eyes, blown by the wind. Your father glares at me, or is it my friend the bear? The sunlight glints off the blade of the dirty knife.

*

The fierce little men rushed around us in their rough fur coats, the first human beings we had seen since leaving the ship. But they would not come close, shouting

11

at us from a distance, words we could not understand. They looked strangely Oriental, comic yet formidable. Do they perhaps change into terrible white Bears when the moon is full? Or like Doctor Jekyll in Mr Stevenson's terrifying story? They threw stones at us before fleeing the lieutenant's pistol shot, speeding off on their wonderful sledges, pulled by packs of hounds. Dogs like wolves, fierce and beautiful.

If only we could travel so quickly, so easily. If only they would come back, and throw more lumps of dried meat at us.

*

Your bridesmaids line up behind us and argue over the loads, complain that their boat is too heavy. I take your hand as Queen Victoria recites the wedding service. Prince Albert whispers a joke to Mr Dickens who writes it down in his notebook, or is it my friend the bear? The fielders line up behind her Majesty, fascinated by the tiny crown bobbing on her head. I try to kiss you, but you move away as I reach for your veil.

You wait for me on the bridge. Beyond, sails lean into the wind on Coniston Water. Although it's hard to see, the wind drives hawthorn blossom into my face, my eyes. The moon glares down on us as my friend the bear wanders off in search of refreshments. I hear the crack of blade through bone or is it a tree branch, snapping in the wind?

*

They look at me, my fellow explorers. Considering. Calculating. I am the weakest of the party, there is no denying it. They stare around for the things I describe, the things only I can see, wishing I would shut up.

They listen to my constant racking coughs, each time producing more and more blood on my frozen gear, on the snow around us. I have almost no strength left to pull on the rope. Our poor fire gives little warmth, barely enough to heat our terrible supper.

*

We walk through the Snowdrops to the Green Chapel. My friend the bear loads our plates with meringues and pours cream on the strawberries. Bubbles froth on a glass of champagne, steam rises from a bowl of soup. The cold has taken all my teeth. I smile with mouth shut as the sunlight gleams off the dirty knife. The wind blows sugar into my face, into my eyes and when I can see again the room is deserted. From outside I hear music and the bridesmaids' laughter as they dance.

*

From the top of the ridge I look south. Only more ice awaits us.

Does Her Majesty still reign? Does Prince Albert still plan great things for the city? I remember schemes for a great palace of crystal, how I should have loved to visit it with you.

*

You beckon from the top of the stairs. I know it's you although your face is in shadow. A grim aunt glares down at me from a picture frame, or is it my friend the bear? In the bedroom you remove my icy gear. The wind blows talcum into my face, into my eyes and when I can see again, the chaps have scratched 'Just Married!' onto my harness.

My friend the bear settles on the floor, rests his head on his paws. You pull sheets and blankets over me and still I can't get warm.

*

No strength remains for writing, and neither pen nor paper. Nothing flammable may be kept from the common store.

I have one more purpose to fulfill. The others stare at me as my coughing becomes uncontrollable, as I become ever weaker; as they become ever hungrier. Think well of me, I had no wish for exploring, no hunger to see a Northwest Passage. Only to make your father smile upon me and give his blessing.

A great cough builds within my chest, it cannot be denied.

*

The bridesmaids help me lie down and take position around me, an honour guard, each bearing the dirty knife like a sword, each now with a scarlet cross splashed across his chest. You lie down beside me and I take your hand as my sight begins to fade.

An eiderdown has split. Its feathers rain down upon us, a pleasant tickling, covering my eyes until I can see nothing. And why should I want to get up, when I am finally beginning to get warm?

13

Julie Wiltshire

The Unwanted Visitor

The night cold and fresh as a new dug grave drops like a stone upon the dank earth. A rogue rain cloud stalks the darkness and whips the stagnant dull mirror in the bottom acre. It cries for the wandering soul who already has a place booked at the gates of Hell.

An old man stung by sorrow coughs and gobs his phlegm onto the glowing fire. It hisses and spits back at the huddled frame. He slowly picks up the iron poker and prods it menacingly with his clawed hand in retaliation of its defiance, bringing the dying flames back to life with a crackle and splutter.

Fred stares blindly into the burning embers, tormented shadows dance across the furrows of his brow and his leathered face, splintered by life. His worn flat cap greasy with age squats on his head like a squashed toad trying to keep his thoughts from wandering. A candle curls its vapours up into a corner of his room and drips its bronze blood over a wooden table in its cremation. Fred is very thrifty. Who needs bulbs? The moon appears once more and fires its arrows through the gaping holes in the yellowing net curtains, once hung with love, and stabs at the cracks of the cell with its fine shavings of bone. Cold tears shine in the corners of Fred's cloudy eyes which are as dead as his grief, and his stiffened ears remain cocked, listening like the wild beasts in the fields for the slightest sound of danger in the deafening silence.

Fred sold his land to the developer who had been chasing him for many years. The fight has gone out of him and all that is left is the flight. All he wants now is to be left alone. Smoke from the candle acids his eyes. He wipes them gently with a filthy stained handkerchief found in his pocket, and coughs once again through brittle cracked lips to relieve his tension. He clears his throat before wiping the dribble oozing from the corners of his mouth.

The shrunken farmer, living his half death, remains huddled in his threadbare chair. Life had not materialised as he had hoped for. Dreams had faded and dropped away into a chasm of resentment. There were no sons, or even daughters, to work the land; he and his wife were not blessed. Maybe that was her problem. She was barren as the harsh top acres. He once again tries to unpick the threads of the past and reweave them into fiction, to justify all the events that had happened. A moth flutters around the candle's flame and touching its fate, singes its delicate glass wings.

Fred recalls the pond in the centre of his land where ducks swam and frogs croaked in their calling site in the ever changing face of nature. Reeds like twisted lanes held a multitude of life. It had eventually lost its fight for survival and died, and became an ugly scar, holding on to the stagnancy of its secret. The developers want to keep the pond to make a feature of it on the estate, after they have removed all the silt and poison from its grasp. What a feature thinks Fred. The old home groans with pain and Fred shivers slightly as the room chills. Armed with the dead weight of the past he pokes the fire again, demanding its warmth, knowing all the while it is him that is burnt out not the fire.

Suddenly he hears it, and stiffens like a stook. Yes, there it is again, a scratching. The wooden boards outside the butter stone cottage creak, snapping their teeth at the night.

"Who's there?" he growls, hoping for a reply, but none comes. He once again clears his throat. The moon disappears behind its buttress of cloud, adding to the atmosphere of panic. A fox's cry fills the lower Cotswold meadow like a child in pain making the old farmer jump.

Fred, haunted by the worst of himself, curls back into the comfort of his chair, as he draws a sour breath. I wonder if they will dredge the pond and restore it to its former glory soon, he ponders. The digger had positioned itself beside the once crystal clear waters, mocking Fred with its harsh hostile wide grin, and bearing its metal teeth. Days it has silently stood, devouring time. Fred did not want to go down to the pond to see what was happening, he could see enough from his window.

Suddenly the scratching begins again. Night after night the visitor comes to his door, ever since he signed the land over to the developers three months ago. A scratching like chalk scraped down a blackboard, long and slow.

"Go away, go away whoever you are," rasps Fred frozen in fright, and asthmatically coughs.

"What do you want of me?" he calls again with words of desperation drying in his mouth. Nails drag down the door, scraping, scraping away at the peeling paint. Fred jumps up forgetting his arthritis. The hairs on his neck stand to attention, as he shivers. He swings around and grabs the iron poker and brandishes it like a sword.

"Come on then you bugger, come on." He hears a whisper or was it the wind, his hearing is not as sharp as it used to be. Shapes of darkness uncoil and dance across his walls and crawl across his ceiling, mocking his fear.

His picks out the murmuring words, yes he can hear them. "Fred, Fred," she calls. He has that voice imprinted on his mind. The cruel necessity of constant nagging had filled his past until he could no longer stand it in his life, and now once again that same voice had come back to haunt him. "Fred, Fred," she cries again.

"Shut up, shut up. Leave me alone," Fred shouts, calling out to the nothingness in the thick smog of his smoky room.

He knew in his heart what was coming next. The latch suddenly clicks and rises, trying to crack the door alive, but the bolt holds firm. He stares down to the chipped quarry tiled floor where the old stable door locks out the evils of the night. There, there it was again sliding under the door. Slowly and menacingly, the ghostly dark fingers slither towards him. The oily slick, black as blindness itself slowly grows larger and feels its way, crawling, crawling towards Fred. The silted dark blood soaks into Fred's slippers.

"Enid, Enid, leave me alone. What do you want of me?" A cackle fills the air and echoes around his icy space. Fred stands alone in his room, where love had lost its way many years ago. He cannot open the door, for he knows he will be staring into the shrunken eyes of death. Terror takes its hold, his heavy heartbeat quickens until it beats outside of itself, louder and louder it thumps.

He draws one last painful breath and crumples onto the floor clutching at his chest as the walls busied by damp close in and swallow him up. A shadow floats between him and the shining light of the moon, and touches his ploughed forehead with its icy immortal hands.

The funeral was a sombre occasion, with very few mourners attending, held between the local church's crumbling grey walls. The manager of Hill Rise Homes turned up to show a fleeting respect.

A few curled-up ham and cheese sandwiches were laid on after the service at The Brown Bear. Mr Edwards' mobile rings as he stands upright in the corner of the pub, clutching an Old Ric. He juggles with his beer and mobile phone. "Hill Rise Homes. Mr Edwards speaking."

"Oh, hi George. What...what are you saying?...Repeat it again. In the pond, you found what? For God's sake, George, ring the police quick. Quick!"

Daniel Gooding

Points to the Eye

The dead man lay flat on his back, arms flung out as though he were throwing a tantrum. From the accounts of various eyewitnesses, the man had just been standing there looking at a painting, perhaps a little more attentively than most, when they had suddenly heard a horrible wailing noise ('bloodcurdling' was the unimaginative consensus). Strangely enough, no-one had actually seen the victim at the critical moment, or even been near him, all seeming to pass through various archways to adjoining rooms just as the incident occurred. The only thing anyone seemed to remember was turning round abruptly to see the man stagger into the middle of the room, with great jagged steps and hands on head in true old-school horror fashion, before falling lifeless to the ground.

Officer Cadden knew the place well. Having lived in the area his whole life, he had passed many afternoons as a child here in the city's museum and art gallery. Most of the paintings and sculptures were the same ones that had always been there, which somehow made them seem older than the fact that they had been created over a hundred years ago. He remembered one sculpture in particular, although not the name of the artist or even much of what it looked like; just some sort of suspended arrangement involving a triangle, aimed arrow-like at a pale sphere. The only thing he could recall was the name of the piece, *Points to the Eye*, and the fact that it was supposed to represent the triumph of life over death. Or something.

While other officers were busy sealing the main doors in the lobby, some of them talking to reception desk staff, and the manager was doing his best to look stoic in the face of everything that was suddenly happening to him, Cadden's job was to guard the body. With nobody else around, this required little effort on his part, and so he wandered slowly around the room looking at the pieces again, some of which he had not seen in years. The *Points to the Eye* sculpture wasn't there, but then perhaps it had simply been on loan from another gallery. Then again, it might just be in another room upstairs.

He turned around to make a perfunctory check. The unidentified figure peered back at him down the length of his body. This wasn't the first time that Cadden had seen a dead body, nor the first time he had been left alone with one; but he had never felt this particular unease before. He told himself that he was imagining things, but at the same time he knew, from the way the eyes glinted, that they were pointed in his direction. Perhaps the killer had stood where he was now standing.

He moved around the room slowly, giving each painting an equally appreciative glance, until he came to the one in the far corner. This one he remembered well. It was dated from 1616, and showed an obviously well-born mother in bed, holding her two infant sons. Presumably the idea was that the twins had just been born, and yet despite this, the woman was shown in full Elizabethan costume. Not only that, the two twins seemed also to be swaddled in material cut from the same pattern. He felt the same reaction to this picture as he had done many times as a child, imagining how sweaty and uncomfortable she must have been in that get-up, combined with the heavy bedclothes and the numerous candles lighting the room. He reminded himself that the woman would have been given the garb in the picture to protect her modesty; but even so, he couldn't help thinking about the residual horrors of childbirth that might lie beneath those sheets, staining the already musty fabric.

He heard a noise behind him, like the sound of a child stifling a giggle. Turning round he couldn't see anything different, nor any sign of life from the raised walkways above. He glanced again towards the body. The eyes were looking straight at him. Decidedly unnerved now, he took a step closer to make sure. The eyes were definitely staring right at him, although neither the head nor any other part of the body had moved. He took one step to the side, then two more in quick succession. The eyes remained locked on his, seemingly unmoving, and yet following him around the room.

Cadden shook his head and went back to the painting. He looked at the matching expressions of the children, identical with the vacant stare of their mother. He realised that of the two babies, the one on the left was somehow fainter than the other; the colour and detail on the face and blanket were faded, even though the rest of the painting seemed fine. It was as though that particular baby had been exposed to sunlight for a long period of time, while the rest of the picture had been kept in darkness.

Cadden heard a scuffling sound from the doorway, the squeak of soles on a wooden floor. He turned his head, expecting to see Richards coming through the archway, but nobody was there. He looked around again for another quick check on the body. It was gone.

He turned round in a complete circle, and immediately felt stupid. Then he heard it again: the sound of a child suppressing laughter, only louder this time. He looked up again towards one of the balconies that overlooked the main gallery. Suddenly there was a harsh guffawing from the opposite side of the room; this time it sounded like an adult, but there was something forced and unnatural about the noise, as though the person were trying to laugh for the first very time. There was a loud, stilted clumping noise, and Cadden turned to face the opposite walkway, just in time to see a figure of some sort lolloping out of sight behind a pillar. There was something horrible about the way it was moving, as though it wasn't used to those legs.

Cadden felt his own legs growing equally unstable, and felt like fleeing the room himself, but thought he would merely stumble and fall if he tried. He thought of reaching for his radio. Of course, that was what he *should* be doing for Christ's sake. But any movement would only draw attention to himself, though from whom, or what, he didn't want to think about. Instead, he turned slowly back to the painting. He looked at the faded infant, and at the brighter one alongside. The latter one now seemed to glow in comparison, throbbing imperceptibly.

Despite Cadden's terror of moving, he thought something in the painting would be able to help him, to provide some sort of answer. Slowly, he moved towards the portrait, trying to keep the rest of his body as motionless as possible as his legs pulled him towards the canvas. He looked at the brighter child; the eyes were looking directly at him, and yet as his own eyes moved minutely around the small figure its gaze seemed to flick aside in a similar fashion, as though trying to indicate something to him.

He turned to look in the same direction, but could see nothing different; another peculiar slapping of feet came from upstairs, but further away this time. He looked again at the child's face. The eyes were definitely staring now in that one direction, but not quite from the same angle.

Cadden gingerly stepped over the thin line of black cord that guarded the painting, half expecting an alarm to be triggered somewhere. He stood as close to the canvas as he dared, and turned again to face where the infant seemed to be pointing. Still seeing nothing, he crouched down to the height of the child's head.

He felt a faint movement in the air, like the billowing of a musty curtain. The museum smell suddenly intensified as two tiny ice-cold hands covered his eyes, his own screams distorted in his mind by the new-born-like crying that seemed to drown them out. He ran forward, immediately stumbling over the dividing cord line and falling face first to the ground. He felt the impact of his head striking the wooden floor, but before the pain could register he had already been tuned out, like a television turned down quickly at a loud part of a film.

It looked through the new, glassy eyes at the strangely black-clad figures running into the room, who now peered down at the new body and pressed fingers against its neck. Still trying not to giggle, it stretched out in its new body and lay down to wait. To wait for the funny men to leave, so it could go and find its brother.

Simon Piney

The Ghastly Rolling

You asked me for an eerie story. I can tell you one which I know to be true because it happened to me and still haunts my dreams so many years later. I warn you it is not a pleasant tale, nor has it a neat and tidy ending which explains all away.

*

It began many years ago when I was young and foolish. It had been a hot day in May and I had spent a bibulous evening with some other young bloods at a hostelry in Cranham woods. In those far-off days, pubs closed their doors at eleven o'clock and, some minutes after hour, we found ourselves outside in the fine sprint night.

It had been our intention to take part in the next day's Cheese Rolling event which has taken place since time immemorial at Cooper's Hill. I had decided, the weather being so clement, that I would sleep that night under the stars, but, much to my astonishment, none of my companions was disposed to accompany me. Indeed, they seemed bent on dissuading me from my endeavour.

Emboldened by many a pint of local ale, I left them to make their way home while I struck out towards Moorend and Prinknash, cutting up the wooded slopes. The walk was pleasant; the moon was full. I was carrying no more than my bedroll and my heart was light.

In no time at all, or so it seemed to me, I reached the heights and entered Brockworth Wood, where I planned to find a favourable spot to sleep for a few hours, it being now around midnight. Hardly had I unrolled my sleeping bag under a tall tree than I heard the sound of music. It came, piping and drumming, from the direction of Cooper's Hill itself, and, through the trees, I caught a glimpse of a bonfire.

"Aha!" thought I. "Others have gathered to celebrate the Rolling. Perhaps they will let me join them round the fire."

Indeed, the air had taken on a distinct chill, or, perhaps, the alcohol I had imbibed had cooled my blood. Taking up my makeshift bed, I wound my way between the trees and up the slope. Before ever I emerged from the wood onto the open grassy top that crowns the hill, I was astonished to see, around the fire, a crowd of what I took to be men and women in fancy dress.

Here were Roman soldiers, there Saxon peasants, doublets and hose, stove-pipe hats, even a few monks in habit and hooded. Every age of Britain's long history was present. All were bedaubed and streaked with dark stains, which, as the figures moved nearer the fire, I saw, all too clearly, was the vermillion as of blood.

In their midst and kneeling, bound hand and foot and blindfolded, was an enormously fat man. He was stripped to a loin cloth, and his head appeared to have been shaved and polished to a high gloss reflecting the dancing flames. All the while the piping and drumming grew louder and more frantic. I stood, rooted to the spot, gripped by a terror I could not explain as the strangely-dressed crowd pressed on either side nearer and nearer the obese and sweat-stained man.

As if at a sudden signal, the music stopped. Silence fell. All the figures turned to look beyond the bonfire, and, as one, fell to their knees.

There, to my horror, rose, beyond the flames, what seemed to be the figure of a monstrous toad, all warts and glistening slime. Its eyes glowed red and its maw opened to emit a foul croak. At the sound, one of the Romans, a centurion, rose to his feet and stepped forward.

At a second eldritch croak from the horrid creature behind the fire, he drew his sword, and, with one stupendous blow, cut the prisoned man's head clean off its body. At this, the crowd set up a low and rhythmic chant. The centurion bent and picked up the dripping head, blood running down onto his breastplate. Swinging back his arm, he sent the grisly object down the hill, leaving a trail of blood and tattered flesh behind it as it rolled.

The assembled crowd now began to run after the head, whooping and shrieking, while the toad croaked its obscene encouragement.

As the crowd began to tumble down the hill, my worst moment was still to come. The toad turned and looked straight at me where I stood. It crouched, and, as it sprang over the dying flames, it opened its jaws to reveal row upon row of sharp teeth dripping with blood and scraps of flesh. The stench of its fetid breath overcame me and I fell, senseless, to the ground.

How long I lay in a swoon I cannot tell, but I woke to bright sunlight and the sounds of cheering. Fearing the return of the foul masked crew, I lay still and peered through the undergrowth. No bonfire met my eyes, but a crowd of people tossing a cheese-like ball down the steep slope. It was the start of the annual Rolling. No sign remained of the gory horror I had witnessed.

*

There is little more to tell. I got home as fast as I could, shaken and trembling. I lay on my bed in a fever for a fortnight. To this day I cannot pass along the road from Painswick to Cheltenham without a shudder, nor are my nights always quiet.

Ask me no more. My tale is told. Such stories are unfit for dark nights.

But listen! Is that not the sound of a rattling drum and a foul piping? And can you not hear a ghostly croaking borne on our dark, winter Cotswold winds?

Elizabeth Murphy

Breathing Exercises

If I were not me, I would be rendered speechless! You make such a mercurial Hamlet. Your delivery is so intuitive and the nasality of your Camden boyhood has all but disappeared.

It is such a pleasure to be working with you again. Too many years have passed since our last collaboration. Of course, I have continued in my servitude to the theatre. Sadly you did not appear in any of my productions. You dropped out of my directorial realm so suddenly.

The advent of children necessitates the mundanity of seeking a regular revenue stream but you were so close to making it big. I know it is difficult to make a living treading the boards, but did you really have to tread the pavements instead? A career as a postman is so utterly pedestrian. All is not lost. If we combine our talents again, we can create something life-altering.

I remember when I first directed you, in your 'salad days'. Your raw talent won you a rare grant-funded entrance into The Academy, but left you painfully exposed when compared to your more formally-trained fellow students. It must have been so tiresome returning to your parents' council flat each night. It would have been like spending all day in the company of the Bard but returning to sleep with Sheila Delaney. Your dreadful parents thwarted your big opportunity, siphoning off your grant cheque before the nascent term had even started. The shame of being asked to leave for not paying your fees was unbearable. You must remember that your departure was not from lack of talent, just lack of funds. Perhaps you should have considered hitching up with one of the older actresses? It would have provided funding and a wealth of untapped experience and contacts.

We probably need to discuss the night you were arrested. I encouraged you to immerse yourself in the actors' world. I told you to make friends now as friendships are needed to get the parts, or your gift would remain veiled and unappreciated. Your fellow students wanted you to join them. You were invited. Your financial shortfall was becoming such a drag and I was almost certain that someone would pick up the cost of your taxi fare once you got to the bar. That damned cabbie wouldn't be persuaded about your friends inside with money. He just locked the doors on us and drove us straight round to the police station. It was obvious to the constable that you were not criminal class (although I am sure you could have played that part very well should you have wished to do so). He, in turn, drove you round to that hospital where it was made clear that my company was unwelcome. Blasted pills! We didn't speak for years.

Without me, you were discharged out of hospital, straight onto the path to mediocrity. You met your wife at a dance hall. She treated your acting as something of an embarrassment and was not impressed that you were 'between roles'. She had no understanding of vocation and your calling went unsupported. She encouraged you to stay in your steady job in the postal service. Lumbering along the same streets every day, delivering endless brown envelopes containing demands for gold and postcards from other people's holidays which you could never afford. She didn't approve of your Catholicism, which to my mind is such a beautiful religion; the sweet oscillation between the lows of guilt and the highs of absolution.   She dreaded seeing your car parked outside the local church; it was a bad sign. 'Mortifying' was her description of your Passion Play production. The procession through the town was not observed by any of your family. The chill wind excused them from watching you get nailed to the cross on the local recreation ground. You died beautifully.

I managed to get through to you for a short while around your mother's passing a few years back, but your wife soon blocked me out. Further separation would only be detrimental to both of us. Our endeavour is too important.

So, you have been laid off from your postal rounds. Erratic deliveries and questions over missing items exposed your eccentricities to unsympathetic souls. Your wife has taken on further drudgery which, on the positive, means that she is absent from the house much more. Now we have time to cultivate your craft. You can finally dispense with the essence-quelling pills outside of her scrutiny. You are free which means that we can toil together again.

The major drain on your time has been the children. What a fete of acting the last six years have been! No one could have ever guessed that the tears of happiness, the knitted brows of anxiety, the roars of laughter covered up a feeling of nothingness. Looking at those children stirred no more real joy in you than that desiccating job you have been carrying out daily. You worried that your wife saw though it, but she was so absurdly wrapped up in those urchins that she was blind to your indifference. She even believes that you should look after the imps while she works. This irritation is beginning to ooze into our rehearsal time.Your cacophonous children's interruptions are becoming too wearisome. Surely, they can get themselves some provisions from the cupboard. I'm sure they are capable of slavering some margarine on a cracker or two to stave off their incessant hunger. How will we ever get this play off the ground with this insistent chatter? Do not respond! Light a cigarette! Look straight ahead at the television. Ignore, ignore, ignore. Do not get out of your chair! Well done. The moment has passed. We can get back to our run-through, but we might have to consider a more permanent solution to limit the disturbances.

So how about moving today's rehearsal to the garage, or as we shall call it from now on, The Studio? We can start to set the scene properly and work with the props. Quickly now! Shut and lock the door before those irritating pucks start to bother us again.

I knew it wouldn't be long. Who knew that such small paws could bang so loudly? Don't go to them. Well-played! Your rage is like a young Burton performing Osborne. You really haven't lost your touch after all these years.

27

It is impossible to concentrate here with those mosquitoes of yours buzzing around. We should consider finding somewhere else to go. Turn on the car engine and let it run while we think of a place where we can find peace. We need rehearsal space and time; unrestricted and unlimited by your lacklustre surroundings and dreary ruminations. We must head towards the denouement. Let us practise our breathing exercises. Are you tired, my muse? Sleep has been so difficult of late. Well, sleep on. In our dreams, we are inseparable.

Graham Bruce-Fletcher

Thrown Together

A sharp elbow repeatedly jabbing into his ribs was a far from welcome summons to consciousness. Erik was disorientated; angry. Then he began to panic.

The familiar explanation would have been his sister trying to take more than her fair share of the palliasse, but such comfort was denied by the sensation of jolting movement, the constant hollow rumbling and the overwhelming stench – far worse than the usual reek of his home – coupled with what seemed like bare boards beneath him and the pressure of ...

...of what?

Erik struggled to free his left hand, to explore the origin of the weight bearing down upon him. His eyes could discern nothing but the occasional flicker of a torch-flame, intermittently revealed and concealed, as something shifted above him in the darkness. Perhaps the roof had collapsed? Or the whole building? A thunderstorm seemed to be raging around him. Maybe the cold, slimy flesh his fingers were now probing was of the pig from beneath, crushed to death, burst by the fall of this upper part of the hovel the Lord of the Manor grudgingly provided for his serfs? But this miasma was more than could be due solely to the ruptured gut of a dead swine.

There was no doubt about the elbow. Human; female. He pushed at it. It was warm but slippery; the heel of his hand skidded over the arm as it straightened, and his palm came to rest over a naked breast. This was neither his sister, nor even his mother, whose feet, because the family slept alternately head to toe, would, as they had been all his life, have been far away, beyond his sister and father. This breast was heavier than his sister's, less flaccid than his mother's. A stranger's. His hand sought more information.

Beneath the smooth but pus-besmirched skin of a well-fed belly, he felt her heart beat.

The unfamiliar sound he'd at first taken for thunder ceased for a moment. He heard muffled voices, and a sudden redoubling of the weight pressing down on him. There was a fart, a groan, and a stink which brought his mind to a full understanding of his situation.

Dead pigs – nay, even live pigs – have no hands. It was, without the slightest doubt, a lifeless hand which pressed curled, rigid fingers to his cheek as the crackling rolling wheels began to turn once more.

Erik realised he was – together with the strange woman – beneath the ghastly nightly harvest of corpses destined for the pit into which so many of the villagers had been cast throughout this year of Our Lord, 1348.

The elbow jabbed him in the ribs again. His hand reached for the stranger beside him.

"Touch me not, villein!" she said, almost inaudible through the growing cairn of cadavers. Erik realised: the stranger was Therese, the Lord's daughter. This sickness had levelled all classes.

"I beg pardon, lady, but we are both brought to the depths together. I have, I now remember, suffered with the sickness these past few days, and am relieved that I may now believe myself delivered, as it must also be for you. Your father in the Hall, and mine in the village, must have taken us for dead."

"Then you shall be my saviour, and gain reward," she said.

Erik used the little strength his illness had spared him to burrow beneath the mound of victims, inching beneath them, aided by the shocks, each of which bounced them from the boards of the cart, until he was able to cover her, bracing his arms and legs to relieve her entirely of the pressure of their neighbours.

"Aren't you the ploughman, Erik?" she whispered.

"Aye," he grunted, wondering how long his weakened muscles could lock his body to form a bridge over hers.

Therese giggled. "I've watched you these past years. A well-made man, such as any woman, even a lady, would take as a husband."

30

"My lady, would it were so. I have banished such desires from my mind. Though I confess I have often dreamed of how it would be to win your heart."

Therese giggled again and pressed her hands to his chest. "Then kiss me now and seal our pact. My father shall release you and let you have your just desert, for you shall truly be my champion."

Her mouth was sour with the sickness, her skin and hair sticky with the humours running from all who surrounded them, but Erik felt he'd been reprieved from Hell and redeemed unto Heaven. "Amen," he said.

When the noise and motion stopped, Erik drew a painful breath, preparing to shout and be discovered with his future bride, so they could regain the life this miracle promised.

Only the sound of the men heaving their deadly burden into the pit interrupted the cold, dark silence. Erik resolved to wait until he could safely rise without causing any foul creature to fall upon Therese, and give his lungs the freedom to cry out and save them both. Bloated with the gases of putrefaction, the dead let off sighs, groans, moans, farts and belches as they were stirred by the carters. His face and body smeared with their fluids, he must be sure to make his words clear and loud.

Wisely, the cart men used pitchforks to unload the wretches. It kept the exudate and bloody flux away from them, otherwise they should needs wash their clothing, and be forced to put them on again still damp, for they surely would not dry in this inclement weather before another night's collections.

Erik did not understand when, having been relieved of the burden of the final corpse from his back, he felt a fresh assault of pain, piercing him and whirling him through the air. As he lay in the pit, his life dribbling from him, he heard Therese shout, "'Hold, villeins. God has spared me for my beauty and nobility. I alone still live and will have you despatched if you should harm me! Take me to the Hall, and be quick about it, for this night is cold, and I must bathe to rid myself of the stench of these common dead."

In his final delirium, Erik had a vision of the doom painting on the walls of St Michael's Church; a demon goading a beautiful young woman towards the fiery maw of Hell. Turning his head as an angel led him to paradise, he felt assured that he would indeed have his just desert: in eternity.

Judith Gunn

The Ghost in the Classroom

L204 was not a particularly prepossessing classroom; it was separate from the rest of the IT block. It had been the first wired classroom, an early adopter, but now a smart new block dominated the school, filled with clean and well-appointed PCs. L204 was a cold classroom, damp and smelly. Paul could not quite define the smell, although he had discovered that the collective scents of Lynx and female hairspray did not quite cover a nagging hint of decay. He opened cupboards, looking for the source of the odd odour. It emanated, he thought, from one particular terminal, the one next to the printer. Someone had scratched 'Mr Evans is a wanker' into the plastic desktop, later more had been added. The original had been struck through and some wag had written 'See me Peters'. Paul chuckled. Mr Evans, his predecessor, had been a bit of a tartar. Paul knew little of him, except his tragic end and his penchant for a tidy classroom.

"Peters? Oh, Peters is dead, hit and run, and good riddance to bad rubbish. I'd have run him over myself given half a chance! After what he did!" Mr Roberts doodled on his iPad as they suffered a fruitless training day. Paul had spent some of the day trying to exorcise the smell and remove the ever increasing repetition of the name Peters from various desktops, keyboards, chairs and, for some reason, the floor under his desk.

"What did he do?"

"Nasty little git, he made accusations, did it at a parents' evening. Started sobbing at the table. Said Evans had fiddled with him during detention. Evans always came in for it from the kids. He was not great in the classroom."

"And did he?"

"Did he what? Oh, that, God no! He made the mistake of detaining Peters on his own that day, but we have cameras, precisely for that reason. Nothing went on, looked like Peters was asleep for most of it. Father believed him though, clambered over the desk and thumped Evans, knocked a tooth out! I s'pose that's why the poor sod hung himself in his shed. All nice and tidy. He always was tidy, left a note so everyone was clear."

"What did it say?"

"It just said 'Don't teach'. Can't argue there - at least in his case."

*

"Pozlaski, Peters.....Peters?" he had a received a reply for every name except Peters.

"He's not here," someone said.

The penny dropped for Paul. "Oh shit!" He thought he had muttered it, but the class heard and a collective "oh" growled out from them, accompanied by banging on desks.

"All right, enough!" To his satisfaction they stopped immediately. 'Still got it,' he thought.

*

Email

Subject: Unmarked Register

There are several missing marks on your register for the week beginning 06.12. Please amend.

A machine bred reproach, typical! Paul phoned again. "Lloyd, I am forwarding the email that is telling me I have not done my register for Peters. Please can you remove his name?"

"Well, I am looking at the register now and I can't see it."

"It's a mystery then because I am telling you it is there!"

"Are you gay, sir?"

"What's it to you?"

"Well you might be bit weird, sir, like Mr Evans." The conversation was designed to distract from the task of entering data into Excel. Paul had some sympathy. It wasn't quite the IT syllabus he had hoped to teach.

"Yes, I am normal and I am gay." Silence. "As for Mr Evans, he was not weird either. He was maligned, viciously maligned and what happened was tragic."

"It's on Facebook," someone ventured.

"What is?"

34

"That you're gay. It's on all our walls."

"Well, we'd better find out who put it there, my private life is private, not for Facebook."

"You did, sir."

"What?"

"It says you did, sir. There's a picture of you. Look!" Again, there was sniggering as other pupils produced their phones and held up the picture, a very private picture of himself and Andrew, not pornographic, just a selfie of them at home, happy, a private picture. He was very rigorous with his privacy settings. This was not a profile picture.

"Snail mail, Paul, snail mail, you should try it some time," the Head commented after he apologised for the picture and gave up trying to explain how it might have happened.

*

He liked the Year 7s. They were both easy to scare and easy to please.

"Settle down, settle down, remember the rules of this room. No one switches on until we are seated and tidied. Bags under the table, phones off and in bags! Everybody ready? Good, okay start up, but don't open anything until I say. Turn and face the smartboard when you're ready."

He was not prepared for the screaming, the tears, or the terrible, terrible image. On every screen around the room, on the smartboard above, was the grizzled, hanging form of the half decayed Mr Evans, a slideshow of gore for 7E. He panicked. He forgot how to switch anything off, he was transfixed by the images, appalled and fascinated, unable to move until Sophie Linnet fainted.

*

"The machines are not networked, the internet is switched off, the only way that could have happened is if someone got in and went round every computer and applied that screensaver."

"Or you did it." Site management was defensive.

"Well, we can review the tapes," suggested the Head.

"No we can't. Camera's broke. I just checked."

35

"Oh, you are kidding!" Paul was exasperated. "Doesn't that tell you anything?"

"It is suspicious, I agree, but you are in the frame, Paul. If not in my mind then, in the class of Year 7 and their parents."

"Great!"

*

The smell was oppressive. It covered him as he set up the camera, connected the router, tested it, switched it on, left the classroom spic and span, locked up, took the key and went home to watch his dedicated L204 channel.

Nothing happened. He poured another glass of wine. He sat down, tore off a piece of pizza and drank some more. The lights went on.

"I knew it! I bloody knew it! Someone on a campaign, a relative, some kid, some friend of Peters...or the Head?" He dismissed the idea...the wine. "Where are you though? The lights are on but nobody's home." The camera scoured the room but it didn't cover everywhere. He crept closer to the TV looking for hints of movement: papers moving, lights on the computers, screens coming on. He got right up close to the screen, investigating each inch.

Suddenly 42 inches high in his face was a face! Angry! He screamed and leapt back, spilling his drink, scattering his pizza. He looked again, nothing there. "Oh, that's just a joke! That's just one of those stupid internet frighteners. Oh, we can do better than that, surely."

He looked again, this time the figure was evident in the classroom, an adult, not a student, someone wearing a suit. He was switching on a computer, the one by the printer, the one near the smell. Paul grabbed his coat, the car keys and, unwisely, took one more swig of wine. He raged as he drove. He crashed open the door, the alarm screamed, secrecy and stealth seemed irrelevant, the idiot knew he was watching. Surely he would either wait for a confrontation or scarper. He reached the classroom, the lights were off again. He struggled with the keys and, as he did so, a slight sense of uneasy recognition entered his soul that face, the face on the screen, wasn't that...? The key turned in the door he hesitated. Was this wise? Probably not. He switched on the lights. Nothing. No one. "Bugger!"

The classroom was as it always was, cold, smelly, normal. Never mind! He had the evidence, evidence on the computer. He felt cold and suddenly stupid. Had he been duped? He turned to leave but the computer by the printer kicked into life. A remote switch on? The screen lit up and tempted him closer, it was typing, repeating text. The printer whined. The words grew bigger on the screen, animated like a tag cloud, two words, two words he knew. He peered closer, the words danced, demanding, the printer started to print. That face again! Sudden, filling the screen, angry malevolent as never before. This had gone too far, it wasn't just a bad joke. It was some form of stalker. A stalker who looked like the decayed vision of...Whatever, time to end it! Time to switch off the computer and report it all to the police.

He reached out to the PC to shut it down...but...it was live. He touched it and it shunted him full of volts. He contorted into a helpless, silent scream. The printer printed. The paper spat out and floated to the still twitching body...

And on the paper...

In capitals...

'DON'T TEACH!'

Andrew Stevenson

A Good Old-Fashioned Copper

It was going to be a tough case. I'd been working all night. No breaks. No leads. No ideas. Just a body. A body on a cold steel slab.

Maybe forensics would have something. Maybe. There are a lot of maybes in police work. I wasn't expecting much. I don't hold with forensics. They're the ones who get all the glory in those TV series instead of the good old-fashioned coppers.

I pushed open the door to the morgue with my foot and yelled at the pathologist, "What have you got for me?"

Dr Axelby picked up his skull chisel. "Male, twenty-eight years old." He pointed to the left forearm of the body. "A tiny puncture mark just here. Died at three forty-seven and nine seconds yesterday afternoon." Axelby prised off the top of the skull with a neat flick of the chisel.

"Can you tell me anything about the murderer?" I doubted he could. It's not forensics but good old-fashioned police work that gets the job done.

"I've run a few tests." Axelby put down the skull chisel and picked up a printout from his computer. I don't hold with computers but he was keen and I was willing to humour him.

"The murderer is also male. Thirty-seven years and twenty-six days old. Sagittarius. He's wearing a dark blue wool and cashmere-blend suit from Hardy Amies of 14 Savile Row, sold to him by Peter. The suit, worn over white boxer shorts with navy dots, is complemented by a blue tie with muted yellow stripes, red socks and black Oxford brogues by Loake. He banks with HSBC, likes progressive rock music and supports Arsenal."

"Is that all?" I was getting impatient with Axelby.

"He is at present walking in a north-easterly direction through Hyde Park. In twenty-one minutes and seventeen seconds, he will enter the kitchenware department in the basement of John Lewis at 278-306 Oxford Street. Here he will buy a one-and-a-half litre capacity Russell Hobbs kettle and a Morphy Richards steam iron in white with purple trim."

"What colour will the kettle be?"

"He hasn't decided yet, but I'm betting on cobalt blue."

It was conjecture but I let it pass. "Anything else?"

Axelby removed the brain from the skull and slid it carefully into a stainless steel dish.

"John Lewis is experiencing a problem with the debit cards of HSBC customers due to a fault caused by Jason in IT who was kept awake all night by noisy neighbours. The fault will delay your man for a further nine minutes and forty-three seconds. During this time, he will browse the food processors, which are located at the foot of the down escalator from the ground floor."

"To the right or to the left?"

"Six feet exactly to the right."

"We work in metric these days." I spoke softly. Axelby was new and needed encouragement.

"The distance from the escalator to the food processor stand is 1.82 metres." Axelby opened a freezer box suitable for brains, hearts and livers. "I can give you more decimal points if you need them."

I shook my head. I didn't need them. I don't hold with decimal points.

Axelby picked up the brain. "Oh," he said, "and watch out for the slippery bit by the Magimix display."

I looked Axelby in the eye. "I'm sure you're doing your best but call me as soon as you've got anything I can use."

I took the brain from him and squeezed it between my hands to test for damage. There was a compression injury he'd missed. I told him to pull his socks up. He might be new but I'd made enough allowances for one day.

I reminded Axelby that it wasn't forensics but good old-fashioned police work that would get the job done. Maybe not today. Maybe not tomorrow. Maybe not this week. Maybe not next. That's what good old-fashioned police work is. A lot of maybes.

But however long it took, I was going to get my man. If it was a man. Maybe it was a woman. Another maybe. I threw the brain back to Axelby. He nearly dropped it.

As I said, it was going to be a tough case. And with Axelby's skull chisel piercing the skin of my neck, it had just got tougher.

Los Muertos
April 2016

Rommy Collingwood

Dia de los Muertos (Day of the Dead)

It was a very small death notice considering the big love we all had for the man. Alice never did see it. Actually, when Alice came out of her coma, our beloved Rio Zamora, her best buddy and partner-in-crime, was already dead and buried. We all went to the mass at St Francis. The sky was blue and perfect, the Daylilies were gorgeous and there were bunches of Irises all over, in bloom, in vases as pretty as the stained glass. Everyone agreed it was a glorious send-off. The low-riders even did a ceremonial drive-by honking their horns all around the Plaza, before they took off to smoke some bud in honour of his passing.

It was a shame Alice didn't make it, though she still had the greatest friends alive. One sweet man gave her the best piece of advice ever about how to face the future. Jesus Martinez told her not to waste time tormenting herself asking what if. That way lay madness. Just accept it as an accident and move on. Not that it would be easy. The hardest thing would probably be seeing Rio's parents and offering condolences. But if she got down on her knees and begged forgiveness...Alice was forever grateful. Later on. First came her creeping realisation that life had changed forever. Then understanding.

Jesus and me agreed: Alice had big problems. For a start, she was broke. Of course, she was already homeless and had lost her job. But worse than all that, she had no car, and without a car in America, you're royally screwed. Ironically, she was late with her last car payment because she was unconscious in hospital. Jesus said, privately, that Alice should feel especially grateful to have retrograde amnesia so she was spared the horrors of remembering her shitty life.

Of course, gratitude for Alice came later. First off she had to learn to feel. There were weeks and weeks of feeling numb, and she couldn't say Rio's name out loud without crying. It was always 'my friend' or 'that rascal'. She couldn't recall a thing after she gave Rio a ride about 1.00 pm the day of the accident. She'd picked him up outside his cousin Tony's shop on the east side; Tony with the wall-eye. He waved them off, all smiles. 'Course, I'm not sure how Tony feels about Alice now.

Anyway, they were driving to 'Burque to a concert. Alice was beyond excited because they were going to a Tina Turner concert. She was a big star at that time. Mega. Though she's not so huge anymore. Alice never knew what happened, and all we knew was that rush hour traffic on I-40 East was snarled up for hours. 5-0 was there of course. Then the jungle drums started. Somebody said something to somebody. Possibly recognised Alice's car on TV. Whatever.

Before too long, we were all in our cars on I-25 driving south to see what was up. The community, man. Those of us that bothered held a vigil at her bedside. Jesus said he'd never forget the white walls, and the way the nurses were in their white uniforms with their built-up shoes. He reckons what saved Alice was the power of prayer, and Nuestra Senora de Guadaloupe.

Alice looked so fragile. It was in all the papers, and, some folks found out that Alice had been lying about her age! Not that that mattered much: after all, she was in a coma and in critical condition. And, boy, was she pitiful those first few days! It was clear she'd been behind the wheel, but, because Alice had no memory of the crash, Jesus very kindly reminded her what happened. He kept all the articles for her to read, which, personally, I thought was in poor taste; but I suppose it was the biggest news in that *maricon's* life since he got busted for smack and went to county. All of Alice's real friends, some of whom were Rio's friends as well, prayed over her and waited to see if she had sustained brain damage and become a vegetable. And some of them, you know who you are, stayed on to catch a glimpse of her lush naked body. Some people don't know when to stop.

Later on, in recovery, Alice sat in a chair with a glazed expression in her eyes, staring at all the get well cards on her tray table, probably wondering what happened. It wasn't all about her -

somebody died is what happened. I lost my best buddy, a brother from another mother. All Alice got was some kind of chipped tooth. Her doctor came by to check on her, wearing his thousand dollar suit. We all heard him tell her, straight out, I was worried about you for a while there, girl. Your head injury was giving me some cause for concern. Alice didn't blink. Just nodded at his words. Didn't have a clue what he was talking about. She told me later she was worried about having bad breath, what with being unconscious and all and not brushing her teeth. Fact is, she was struck dumb and stayed dumb for quite some time afterwards.

Anyhow, thanks to friends like me and Jesus, dear sweet Alice discovered what went down. Apparently, *mi hermano* passed away where six lanes of traffic join up, a notorious black spot. All those crazy drivers getting in lane or changing lanes to go downtown, which is kind of nuts, now that I think of it. Even as Jesus and I were gassing, the rumour mill was working overtime. People in the barrio were saying, *Alice was loaded, probably high on Sensamilla. You know what she and Rio were like. Maybe even had a couple of margaritas.* Who knows what really went on; it's between her and the cops.

I believe I mentioned the funeral at the Cathedral? There was the service with a lovely eulogy by his *novia*, and then we crossed the road to La Fonda and drank ourselves stupid way into the evening when we ran out on the bill, just like Rio used to do. The stories we shared. We laughed and we cried. Rio meant the world to me and I can truly say that he loved me as only a good Catholic boy can love. And I know for a fact Rio was a slave to love, with all the bells and whistles. Jesus said he was proud to have known him. I'm not sure if he had carnal knowledge though. Once Rio took up with that hustler, *Raymundo*, nobody got to see him anymore, and he was pretty much lost to me. Alice barely stayed in touch. But that's the way she rolls: she's all about the dirt and the downlow.

Some might say it's a wonder Rio had any time to be himself, what with all the action that came his way. But we knew his faults. Okay, so he was a voluptuary. So what? The Jesuits had a big say in his life. And I think it's fair to say that the glamour of the church left an indelible impression on his ass. After countless communions, with all the smells and bells, Rio always figured that divinity could be found in the carnal as well as the spiritual. I'll never forget the time he told me that he'd seduced a seminarian. What can you say? All I could do was laugh at his shamelessness. It didn't matter, we all loved him anyway. We didn't care about his shoplifting or any of his shit. He always shared the wealth and brought me presents, and I know Alice still keeps the valentine he gave her. It was just his way. His mind may have been in the gutter but his head was something else.

Only Rio could tussle with the priest about mortal and venal sins. His problem was that his moral compass pointed south to his pleasure zone and he found absolution in confession. One minute his mind was in the gutter, the next he was making a wreath for Nuestra Senora de Guadalupe. The sweetest altar boy cum hustler cum felon. And the way he used to talk your money into his wallet. That was something else. Then he married a wonderful girl and had two adorable children. It was only after he got married that he came out and got into gay porn.

Yeah. It was me. I turned him out. Alice sussed it. Naturally, I was all over her, that *puta*. This was just before Rio graduated - summa cum laude, I believe - and it wasn't because he went down on the dean. I know who he was, and Alice will get over it eventually. He was one of a kind but she doesn't need me to tell her that. Her scars will last a lifetime. And serves her right. We'll see you.

Jan Petrie

Half a Chance

It's quite a shock when she sees him through the glass. Her legs weaken and she has to clasp at the doorframe for support. For some reason he's looking over his shoulder, back towards the gate.

But then he turns.

Now that she's staring into his face, the differences are clearer. His brow is heavier so that his eyes seem darker and his hair's much longer and way lighter - especially at the front.

She opens the door and cold air rushes in. "Hi," she says. Just that. What else is there?

He offers her the briefest of smiles, the low sun glinting off the stud in his left ear. "I was walking right past. Thought I'd, um, just call in, say hi. But, if you're working I can always…"

"Come in," she says, holding the door open a fraction more and stepping well back

He doesn't know whether he should kiss her on both cheeks in that city way she brought down here with her, but looking at her bird-brittle arms he decides against it. Instead he nods a greeting. "Really good to see you again," he says. The first lie.

Already, he's wishing he hadn't come; should have left well alone, although that's hardly the case. "You're looking, um, better."

"Really?" The word is heavy with disbelief.

Remembering her manners, she offers him a drink, "Tea, coffee, something stronger?"

"Tea would be great," he says, though he'd prefer a beer.

She gestures towards a chair. Is disconcerted when he follows her on through into her cramped kitchen.

When she reaches for two mugs from the shelf, her top rides up to reveal her scrawny midriff. He looks away. "Thought I'd come to say goodbye," he says. "You know, before I go."

47

"Ah yes, I heard you were off abroad again. New Zealand someone said."

"Well, I got a job offer and I figured - you know, why not? I mean, there's nothing for me here. Not now." He shrugs. "You only live once, eh?"

She seemed to flinch at that last part and now he wishes he'd expressed himself with greater care.

Busying herself, she remembers to drop two bags, not one, into the pot. Impatient for the kettle to boil, she spills the milk. Her fingers burn against the china as she carries their drinks through into the other room - into a space that will enable her to increase the distance between them.

He sits down, then worries he may have chosen the wrong chair. To fill the next silence, he asks: "How's the painting going?"

"Okay. Got a new show starting next week. I'm just sorting through what to take."

Forcing herself to look directly at him, she registers each small discrepancy. His way of sitting, his whole physicality is different, and yet, if she half-closes her eyes, it could be like before, with him sitting beside her once again.

The idea develops while she's sipping at her too-hot tea. "Could you help me move some of the bigger canvases?" she asks, already despising herself for playing this weak woman card. She won't think it through too much though. Let what happens, happen. Isn't that what her therapist keeps advising her to do?

Of course he agrees. How could he refuse?

He likes it in her studio, likes the smell of the paint and that. It reminds him of something or somewhere though he's not sure what.

She lets him find it for himself almost at the back of the stack she'd pointed to. The ones she's no intention of exhibiting though he won't realise that.

"Oh, good God," he recoils. "It's Mark," he says; words inadequate for the shock he feels looking at his brother's remarkable likeness. To cover his emotions, he states the obvious, "I didn't know you painted portraits."

"I don't normally. This isn't...wasn't...normal."

"You've not finished it."

"No. I didn't have time to, you know, before…" She shakes her head, doesn't need to say more. Not to him.

"You know," he says, and it's the only time he's admitted this to anyone. "Since it happened, all the time, I feel like half of me is missing - like some vital part's been amputated."

"I understand." She touches him then for the first time, just his hand. "Like you're walking around half rubbed-out."

He looks again at her work - at the way Mark is staring right back at him. His face so animated, and yet with his neck and torso reduced to charcoal outlines still waiting to be fleshed out.

A deep breath. "Would you sit for me before you leave?" she asks. "You know, so I can finally finish it."

Struggling to hide his shock, he says, "Yeah, okay," before he can regret it. Such a strange, inappropriate request but how can he refuse her? "If there's time before I go."

"I can fit in with you, once my private view's over with." For politeness she adds, "You're welcome to come to that, if you'd like, if you're free next Friday evening."

"Maybe I'll pop by," he says, with no intention of turning up to look at an array of her twitchy artworks.

Soon he begins the retreat. "I'd better be going." At the front door he pauses like a guilty lover. "I'll ring you."

They're both surprised when he does just that. Now back from seeing old friends in the north, he even repeats his willingness to pose. Out of loyalty to his brother, he should spare her half a day. No harm in only sitting, is there?

This time there's a heady smell to her studio - the stench of turpentine overpowering the trapped air.

She puts on a paint-splattered overall then pours him a glass of red wine. "To relax you a bit," she says, standing at a professional distance. "Helps the pose look more natural."

He thinks it would be churlish to complain about how rough the wine tastes. She's right - this whole thing's making him tense. Especially having to strip to the waist as Mark had done.

There's a small couch wedged in one corner positioned near the window. "Sit there." A pause before she adds, "If you wouldn't mind."

Though he hasn't drunk that much, she tops up his glass before turning to busy herself with the paints - preparing her palette.

The wine is already beginning to loosen him up. Now he doesn't mind so much her appraising gaze; the way she's taking in every inch of his torso like he's a specimen under glass.

He's becoming light headed - so unconcerned he thinks he might actually be falling asleep.

In his dream, she leaves the room and then, after a short while, she's back. This time naked from the waist down. Odd, that combination of her being dressed and undressed. Like he is, but in reverse. Odd too, that he's never, for one second, thought of her like this dominatrix now taking charge of him, not letting him touch her, while she uses his body to extract every last drop of painful pleasure.

When he wakes properly, she's no longer in the room. It's almost dark. He's slumped across the small couch, his whole body sore and aching. Heavy headed, he looks at the portrait of his brother on the easel and sees that it's no further forward.

He finds her standing in the kitchen, looking out at the gathering night.

"You fell asleep," she tells him. "I couldn't finish the painting after all. P'haps it's just as well." His fringe is sticking up in a way that makes him so like his twin she has to glance away.

"I'm really sorry." He's still struggling to rid himself of her dream image.

"Don't know why that happened. It must have been the wine; all that travelling yesterday."

"That's okay," she assures him, still averting her gaze. "It was probably a really bad idea in the first place."

She seems calm enough, betrays no disappointment. "Would you like some tea or something before you...?"

"No. No, thanks. I think I'm okay." His watch is showing him all the time this has cost him. Perhaps the long walk home will clear his head. "I should get going. Things to do and all that."

They part at the door. "Will you be alright?" he asks her. "I mean, I know Mark would want you to get better; to feel whole again."

"Thanks," she says. "He'd say the same to you. I really hope you find everything you're looking for in New Zealand."

He's already outside, zipping his jacket against the cold. She touches his arm, detains him for one final minute. "Grief can make you crazy, but I think I'm over the worst," she tells him. "Maybe, you know, with luck, we can both start a new life."

Jane Gordon-Cumming

Settling In

When Sarah met Gwilym, she realised he was everything she'd been looking for. He had long, slightly greying hair tied back in a ponytail, and sensitive, earnest eyes, and it was clear he Believed in Things. Precisely what, she wasn't sure. Druids or World Peace or free range poultry. Plenty to be going on with, anyway. Although he had a job, teaching at the local FE College (woodwork and ceramics), she got the impression he was a man of independent means. He lived alone in what was obviously a large house, in the countryside near Horsley, with enough land for some kind of small-holding, which he ran on ethically principled lines. Gwilym was exactly what she'd had in mind.

Sarah had recently moved to the area, as one does, with *Escape to the Country* visions of herself in a picturesque old farmhouse, surrounded by a productive vegetable garden and a selection of attractive livestock. Unfortunately the tiny cottage perched on a cliff-face, which was all she could afford, had a garden so steep that any livestock one put into it would fall straight off, and nutritious, organically grown produce meant a trip to Waitrose. But Sarah was a woman who preferred to change unfortunate circumstances, rather than bow to them. She might not be rich, or particularly beautiful, or blessed with some outstanding talent to bring her fame, but Sarah did have a talent nevertheless, and one arguably more useful than playing the violin. Just as a potter moulds clay or a mason shapes stone, the material she worked with was people. She knew the medium, and how to use it to create the effect she wanted.

Keen to fit into her new community, Sarah had done all the right things. She'd joined a Sustainable Choir, Empowering Women Pilates and a Mindful Weaving Workshop, and on Saturdays she went and cut things down on a rather bleak common with a group of rather bleak people, which is where she met Gwilym. The more she saw of him, the more convinced she was that Gwilym was The One. His rugged, not unattractive face suggested a man who had Seen Life, and there was a touch of intriguing aloofness which placed him a little apart, and higher. With the mesmerising gaze of an Ancient Mariner, and an intense, low-toned voice which made everything he said sound weighty and significant, even "pass the shears", he came over as someone who had the answers. This, one felt, was a man who *knew*.

She began with a little modest worshipping. While they were making homes for butterflies, she encouraged him to talk, and nodded at everything he said. Sometimes she'd repeat it back at him in a slightly different form, as if making a new point of her own. The first week, he said what an interesting woman she was. On the second, he invited her back for coffee.

Gwilym's house was just what she would have chosen, a somewhat dilapidated Victorian mansion, discreetly placed at the end of a long farm track. He kept goats for their milk, ducks for their eggs and a small flock of Jacob's Sheep, and on the excuse of finding the loo, she counted seven potential bedrooms. It was absolutely perfect for what Sarah had in mind - a nice little, well-run cult.

She didn't feel the need to share her plans with Gwilym. No point in making the man self-conscious, and someone of his integrity might have had objections to raise. Better for such things to appear to arise naturally.

The next step was to let people know that Gwilym was there. She made her selection carefully. Veronica and Lilian from her choir, the intense young man who served her at the green greengrocer's, and drew them out. Having learned their particular concerns - body image, toxic rays from Wi-Fi, the European Union - she proceeded to convince them that Gwilym's views coincided with their own.

"Well, of course, Gwilym says women look sexier with a bit of weight on."

"Gwilym thinks we'd be better off staying in/coming out."

53

"You haven't met Gwilym? Oh, you should!"

Having acquired a solid band of interested lost souls, it was time to exhibit their leader to his potential flock. "You should give a talk, Gwilym," she suggested. "Such an interesting subject!" What had he been talking about? She hadn't been listening, but it didn't matter. "People would love to hear your views. Where? Oh, right here, in your house. It's such a lovely setting. I can make a few refreshments."

She made what she called a fruit punch, and added a good slug of Cointreau. It was a bit naughty, because most of them were driving, but it had the desired effect. They listened in a contented haze, unable to recall afterwards exactly what Gwilym had said, but knowing it was wise and inspiring.

Word spread, and he was easily persuaded to turn it into a series. Space was limited in Gwilym's front room, but she didn't make the mistake of suggesting they hire somewhere larger. Instead, places had to be fought for. A small non-refundable booking fee would reserve one. It was necessary to sign up for the whole course, and one was advised to do so early. Sarah took care of all the administration. She also devised suitably versatile topics: Self-Discovery Through Creativity and Natural Riches of our Countryside, enabling Gwilym to talk about virtually anything he felt like, and maintain his wide appeal.

She left it to Veronica to suggest making the courses residential. Far better to have this, the crowning stage of a carefully constructed plan, appear to have come unbidden from somebody else's head. "Such a pity," she said to Veronica, "that Gwilym can't show us exactly how he means life to be led, in a practical way, just as he leads it here. I know he would have so much more to teach one than can possibly be learned in a day."

And when Gwilym came back to her with Veronica's suggestion that he might run a residential course, she appeared to consider it carefully. "Well yes, it should be feasible, if you ask people to share rooms, and take a turn with the cooking, as well as contribute a bit to your expenses."

Sarah worked Gwilym's expenses out for him. It was surprising how much they came to, what with wear and tear on the furnishings, and potential compensation if anyone turned out to be allergic to home-grown quinoa. But nobody minded paying a bit extra for the privilege of being shown Gwilym's method of preparing gluten-free chicken pellets, or learning the songs he sang to the bees. The first course was such a success, they had to run another, and then one almost every week. Soon, for the core of regular, loyal participants, it wasn't worth going home. Sarah closed up the little cottage on the cliff-face, and moved into Gwilym's best spare bedroom. As Principal Pathfinder, she wasn't expected to share.

One morning in late summer, resting on Gwilym's rather comfortable sofa, listening to his followers toiling away happily outdoors and in, Sarah looked round and realised she had everything she wanted: a home in a nice old house, with nothing to do but wait for the next delicious home-grown, home-cooked meal (the Principal Pathfinder wasn't expected to cook), and a little money in the bank (the Principal Pathfinder was paid a small honorarium). She also realised she was bored. It was time to move on.

When she broke the news to Gwilym, he surprised her - she who was never caught out by the unexpected. He asked her to marry him. Sarah contemplated for a moment a future married to Gwilym. Pretending to believe all that hippy dippy nature-is-wonderful crap? Wearing scarves round her hair, and eating nut roast instead of a decent steak? Every day, for the rest of her life? She didn't think so!

She thanked him politely, and said something about different paths and needing to explore her own karma, and packed her bags. Onward and upward. Her talent for directing people - one hardly liked to call it manipulating - sought a new outlet, and Sarah fancied it might lie in the art world. If ever something relied on the perception of the beholder, it was Modern Art. Easy enough to throw some paint together, and Sarah was so good at directing perceptions.

Rick Vick

The Execution

As I was walking homewards from the Tower, I looked back and saw the ravens, aerial sentries gliding in a descending gyre, loudly celebrating their anticipation of eyes and coils of innards.

It had been a splendid spectacle – all three of them Papists, who had, we were told by the Lord High Chamberlain, confessed to a plot to overthrow the Queen. "Under torture, thumbscrews, rack and fire," I heard murmured amongst the mob gathered by the river. An old fisher woman, I deduced by the reek wafting from her, told, in a delighted screech, that their screams could be heard beyond the tower walls.

The man, a tall fellow, led out first onto the scaffold, newly strewn with straw to soak up the blood that would soon flow, was dressed in a dark red ermine cloak. He held his head high though his hands, bound before him, were bloodily mangled. His wife, in a torn white gown, was weeping piteously, blood running down her legs. She had, I suppose been a fetching woman, but now her face was blotched and tears ran in bloody rivulets down her ravaged face. High born both, from the north, my neighbour told me, de Mont something or other. Her guilt, once displayed to the baying mob, she was taken back within. As a woman, it being deemed inappropriate to expose her nakedness, she was spared noose and knife, and would, in the hungry embrace of the flames at the stake, meet her maker.

Their son, a mere boy of 15 or 16, came last on his knees, dragged like a whipped cur by the gaoler. He wailed over and over in a shrill voice. "I'm innocent. Innocent." The crowd, momentarily hushed by the sight of the broken lad, began booing and the fisherwoman bawled out. "Do for him and make it slow." Heartless crone.

It was a muggy afternoon, black bulging bladders of clouds hung portentously. The tide was low and a host of gulls screamed and squabbled on the stinking mud.

The boy - last out, first in - the noose about his neck was hauled up to dangle him, his feet kicking, a few inches above the boards. The executioner, Dan Drury it was, much loved by the rabble for his showmanship and adroit skill with the disembowelling knife, had the lad split from neck to crutch in a trice, coils of innards spilling out. With one deft slice, Drury severed the boy's genitals holding them up above his head to a roar of approval. What a sight it was, and the boy's cries, I swear, reached way beyond the range of the human voice. I saw a giggle of children, playing a game of peek-a-boo, covering their eyes and ears then uncovering them screaming delightedly.

I wonder sometimes about human desires. Sex I understand, mostly; that compulsion that leads one again and again to seek out the erotic mystery of the woman, which is not to say that it necessarily requires that complicity with one's wife. I have had many most satisfactory humpings with whores. But this spectacle, witnessing of the extremes of human suffering, is edifying. All the senses provoked to such extremes I feel a sense of giddy elation. The smells, the expectant rapt expressions on the faces of the mob and their cries and hoots, here by the river flowing in and flowing out. The sounds: the groans of the man, the screams of the boy mingling with the sky high kaws of the ravens, combine to encapsulate the extremes of human experience.

The father was next. He had held out his bloody hands to his wife when she was dragged away to the stake. The expression on his face was piteous. What could be worse than this, I wondered, knowing with grim satisfaction that we were yet to witness such humiliation and agony that would fill us all with dread and exultation, that it was not one of us about to be so dexterously dismembered.

We were not disappointed. With cool precision Mr Drury brought the man, like his son before him, to within a whisper of suffocation; the knotted rope tight about his neck, his eyes starting from his head, as he was sliced and adroitly divided - like one would a roasted chicken, the limbs from the torso. As they were both drawn higher on the gibbet it amazed me how they still hung onto life. The boy was past screaming, his face was all rounds, eyes, mouth as if he had reached some pinnacle of pain that no sound could possibly give cry to, 'though I wondered if there was yet sufficient air in his body to give vent. There they hung dangling, slowly strangling, swinging in the fetid breeze from the river.

I had a fierce appetite and decided to stop at my favourite pie shop. When I next glanced back again at the scene, the ravens had descended and were at their squabbling business pecking vigorously at the corpses; so I presumed them now to be. One atop each head, two cowl black birds stabbed at the eyes, and others on the shoulders bobbing and crying as they dipped their heads into the bloody cavities.

Accompanied by a jug of rich ruby claret, I wondered, as I savoured the succulent beef pie, which of the entertainments on offer in the city I most enjoyed; theatre or execution? I could not decide. There would be no public killings for a while so it would next have to be the theatre. There was a new play at The Globe I'd heard by the up-and-coming penman, William something. Macbeth, I had heard, by title. A bloodthirsty yarn by all accounts. That was something to look forward to.

I decided I would to The Globe next day, via the tower, to see how much remained of them.

Ali Bacon

Silver Harvest

It's Sunday, and the other women are readying their bairns for the kirk, but I am drawn to the shore. On my way across the market square, a fractured sun picks out the scattering of fish-scales in the cobbles, bright as new bawbees. On the rough beach I look up the firth to the open sea but there will be no boats home today. They have gone north and will lay up at anchor, praying for a good catch and a safe return.

A gannet with a scrawny neck bobs and dives as the waves creep up the shingle and nibble at the turf. The tide at least is predictable, unlike the herring or the money coming in. But when the church bell calls me back I take my place in the pew and give thanks for what we have.

After the kirk, I take a chair to the foot of our outside stairs where the street is set off by gatherings of lace-capped girls checking sails or mending nets, talking amongst themselves while their hands are busy. Jeannie Crawford waves and comes to sit by me.

"Where's Susan?" she says.

"The sun gives her a headache."

Susan is my mother-in-law. Neither of us is sorry for her absence. Jeannie's laddies, three of them, will be down at the shore, skimming stones and plowtering in the boats laid up for repair. Bairns slip from her as easily as herring from a creel. But no matter how often Willie plants his seed, my womb fails to quicken.

Jeannie looks up. "We have a visitor."

Down here we are well-known for our steadfast ways and the good order of our homes. The figure who's approaching might be a councillor, or a writer who'll set down in some magazine what he thinks is the secret of our sobriety. But it's no secret that cleaning

59

fish and carrying them two miles up to Edinburgh leaves no time or energy for loose-living.

Jeannie gets up. "I'd better see what the boys are up to."

As she leaves, the stranger lifts his hat to her. He has a worldly air, but not a haughty one. I concentrate on the sailcloth. Let him speak first if he must. But after a minute he is still there, no closer, no farther off, as if there is something particular about the space between us.

I look up and he comes forward. "I'm sorry to have disturbed you."

Although the sun is over his shoulder, I can see he is in his middle years and handsome. "We are often disturbed of a Sunday."

"Would you rather I left you in peace?"

Peace is all very fine. Sometimes company is better. "Did you want to ask me something?"

He holds out his hand. It's smooth and warm on mine. "David Octavius Hill. The artist," he adds, as if this is something I should have known.

I introduce myself. "Mrs Johnstone Hall."

He nods, as if two names apiece put us on an equal footing.

"I'm planning a series of studies of the fisher folk. I wonder if you would sit for a portrait?"

He wants to paint me. My hands ache to straighten my cap and feel for any hair coming loose. But I stay still and keep my eyes on my needle, although it has come to the end of its stitching.

He lifts his coat and sits on the bottom step. Glancing back at the way he has come, past the other women, I wonder if I am the first he has asked.

Then Mr Hill draws a sheet of paper from his pocket and shows me a painting, or maybe a drawing, I can't tell, of a man who might have looked in a glass and had the colour sucked from his cheeks. I don't know what to make of it, but I would know him again, this man with sullen features and a heavy brow.

"You don't like it?"

I hear disappointment in his voice. "How is it made?"

"By the light of the sun."

This is too glib. If it's such an easy thing these pictures would be everywhere. "What else does it need?"

He frowns and thinks for a minute. "Silver," he says. "The light reacts with silver salts."

The picture is a mottled brown with no trace of silver in it. But the likeness, I agree, is very good.

*

"What do you think?" I ask Willie when he comes home. "Would you mind if I sat for a picture?"

He is looking at me across the table, flattered that he and the artist have made the same choice. "You are the best of them, Lizzie. You always were. Besides, they say these pictures only take a minute."

I hide my disappointment by getting up to clean the range.

Susan makes no comment. This morning she asked me if Willie and I were still trying for a bairn but I didn't answer her. What we do under the blanket is our business.

Mr Hill comes again on a weekday afternoon. He has a younger man with him and together they push a cart from which the artist takes a good padded chair. He invites me to sit in it and walks around me at a distance. His assistant sets up his apparatus, a box with a glass eye.

Where Mr Hill has placed the chair I am squinting into the sun.

"Excuse me," he says, and, coming closer, tilts my chin away from the light. His hand on my face is a shock. I can smell the hot felt of his suit and something of lemons in his hair. "Keep your eyes cast down," he says. "We can afford a shadow or two. Just stay as still as you can."

News has travelled up the street and a small crowd has gathered. When a message boy comes whistling up from the harbour somebody says 'wheesht' and an arm is flung out to hold him back. Just as I think I am turned to stone, the young man makes a flourish and says, "We're done!"

Mr Hill gives me his hand to raise me from my seat and the crowd claps, even though there is nothing to see.

*

He doesn't come back, but one day I put on my Sunday clothes and walk up to Calton Hill where he has his business. No one answers the front door, but through a garden gate I see a single-storey outhouse. As I draw nearer men's voices can be heard in a friendly argument, disagreement giving way to laughter.

I shouldn't have come here, certainly not alone. But before I can turn back, the door of the outhouse opens and he is standing there, covering his surprise with a smile and an outstretched hand.

"Mrs Hall. What brings you...?"

"I'm sorry. You're busy."

He opens the gate and invites me in. "Would you like to see what we made of you?" He turns and calls, "Robert! We have a visitor!"

Inside, the assistant is flitting about in the darkness, one of many shadows in the room. Tacked to the wall there are dozens of pictures, men, women and bairns. I recognise the beach and the great buildings of Princes Street.

"Look," the artist points to a high corner of the wall where I see myself looking down. "What do you think?"

My face is not how I have seen it, even in a glass. Is this the woman I have been or the one I will become?

He answers my silence by opening a chest and taking out an armful of pictures which he lays down awkwardly so they slew across the table. They are all of me, the same picture, many times over, in shades of grey, brown or violet, some misty, some sharply drawn.

"It took us a while to get it right." He nods to the one on the wall, "But this is the best. We'll copy it exactly."

My picture will be in an exhibition, he says, on Princes Street, and after that in a book, many books. He picks one from the pile and offers it to me. "For your family."

*

I carry my portrait home but keep it hidden until I can show it to Willie, who lays it on the chest of drawers.

"It's a good likeness," he says, and closes the bedroom door.

As he takes me in his arms, I close my eyes and see the all the pictures, calotypes he called them, shifting in the gloaming like a shoal of herring.

Something is loosened inside me.
A rising tide. A silver harvest.

'Silver Harvest' is chapter eight of 'In the Blink of an Eye' - a novel in ten voices by Ali Bacon, published by Linen Press in 2018.

Sarah Hitchcock

New Glasses

"Ta Da!"

"Oh my God! Maisy!"

"Maz."

"Maisy, what've you done?"

I shake my head to feel the short curls bounce around my ears, trying to recapture the elation I felt walking home.

"Had my hair cut," I say. Inside I'm fighting the urge to punch her.

"All those beautiful golden curls – your crowning glory – how could you?"

"It was ginger frizz, Mum."

"And what are those? I preferred your old glasses; those make you look..."

"Trendy. I'm starting my new job Monday and want to look…"

"Trendy!"

Mum snorts and turns on the telly. I stare at the back of her head. Why does she always do this?

"Make us a cuppa, love, my favourite show's starting."

Make your own, you lazy cow. "Yes, mum."

On the way to the kitchen I look in the hall mirror. I look bloody brilliant and somehow that makes me really angry. I want to run to my room and slam the door – bugger her tea! But that would be childish, and anyway *I* want a cuppa.

There's a burst of applause from the telly, *"On today's show we'll be meeting Charlene whose fiancé slept with all six bridesmaids on the night before their wedding. He's now the father of twins by the maid of honour and he expects them all to live as one big happy family."*

God! Why does she watch that crap? And she hasn't bothered to get dressed. She just slobs around in that bloody onesie watching

64

shit daytime telly. I can't wait to get out. This job with the insurance firm is my ticket to freedom; my chance to really be me – a new me – the me I want to be – different and exciting me! Stumping back to the lounge, I slop tea on the hall carpet. So what? I don't care – it's a shit carpet – I'll mop it up in a minute. I push open the lounge door and drop the tea!

"Maisy..."

"Maz."

"You clumsy idiot, get a cloth!"

I can't move. I'm transfixed! Mum pushes past, grumbling all the way to the kitchen. I can't tear my eyes from the telly. Can't believe what I'm seeing! Mum pushes me out of the way again and dumps a pile of tea towels on the floor. She stamps on them to soak up the tea. I sit on the coffee table and lean forward to stare at the show's presenter.

"What the hell? Is this the Halloween special? Why's he got tusks?"

Mum slumps on the sofa, leaving the tea towels in a soggy brown heap. She pokes me in the back with her toe to get me to shift.

"What're you on about? He's no different to normal. Maybe a bit more orange, and he's had his teeth whitened."

"Are you kidding me? He's bloody green!"

"Language, Maisy!"

"Maz! Look at him. He's green with tusks and hairy warts! He's a flippin' ogre."

"Oh for pity's sake, give it a rest! I know you don't like this show, but there's no need to spoil it for *me*. He does a great service: really helps people."

I look at her in disbelief but can see she believes what she's said. Back on the screen the audience is screaming and the couple have started fighting. They're being pulled apart by huge men in black tee shirts – except they're not men! Trolls! Bloody trolls and ogres! The host grins and gulps, his fat neck shudders and balloons.

"He's feeding off their emotions! Can't you see?"

"Stop it! Just stop it! You always spoil it. Go away! Go on, get out! Miss High-and-bloody-mighty-I'm-better-than-everyone-else,

65

take your new glasses and your bloody *trendy* hair and go lecture some other poor sod!"

I feel the sting of tears so pull my glasses off to rub my eyes before she can see. I point at the telly as I fumble them back on, about to argue. Oh! The host and bouncers look normal! My stomach lurches; heat whooshes up my chest into my face – I'm going to throw up."

Been on my bed since I chugged up. It's dark but I haven't turned on the light. I'm trying to convince myself I'm not going mad. If it's not me, it's Mum, which makes more sense. After groping for my new glasses, I stumble to the window. There's still a little light in the sky and the houses opposite are black against deep violet. The street lamp makes the pavement orange. A moth stutters and stoops in the artificial glow. It's a big moth. Really big! Christ Almighty, it's a bloody fairy!

I bang my head trying to get a better view and knock my glasses off. By the time I fumble them back on, the moth – or fairy – has gone. It's me then who's crazy. Bile burns my throat. Don't *think* I'm mad. Maybe it's my eyes. That's it! I pull my new glasses off and squint at them. Come to think of it, the lady who served me was pretty strange. The first thing she said was, "Don't get many of your type in here." I thought she was calling me a lesbian because of my new short hair, but maybe she meant something else. And how come I was able to walk out with new glasses? It usually takes weeks. I look at the glasses. I do like them! I put them on and see my dim reflection in the dressing table mirror. Wow, I look good. What was it I was just worrying about?

"Maisy!"

"Maz," I say under my breath.

There's a tentative knock and the door opens before I can say come in or go away. Mum snaps on the light and puts a mug of tea on the bedside table.

"There you go, love, you've been up here ages. I've brought you some Custard Creams too. Oh, and I found this photo. It's me and your Aunty Sharon. Thought it might make you laugh. That's Margate seafront a week before you were born. Was s'posed to be there with your father, but he ran off the Wednesday before. Went with Sharon instead, seeing as I'd already paid for the B&B. Anyway, thought it would cheer you up."

Mum slips the photo under the biscuits. It's her way of making everything alright again between us. Half way down the stairs she calls back, "I'm doing Hawaiian pizza and garlic bread for tea – that ok?"

"Lovely," I call back.

She won't put the pizza in. I'll have to do it. Picking up the photo, I brush off the crumbs. Mum and her sister look so young! They're wearing flowery dresses and mum's belly is enormous. They're grinning but it looks forced. My eyes fill up. I scrunch them shut. When I look again my heart stops: there's a man with his arms round Mum, one hand on her belly; on me! It has to be Dad. He's just the way Mum always describes him; a young David Essex, with the gold hoop ear-ring and… pointed ears? That can't be right! The Polaroid slips out of my fingers and spins away. I take my glasses off and jam my fists into my eyes. When my insides stop doing weird things I crawl under the bed to get the photo.

He'll be gone when I look again, of course he will. He wasn't there in the first place. None of the things have been there. I'm just anxious because of the new job. I look at the photo. Shit! He's still there, and now he's winking. I chuck the photo across the room followed by my new glasses. The damn things smash into the wall but aren't even scratched by the impact. Got to get rid of them! Stamping on them hurts my foot. Shit, will have to hide them then. In the wardrobe is a box bought to conceal love letters that I never got. I put the picture in with the glasses, lock it and jam it behind the dressing table, then drop the key through a gap in the floorboards. It's where I shove things I need to forget about. There's a diamond ring down there I pinched from Gran's jewellery box and a school report that said I had great potential and should be thinking of university. Done! I can breathe again. I find my old glasses and stare at my reflection. Won't take long to grow my hair out too.

"Maisy, our favourite programme's starting. If you don't hurry you'll miss the first murder. Maisy?"

"Yes, Mum, I'm coming."

Under the floorboards, in a thick layer of dust and cobwebs, there's a diamond ring and a shredded report card. Behind the dressing table, there's an empty box. Downstairs the telly blares and the smell of garlic pervades the house. Outside fairies dance unobserved.

Melanie Golding

A Small Change

Ben is walking from one end of the bus shelter to the other, the fingers on his left hand twirling, fanning open and shut, open and shut over and over by the side of his face. The sound he is making is all vowels, ah-oh-ah-oh. Every fourth step, he taps the knuckles of his right hand twice against his forehead. People are staring, of course they are.

It's just started raining, and the persistent April wind is whipping it up into our faces. The shelter is failing to live up to its name. There's no shelter here, and no proper seat. My hip is starting to hurt now, as it does these days when I stand too long. I try leaning on the narrow tilted shelf they've put in but it makes the ache worse somehow. The danger with providing a shelter, you see, is that those who need shelter will take shelter there. The homeless, the destitute, refugees. Other undesirables, including Autistic boys for whom the rain and wind feel intrusive and violent as an assault.

"Come sit with Granny," I say to Ben. He keeps going round the little circuit he's made, never breaching the edge of the shelter. They call it 'stimming'. Repetitive actions that soothe in times of anxiety. He can't help it. Most people are understanding, but you do get the starers. And the frowners. I have a special smile for them, but actually I would like to give them a slap. Of course, I never would.

The weather had been fine when we set off from the house. Saturday morning, we always go to town together, usually in my little red Ford. Ben had started stimming as we walked past the familiar parked car and on down the road.

"We're getting the bus, today, Ben. You know, the bus?"

He loves buses. He's got a whole box of them at home. He lines them up against the skirting in order of size, for hours. It's hard to stop him, once he's started, so you have to think about the timing. Don't get the buses out when it's nearly time to eat, for instance. When it's all finished and perfectly aligned he'll move onto something else, but he won't have forgotten them. I know now not to try to tidy those buses away until he's gone to bed. Once I swept them back up into the box during lunch; wasn't thinking. The sound of him banging his head and screaming, and not knowing what was wrong, well. We learn the hard way, me and his mum, which things set him off. Then, we avoid those things, which is only sensible. Or so we thought.

Stefanie, my daughter, told me that the psychologist said we have to start trying to challenge the limits for Ben. I don't like the idea - I just want him to be happy. But his world is shrinking. The number of foods he'll eat is already limited, and he won't eat carrots any more. The only veg he'll touch now is broccoli, and you have to cook it just so. The sounds he will not tolerate are numerous, and the list is growing. But it's heartbreaking, watching him worry. And unbearable, seeing what Stef has to go through every day from the second he's up to the second he's wrestled, struggling, into bed. He sleeps a lot less than a neurotypical child - a lot less than Stef did as a girl. Everything I learned as a parent is useless. Living with Ben, I mean he's such a joy, in his own way, but it's not comparable. She can't get him to sleep until midnight some days.

That's why we have our little Saturday morning routine. Me and Ben, Granny time, bit of space for Stef to have some peace, have a bath, not worry about Ben. I know she has to help him try new things, but I also know she's clinging to sanity and the last thing she needs are extra meltdowns. Which is why I thought I'd give it a go on my time. A small change to the routine. It might be an adventure.

"Look, Benny, it's the bus," I say. He doesn't stop the pacing, but I see him tip his head towards the sound of the squeaking brakes. He starts copying the high piercing sound, almost as loud. The other people at the bus stop - a man, two women and a young girl - all turn to look at Ben. Then the young girl puts her hands over her ears and screws up her face.

I smile at the little girl and the mum, sorry, sorry. The mum smiles back at me, uncertain. And then the bus stops and Ben stops making the noise and I think, ok, it might be fine actually. He looks sideways at the bus.

"Right then, let's get on." I know not to try to hold his arm and lead him, but I make an ushering motion. He jumps on board and runs to the back seat, where he starts to rock forwards and backwards, hitting his knuckles lightly against his head and making his happy sound, oh-oh-oh, from the back of his throat.

"Two to town, please."

The driver is giving me a look I refuse to interpret as disapproval. I smile at him, a nothing-to-see-here sort of a smile.

"Is he alright?" he nods over his shoulder at Ben, whose voice has become so loud.

"Yes, thanks." I just need the tickets. My smile becomes a mind-your-own-business sort of a smile. I can't help it.

The man behind me is impatient to get inside out of the weather. "Come on," he says, irritably, and the driver takes my money. He gives me a look.

Oh-oh-oh, the noise is growing higher in volume and pitch, and Ben has started jumping up out of his seat, bouncing on the unfamiliar sprung upholstery. Bouncing is one of his favourite things. I sit next to him and take his hand and he pulls it away, his excitement almost unstoppable. I need to calm him or it may tip over into anxiety and meltdown. I stroke him gently on the back and say shhh, shhh, shhh, my Benny, shhh. He loves that sound. He starts to shhh too, and the bouncing slows, and he leans into me. Shhhh, he says, oh, oh, oh, shhhh.

He watches the rain running down the outside of the windows, the droplets slowing, then joining each other and racing in rivulets to the bottom of the glass and out of sight, mesmerising us both.

Then the bus pulls away and something about the movement must be too much because Ben is screaming, screaming, flailing his arms and running down the aisle towards the doors, falling over with the motion as the bus pulls out into traffic, banging his knee and his head on the metal of the handrail on the way down. He gets up again, scrambles away and throws himself at the closed door and screams, banging his fists on the glass. Someone's shouting, "Oi, you, stop that." But the bus won't stop. The driver is grimly concentrating on the road.

"Can you stop?" I say. "Please, just stop the bus." I go to Ben who is curled on the floor on the bottom step, wedged into the tiny space by the door and I stroke his back and go shhh, shhh, shhh, my Benny, don't worry. But Ben is still screaming into his knees, I am kneeling on the floor of the bus next to him, the shhh not working, but I'm not going to stop trying because it's all I've got.

"Off," says the driver, as if we need telling. With a hiss, the doors fling themselves open and Ben uncurls himself and jumps onto the pavement. I get up from the floor, with difficulty, people watching but no-one helping. The second my foot hits the asphalt the bus pulls away screeching.

We're not far from home, only one stop along. Right outside the Turkish Café. Bulent waves at me through the window, then he frowns and comes outside.

"Mrs Underwood, you are ok?" he says. I wipe my face on the serviette he gives me. Ben has gone inside, is sitting at his usual table in the window, lining up the cutlery.

Later we walk back to the house. Stef is in the kitchen, reading the paper in her dressing gown.

"Did you have a nice morning, love?" I say. Her tired eyes are soft with gratitude. She looks less worried, today. The kettle is leaking steam, as if it's just boiled.

"Yes, thanks, Mum. How about you?"

And I'm not good at lying, so I open the fridge to get the milk for tea so I don't have to look at her.

"Not too bad, love. Not too bad."

I hear the sound of the toy buses being tipped onto the carpet in the hallway.

Ken Popple

A Very Special Day

Mr Crumbtray loved his work. He liked to watch people's faces when he told them what he did all day. He liked the fact that he worked alone and in silence. Others in his profession liked to play music, classical particularly, or upbeat pop, perhaps a cheery local radio station to tell them about up and coming village fetes, traffic jams. It kept them in touch with the world, they said, but Mr Crumbtray had no wish to be in touch with the modern world. Anyway he liked to work in complete silence, or dead silence, as he sometimes joked to Mrs Crumbtray. It was more respectful he thought to work like this.

Today he was working on an elderly lady. She lay face up on his cold stone slab and in this way the blood would drain away from the face. If a face was too heavy with blood it would discolour and bloat, an appearance that would upset the relatives, many still raw with grief. He hated it when they made a scene. It really wasn't necessary at all and it upset him for the rest of the day. It was Mr Crumbtray's personal duty to give all his clients (or friends, as he privately referred to them) the impression of simply being asleep. Asleep and peaceful. In that way he considered himself an artist, a magician even. The things he could do with a wrecked face were really very impressive indeed.

Although Mr Crumbtray didn't approve of music whilst he worked, he did occasionally hum to himself. He hummed if he was in a particularly good mood which he was today. He was looking forward to tonight, a special night: little Tommy's birthday. There would be cake and ice cream, just the three of them. Mrs Crumbtray was preparing his favourite meal: Fray Bentos Steak and Kidney Pie with new potatoes and garden peas, ice cream and jelly for Tommy and cake for all of them. They would both be waiting for him when he arrived home, Mrs Crumbtray and little Tommy, tiny and so well behaved. It'd been such a surprise when they'd had little Tommy after all those years together, just the two of them. But oh what joy he'd brought them. What joy.

The next part of the process Mr Crumbtray found the most demanding, the most skilful. After carefully scanning the body for a clean artery he inserted the draining tube with all the respect and delicacy of a surgeon. Although his patients could not complain, he still believed precision was of the utmost here. Respect for the relatives, for his profession. He'd seen the work of others before, careless and bruising, and it made him upset and angry. Mr Crumbtray was always impressed by the amount of blood a body held. Once, in his early days, he had underestimated the amount of blood his patient contained and it had ended up overflowing the tank, the thick crimson fluid sloshing around on the floor, the air rich with its sharp metallic odour. It was not a mistake he had ever repeated. A patient could hold up to fifteen pints, but today was average, just under ten.

As it was little Tommy's birthday Mrs Crumbtray would be sure to dress him up in his favourite royal blue sailor suit. It would be a quiet peaceful party, just the three of them. Mrs Crumbtray always said that the less friends you had the less problems you had. Mr Crumbtray had once pointed out, quite gently he thought, that it should actually be the fewer friends you had, but Mrs Crumbtray had got terribly upset at this criticism. She had cried and moaned softly for a long time, and he had had to spend almost the entire evening stroking her fine grey hair to sooth and reassure her.

Once all the blood had been drained it was time to introduce the embalming fluid. Mr Crumbtray inserted a fresh tube into the open vein and turned on the embalming pump. Into the body he gently fed a mixture of formaldehyde and methanol to be distributed evenly around the patient, ensuring that the tissue would deteriorate no longer and bacteria would not live. It was at this stage of the process, whilst the machine softly hummed with its work and the veins of the patient gently pulsed with the motion of the fluid, that Mr Crumbtray always had a cup of tea and a digestive biscuit. He liked to sit on his stool and watch his preserving fluid flow around the patient, an underground chemical stream finding its way into all the corners and cavities, the flesh undulating and rippling with the motion.

Walking home from work, Mr Crumbtray felt a deep sense of calm and satisfaction. The preserving work had gone well, and the cosmetic work, often more difficult than people realised, had been successful. With older patients the eyelids would often sag back into the eyes and have to be filled out using cotton wool between the lid and the eye to round it out. The mouth also had to be set to a natural expression, to look as if the patient were simply resting. All this Mr Crumbtray did with precision and care on a daily basis.

Mr Crumbtray walked up his immaculate garden path, paused to admire a particularly magnificent specimen of rhododendron, carried on and knocked on his front door. From behind the door he heard Mrs Crumbtray's plaintive, "Who is it?" to which he replied, "Why it's me, Mr Crumbtray." The bolts were slid back and he was in the hallway holding dear Mrs Crumbtray in his arms. She was trembling slightly. She always did when he first arrived home.

"How's little Tommy?" he said.

"Fine, he's in his pram, having a little nap before his party," she replied.

"I'll go and prepare his bath," said Mr Crumbtray. "You bring him up in a few minutes."

Mr Crumbtray loved to prepare little Tommy's bath every night. He wasn't at home in the day so this evening ritual was always very special for the two of them.

Mrs Crumbtray carried little Tommy into the bathroom and handed him to her husband. Mr Crumbtray lowered him very carefully into his bath, his lovingly prepared bath of formaldehyde and methanol, smiled sadly at the tiny, wrinkled, shrivelled form of his only son and said, "Happy 21st birthday, Tommy."

Mark Rutterford

Mayfly

I need to get some new pants.

A new body too if possible, but pants are the priority. In the unlikely event that someone - anyone - should want to shag my brains out, I'd be annoyed if my pants were to talk them out of it.

The elastic used to be taut. In fact, the contents of my pants used to be taut, but it's the leg-hole elastic that's relevant today. Because I bent down to pick up a pencil that had been dropped by someone I admire, and, as I stood again to hand it back, I realised that my right testicle had slipped through the leg-hole elastic and bulged in an uncomfortable and, frankly, undignified fashion.

It's difficult to be cool and alluring with your right ball hanging out of your pants. I blushed and gurned and looked like I had colic.

It is the Mayfly season and more discomfort is on the way.

*

How long have I known you? We've been working together for weeks now and whilst serving the pinot grigios and the patatas bravas, you have grown on me - a lot.

You have a charm. At ease with yourself and easy with others, you just seem to be relaxed. I like that. You face the world with your eyes open wide, a look that signals a welcome rather than cynicism. I like that too.

You're quite tactile with me, but I could see it was with everyone, and I felt relieved in a way. I flinched at first, I know I did. I'm sorry. But I've always been conscious not to invade personal space, so I was nervous when you came into mine. I tested you a few times, by leaving my hand close to yours and picking up that pencil. Sometimes you passed the test and sometimes you failed, in patterns I could not work out and which got me in such a muddle, I forgot what was right and what was wrong.

I shiver at your touch. And look at your hand or elbow. If I'm feeling brave, I look into your eyes, but I can't do that for long, because it would tell you too much about how I feel.

You know you're fit, right? Out-of-my-league fit, but not showy about it. There is nothing as alluring as an un-conscious beauty. I don't mean unconscious as in knocked out or drugged. I mean beauty that is not aware of their devastating effect on innocent bystanders and infatuated admirers. Do I need to tell you, you're fit? Maybe I do. Maybe I will. If I make it to the summer.

You arrived in April. Lots of people pass through this kitchen and some don't last the week, so I didn't pay particular attention to your arrival. I am wary of April showers, the pull of the currents and the promise of…more. I have been caught out before. I have loosened my grip and been swept away downstream. To drown and die.

Here in the café bar, beauty is not in short supply. Take Maria, the manageress - eyes that would hypnotise a statue. Kobi, with his dreads and wispy beard - he could charm a tigress. Then Edie, "Eighty-three, dear," she says, as she orders "a Yankee", instead of an Americano - a glint in her eye as she remembers lovers from the 1940s, with a smile you can't help but fall in love with.

Anyway, I didn't notice you at first. When I did, the calendar had turned. It was May - a dangerous month when spring gets late and the longing for summer is almost unbearable. I feel foolish, reckless, desperate to fly and bugger the consequences. I should have learned from last year, and the year before that. But after each cold winter, I can't help but respond to the warmth.

In the early days of May, I did shameful things. Stupid things like:

- Look for rings
- Look for clues
- Look you up on Instagram

I start to wonder, start to imagine, start to hope!

Such slender threads justify my thoughts. But then I haven't got long in the Mayfly existence of my emotional being. I need to be as brave as potatoes and not dwell on the feint, but heady, prospect of coming into contact with your lips.

Do you think that, because I'm a bloke, I don't feel these things? How wrong you are.

But the fragile uncertainty of acknowledging this - and all that it entails - makes me want to tear out my heart and scrunch it into a ball and throw it away.

I have flown before and been giddy with the thrill of it. But it's been a long while now, and with each year I gain a bit more weight - physical and spiritual. By now, I'm heavy and the prospect of flying again seems ever more remote. I'd almost reconciled myself to my fate...until you came along. I almost hate you for it.

We started taking lunch together. In the 4 o'clock calm before evening.

It was how I got to know you and reveal some of my many flaws.

"From Napoli," you said. A city you had to leave, because your lover's father disapproved, and such disapproval could lead to a throat cut to pieces and a watery grave. I listened in horror, my mouth agape, until you reached across to push my chin closed.

"It 'appens," you said, with a wistful look I wanted to hug better.

I burbled, with a forkful of lamb circling the tagine I was eating, "It doesn't happen here, I can tell you. You'd be hard pressed to trace your father in half of England these days, never mind find one to defend your honour. It does sound romantic though, a midnight elopement with a strong man at the wheel." I dangled the thought.

"He stayed," you said.

"I'm sorry," I lied and squeezed your hand. As you didn't brush it away, I was elated. My heart sang. Not classically romantic...no. But apt.

"But I be done seen 'bout everything. When I see an elephant fly!"

All good, until my lamb fell from my fork and splashed sauce across my white shirt in dirty brown streaks.

"Dumbo!" I cried, and went on to spatter the room with random thoughts that gave far too much away.

"What an idiot. I'll have to soak it now to get it clean. I tell you, I'm a clumsy oaf. I'd steer well clear if I were you. I need to smarten up, lose a few pounds, keep my mouth shut and concentrate on what I'm doing. There's you, all Italian poise and style, and I'm a bloody elephant!"

You looked at me then and your whole face changed. My lifelong resentment of my obvious ineptitude was wiped away by the ecstasy of making you smile. You said, "Oh, your ears aren't that big, Dumbo!"

And Dumbo became my nickname. A precious thing between you and me that made me feel special. How sad is that?!

Over the next week or so, we talked and had a post-work drink or two, and I grew to like you more and more. I thought you were warming to me too, and I was sure that this year, this May, I would get to unfurl my wings again. No matter if I should die after the summer, or be eaten by a predator. To fly with you, that would be enough for me, I was sure of it.

You made an error. A miscalculation.

You left me. For two weeks, to tend to your mamma's ill health.

You know what absence makes right?

Big mistake.

Your youth, your beauty, it astounded me to such a degree that I forgot.

I forgot that I was looking through my eyes, in my head, sitting atop knackered old me.

I forgot that we are not equals and I soared on the hope that my forgetfulness inspired. The flights of fancy of my romantic imagination, they were many and vivid and real.

If I were to crash, I will almost certainly die. Die of embarrassment - for hoping such stupid hopes. Die of shame - for thinking I ever stood a chance. Me! What was I thinking? Die because my heart will have stopped, and it will have stopped because it will be a little broken.

I crashed as soon as you returned and died - of all those things, my dear Salvatore.

I'm sorry, did I not mention it was a man? No matter. I know you'd be cool with that notion and even if you aren't, you'll get over it much faster than I.

You returned with Marco. In your absence, your lover had grown some balls, and no doubt keeps them in fragrant, figure hugging Calvin Kleins. Here!

So, until the Neapolitan mob smash the doors and firebomb us out of business, I shall cling onto the rocks once again just hoping to survive another year. With a little less belief than before, that this Mayfly shall ever fly again...

The Apocalypse Alphabet
&
Other Stories
October 2016

Alex Clark

The Thief

Angela's first thought, when the yelling started, was *Don't turn around.* The sound, a wordless, growling, first-gear sort of yell, recalled her instantly to the autistic boy she'd seen in the shop last month, snagged on his parents' arms as he tried to crumple to the floor. Five people at least had stopped and stared as his mother and father grappled with him; watched, motionless, as the three of them sank to the tiles in a knot and lay there.

She had despised the watchers. She had desperately wanted to stare too – everybody would, people are people – but instead had turned and walked on to the next aisle, where she had forced herself to shop for tins of tomatoes. That was what you did. You probably couldn't help anyway, or someone else would do it better, so you pretended it wasn't happening. It was simple good manners. So now, when the angry roar blared down the length of the café, it took her only an instant to glue her eyes to the food in front of her.

Around her the crowd gave tiny, animal signs of unease. She stared down at the supermarket meal: shepherd's pie with machine-piped mashed potato, sloppily perfect in the way that only machines could be; khaki peas, crunchy-water lettuce. It was her Friday treat, to come here and have a hot lunch before doing her shop. The noise was really intolerable now, and she felt a spurt of irritation. Good manners went both ways: if you were the person making the fuss, you thanked the non-starers by putting a stop to it as soon as possible. Or at least looking embarrassed. There was no embarrassment in the yelling, and it was getting louder. It was a woman's voice, shredded by rage, and it was shouting "GET THE FUCK OFF ME, FUCK OFF GET OFF ME, UGH." The man next to her tutted and shook his head, and Angela decided that enough was enough and she would like to see what was happening now.

The café looked out over the checkout aisle, up which two men in yellow hi-vis jackets were propelling a struggling girl. She was making no effort to walk, just flailing her legs at the ground in fury as the men dragged her, doubled-over, towards the door marked 'Staff Only'. Her hair had fallen over her face and her jersey trousers had ridden down to expose half an inch of garish pink underwear, but she was beyond caring. Angela saw that nothing existed for her any more: not the shop, not the people, not the lights or the food smell, or even the ground beneath her feet. There was only the struggle. The air must have been half-crushed out of her, but still she yelled like she was fighting for her life.

"Calm...down," grunted one of the men as they passed the café. But the girl wasn't going quietly. She twisted and reached for his wrist with her teeth, and in a flash he knocked her face aside and they were through the door, the screaming fading gradually as the white plastic slab swung to and finally, softly, closed.

People shuffled and turned to each other to raise their eyebrows, in the way that British people did when a scene had been made.

"Junkies," said the man at the next table, contempt in his voice. "Terrible problem round here. Criminals. Stealing." He was excited, she could tell, turned on by the drama. He would tell and retell the story for weeks, entranced by its perfect balance of voyeurism and censure. He would probably still be telling the story in a year, when it would bore his wife and annoy his children, and when there was a good chance that the girl in the little white room, the girl who had fought like a mink for her freedom, would be lying dead in the ground.

Wendy would have been fifty next week. Angela realised suddenly, for the first time, that something like this must have happened to her. She was never prosecuted – she was too young – but there had been shoplifting. There had to be money for what she did, an astounding amount. She had stolen first from her friends, then from the till at work, then from shops, and then, last of all, when she had all but stopped eating, from Angela's purse. Angela had taken this as a sign that she had done a good job of raising her: her mother's handbag had been the last place Wendy had gone, and only when desperate.

Angela could not imagine Wendy fighting like that. She had been a good girl, a quiet girl. She never swore, or brought home bad boyfriends, or wore awful clothes. Even the way in which she had gone about deleting herself was so simple and quiet that for some time Angela hadn't noticed. She had been too busy, with the housework and the cooking and the Post Office job, and with looking after Donald, who spent most of his time in the same chair with the curtains half drawn, and when not in the chair didn't do so much as make a cup of tea. There was a monopoly on sadness in that house: Donald had it all. Everyone else's had to exist somewhere else, outside the walls, inside their heads.

She turned to the man at the next table, and said, "Excuse me. What was she stealing?"

"Pardon?" he said, surprised.

"What was it," she said, "in her hand?"

"It was a razor," he said, looking embarrassed. "One of the pink ones."

She found them on the Bathing and Showering aisle. They were expensive, with the little grey plastic tag to prove it. She paid at the self-checkout tills, though she hated the way they shouted their business. It was better than being scrutinised by one of the young assistants, memorised for ridicule at tea-break later.

The police, as she had suspected, hadn't been called. It was a short wait at the bus stop outside the supermarket, watching the stream of people flow through the doors, until she saw her: the girl, a dirty piece of foam scudding on the current, trying to move faster than the heavy-legged shoppers. When she reached the outdoors she shrugged herself irritably from the crowd and began to march, head down, towards the road. She walked like she was beating sense into the tarmac. You could almost see the shocks rippling up through her narrow bones. Angela had gambled on the bus stop, and she had been right: the girl turned to walk in front of her and Angela stepped out, a pleasant-faced elderly woman wearing a half-smile, her hand brought softly to rest on the girl's arm.

"Excuse me," she said.

85

Her grip was not strong, but the girl pivoted in it, describing a little half circle around Angela before turning to her in surprise. Her face, crunched and furious a second earlier, was wiped clean by confusion, giving her the look of one woken suddenly from a long sleep.

"Here," said Angela, reaching into her bag and holding out the razor.

The girl looked at it, then back at Angela. "What?" she said.

"It's for you," said Angela, stretching her arm out a little further. "A present."

"Are you taking the piss?" the girl said, but her hand was already rising to take the shiny packet. She stood for a second, frowning at the old lady in front of her, then shook her head.

"Whatever," she said, and turned to walk away.

"She would have said thank you," said Angela, without rancour.

The girl didn't hear her. She was part way across the road now, her hands rammed into her coat pockets. In a moment she was on the opposite pavement, in another she was obscured by a passing van, and then she was gone: dissolved into the cold grey wasteland so neatly that she might never have been there at all.

Ken Clements

Morning Market Monologue

Rural Thailand circa 1960 (Christian era)

Aw, good morning, Honourable Grandmother. Arun sawat. You're even earlier today than yesterday; my first customer again. Look, the sun is only just rising over the mountains and the morning mist still covers the River Kong. Why, the watch-keeper hasn't even sounded the forth gong yet. Pardon? Yes, yes, I know all about the early bird and the worm. You're not buying worms today, are you? No! I thought not.

Did you enjoy yesterday's fish? You should have done; you managed to get them at a bargain price. You're fortunate your eyes are so sharp that they can spot imperfections that no one else can see. One scale missing from the first fish and an invisible bruise on the other. Aw! Two Baht each, Lah! My husband scolded me severely. He said he spent hours standing waist-deep in the cold water, waiting to cast his net over that pair of beauties and then I gave them away for next to nothing. *What* did you say? I thought so! Aw! Scandalous! Oi! My ears are burning. Never have I heard such talk before. Your tongue is just as sharp as your eyes.

The other traders warned me about you when I opened my stall last week. They said, "Watch out for Grandma Min, she knows all the tricks in the book, and if the tricks aren't there, it's because she tore the pages out to stop others learning them." Therefore, I replied and said, "Indeed, I'll watch and learn, and soon I will be able to write my own book." So, what are you going to teach this novice food seller today, venerable lady?

Oh, thank you for asking mother. Yes, my new son is doing fine, I left him with sister younger so I can concentrate and not be distracted or cheated. And yes, our lead buffalo is recovering from the snake bite. He'll be fit and ready for the ploughing season.

Ah! How nice of you to enquire about my nephew again. No, there's been no change since yesterday when I told you all about his unfortunate situation in great detail.

Oh look, the sun has cleared the hilltop already and it's quite light enough for you to inspect my food stall. I've made sure all my goods are in perfect condition today, madam, so don't be expecting any cut price bargains this fine morning.

See, the cabbages were freshly picked from our high fields last evening and these mangos are sharp and tart. They will surely suit your taste, perfect for aiding the digestive system. No, no, I wasn't saying you have poor digestion, mother, you are well known for your regularity. The watch-keeper even times the third gong by your early morning visit to the bamboo thicket.

Now tell me at last, before you wear your jaw-bone out, what do you need this morning? And don't expect any bargain prices. I'm a fast learner and have been taking notes already.

Oh, you just need six eggs. That's easy. See, the price is clearly marked so there's no room to wriggle around. Here, let me count them out for you so you don't have to stretch. What's that? You have a special requirement? I feared as much. Does the tiger change his stripes? Or the crows learn to sing in harmony?

Oh, I beg forgiveness, learned mother. It's disrespectful to quote ancient proverbs to one's elders, is it? Yes, I realise that you probably wrote many of the sayings yourself in those far-off days gone by.

Now tell me quickly before the sun is at its strongest and all my lettuces wilt; what exactly is your special requirement for buying eggs?

Eh? What? How am I supposed to know which eggs were laid by a black hen? And what difference does it make anyway? But if that's the only kind you'll buy then I'm resigned to indulging you, and learning another lesson along the way. So go ahead and show me the special eggs.

That one there at the back? And the one to its right? Ah, now I understand. Let me guess the rest. This one, that one and those two there, am I right? Yes? See I told you I was a quick learner.

Today I have learned that black hens lay the largest eggs on the stall!

Aw! Be careful, Mama, you are laughing so much you'll crack your ribs. Here, take my stool and sit before you fall over. You are truly a great rogue, taking advantage of my inexperience like that. Be careful on your way back home through the woods, or Hanuman, the monkey king, will carry you off to teach him new mischief.

Now where's my notebook?

Steve Wheeler

Sculpted Bones

Robert put his two-seater through its paces on the empty roads. Wedged and low slung, it wasn't bad for someone not yet thirty. A switch on the dashboard raised up the concealed headlights, slow and disdainful, like the eyes of a waking cat. They were hungover from the night before. They'd rinsed the wine; white then red. They'd ordered large brandies over coffee, then slept badly after clumsy, lazy sex. She'd wanted to sleep but let him. Both of them on their sides, drowsy, his knees inside hers, like spoons.

Mid Wales; agricultural villages and fallow towns. Pebble-dash chapels with pegboard noticeboards straddling plain memorial stones. Battered family farms; fowl scratching amongst cabbages. Edgy sheepdogs patrolling gateways. Working men's clubs with shit-spattered neon signs missing jigsaw pieces of glass. Pubs in palliative care advertising a quiz night or televised football. Nicotined windows with 'Saloon' or 'Lounge' etched in curling letters. Battened down takeaways - The Bengal Tiger, Peking House.

Robert told Naomi of the evening he'd spent in a similar country pub in Wales. The locals had broken into song - Welsh hymns. He'd tasted the strong brew of Welsh hills and valleys, coalmines, chapels and rugby clubs fermented in that pub, but then some boozed up locals had balanced a metal bucket on top of the toilet door which had booby-trapped him, cutting the bridge of his nose. The heady liquor of song had been watered down with a feeling of 'what was he doing in this shithole?'

"Sounds like you felt the falling bucket part of Welsh heritage," Naomi said.

Naomi told Robert of her days as a trainee solicitor in a Valleys town. A mining community falling apart. Of living in a bedsit above

90

a fish and chip shop. No heating. A square of cardboard taped over a hole in the bedroom window. So cold in the winter there were ice-crystals on the bedding where she'd exhaled during the night. The chip shop owner had an unerring sense of when she was going to dash from the bathroom back to her bedroom wrapped only in a towel. He'd be at the foot of the stairs, looking up.

"Didn't you give him a quick flash?" asked Robert. "He might have reduced the rent."

The only businesses that appeared to be open now were corner shop newsagents with meagre tokens of Christmas in the windows. Locals exiting with a newspaper and tobacco. The lottery checked for another week. The dog walked and its bowels moved.

On past visits they'd mooched in the small town antique shops that would have been called 'junk shops' in the city; dusty mixtures of second-hand tat and an occasional find. They'd taken home a half-decent oil painting last time.

"That was an antique shop back there, wasn't it?" Robert pulled the car over.

"I'd rather find coffee," Naomi said.

"More chance of finding a Picasso." Robert got out of the car into the drizzle.

The painting on the earthenware statuette was crude, but the modelling of the peasant boy was lifelike. Long, sensual legs in maroon leggings. A blue ballet dancer's tunic covered a muscular torso. The blond-haired head turned arrogantly over its right shoulder and a tied bag on a stick over its left.

"He looks like a statue of a Greek God," Naomi said. "Adonis."

"He's got sculpted bones, sure enough," the antique dealer said.

The statuette stood on the floor in the back of the car like a child, wedged in with coats.

"That was a steal," Robert said.

"Now can we find coffee?"

"Shout if you see a hotel," said Robert. "I don't fancy Taff's Caff."

"Fucking English snob." Naomi sunk down in her seat with her scarf pulled up to her nose. Closed her eyes.

Robert always felt horny after a heavy night. He looked down at Naomi's outstretched legs. He wanted to touch their litheness, like the tactile limbs of the statuette. He wanted to slide his hand up her short skirt, but he knew it wouldn't travel far. For her it was in bed only. She tended towards the straight-laced. Something he'd have to work on.

"It's not a hotel, but it'll have to do." Robert pulled up outside a stone-built cottage that had been converted to a catch-all gift shop, restaurant, ice-cream parlour, B&B.

"As long as they sell coffee," said Naomi.

A cow-bell chimed as Robert opened the door and ducked under a low lintel armoured with horse brasses. On every surface there were toby jugs, commemorative plates with 1980s faces of the Prince of Wales and Diana, Welsh dragons made in China, dolls in black hats and tea-towel maps.

"Textbook," Robert said.

"Just order."

A waitress came from behind a chest freezer of ice-creams.

"We'll have two double-shot espressos, with hot skimmed milk on the side," Robert ordered.

"Sorry, but we only do black or white normal coffee," the waitress said.

"Two white normals it is then."

The waitress exited through a rainfall of strung beads.

"Do you have to take the piss?" Naomi said.

"We'll both be drinking it soon."

Robert paced the room, lifting plates and toby jugs, scanning the underside. Naomi took a compact from her bag and re-lipsticked. There was a rack of leaflets advertising things to do, places of interest. The coffees arrived. Robert took a leaflet to the table.

"Apparently, the village church has the 'oldest Celtic stone font in Wales', and there are Celtic carvings on the stone altar. Shall we go and say our prayers?" Robert blew on his drink.

"Will they be answered?"

"Only if you're a good girl."

"Unlikely then." Naomi put the compact back into her bag.

Robert waved at the waitress as though he was holding a pen, writing the tab. Naomi hated it when he did that. One down from clicking fingers.

The churchyard was semi-derelict, drowning in vegetation. Bracken, nettles and ivy had consumed all but the tallest of headstones. Many had toppled or been knocked down. Saturday night sport for bored teenagers. The cobbles in the path leading to the church door, prized apart by dock weed.

"There's something about decomposing buildings. I try to see ghosts," Robert said. "Not ghosts exactly, but photographs of the past. Black and white pictures of people, buried under the nettles now."

Inside, the church had been tended to like a grave. Birthdays and sad days. Flowers in mildewed jars, weeded and dusted pews, the grass of disuse mown by the dwindling few. They ran their fingers over the stone font.

"The stonemason who carved this is buried outside. I can feel it," Robert said. "Gives me vertigo."

"You might be standing on his bones." Naomi was reading the moulded handwritten requests for prayer, pinned on a cork board. "They planted the chosen few inside."

Robert was climbing a stone spiral staircase that went up from the nave. Narrow and unlit, his shoulders brushed both sides.

"Come and see this."

At the top, a wooden floored platform overlooking a pit full of nothing but bird-shit and pigeon feathers. Some winged carcasses. Ribcages rising from scraps of putrefying meat. Two vertical arched slits letting in chilled winter light onto a rotting wooden frame. The bells gone.

In the dark space Robert turned, held Naomi's arms, and kissed her. She responded. Their mouths and tongues working each other's. Robert again felt the urge to put his hand up between her legs. To have sex, there, against the damp wall.

Naomi ended the kiss. "Can we get out of this bird's graveyard? It stinks."

Back outside she led the way around the back of the church. There was a shed-sized stone vault with a gothic, scrolled iron gate just visible among the yew and holly. Blood-red berries dropping on the emerald mossed slate roof. Robert pushed open the unlocked gate. On either side of the inner walls were thick stone shelves. On the shelves, decomposed wooden casks.

"Jesus, they're coffins." Naomi backed out.

From the mire inside one of the coffins, its wooden side rotted away, the arm of a skeleton hung down. Robert viewed the arm like he'd viewed the statuette. His eyes close, moving up and down its anatomy. In the bell loft he'd felt a sexual urgency which hadn't dissipated. He felt it now, in his chest, in his shallow breathing. He felt a need to do something illicit, something carnal, to go all the way. To pull the bones into the ordure that pasted the inscribed floor.

He found Naomi back in the car. "Can we go home now?" she said.

Robert opened a bottle of red. He put a glass into Naomi's hand and filled it. He sat on the floor next to her legs. The statuette stood in the fireplace without a grate, its head turned languidly across one shoulder, looking out into the room. "It's Dick Whittington," Naomi said. "Streets paved with gold."

Robert moved his hands up Naomi's thighs. "I'll stick with sculpted bones."

Andrew Stevenson

Letter of Complaint

Dear Madam or other,

While shopping at my local convenience store for sundry vegetables, namely two and a half pounds of Maris Piper potatoes, a medium carrot and three large onions, I noticed a display of Mrs Mullins' Traditional Boiled Sweets and purchased a packet with enthusiasm. These were advertised as being sugar-free, containing no fewer than four hundred and fifty milligrams of vitamin C and of 'Assorted Citrus Flavours'. While finding no fault with your claims regarding Vitamin C and sugar content (or, indeed, in the latter case, lack of it), I do wish to take issue with your use of the word 'Assorted'.

Imagine if you will, my disappointment on discovering that instead of the promised *assorted* flavours, you had supplied merely two. Perhaps now would be the time to draw your attention to the dictionary definition of the word 'Assorted', which is 'consisting of various kinds, mixed together'. Other definitions can be supplied on request, but rest assured that they neither differ significantly in meaning from the one provided, nor alter the basic thrust of my argument.

The flavours to which I refer above are lemon, which - presumably for the purposes of identification - you manufacture approximately in the colour of a lemon; and orange, which comes, consistent with your policy, approximately in the colour of an orange. On the practical matter of matching flavour to colour, therefore, I congratulate you on your faultless logic.

Nevertheless, I feel that, in addition to lemon and orange, I had every right to expect lime and quite possibly grapefruit, of which I had high hopes. For evidence of what can be achieved in a carefully planned assortment, I shall be sending, under separate cover, a study of the rise and fall of the much-lamented Spangle, an account that also sheds an interesting historical perspective on the genesis and social significance of the boiled sweet.

Drawing on my wide and varied experience of sweets both boiled and otherwise, I suggest that in future you may wish to consider adding to your portfolio of flavours not only lime and grapefruit but also tangerine, which, to the discerning palate, differs subtly from that of the orange. Indeed, such an inclusion would add a welcome degree of complexity to a game I devised some years ago, in which blindfolded contestants are challenged to name the flavour of a sweet of unidentified provenance. Please find enclosed a full set of rules.

Now, to return to the lack of variety in your flavours. After purchase, I had anticipated a carefree afternoon's consumption of the promised assortment. Events, however, the unfolding of which I relate below in narrative form, dictated otherwise.

Having exited the shop, I eagerly removed the wrapping of the aforementioned sweets, resting my shopping bag, as I did so, on the head of a small boy to whom I intended to give ten pence for his trouble.

At this point - suspending for the time my initial disappointment in discovering the restricted nature of your assortment, and not wishing to be hasty in my judgment - I considered the possibility that your sweets, although merely *bi*-coloured, might indeed be *multi*-flavoured. For example, and contrary to my initial assessment of your colouring policy which I outlined above, I speculated that some of the sweets, initially identified as orange by their hue, might be harbouring the taste of a lime or grapefruit. By a similar thought process, I reasoned that a lemon-coloured sweet might conceal the taste of the suggested tangerine, or even that of a more exotic fruit such as the oriental yuzu (when seasonally available).

With this in mind, I sampled each sweet, passing them, after an initial appraisal, to the now securely blindfolded small boy for a second opinion in lieu of the promised ten pence. I had just inserted into his mouth a sweet of the lemon-coloured variety when his mother appeared from within the store and inexplicably began beating me about the head with her own shopping bag, which, by an astonishing coincidence, also contained two and a half pounds of Maris Piper potatoes, a medium carrot and three large onions.

To conclude, I hereby return the sweets, partially consumed but otherwise in good condition. You will note that one is missing, which is the one that was in the mouth of the small boy at the time of his mother's outburst, and which she refused to return to me on the advice of a large policeman. I have calculated that, therefore, I am entitled to a ninety per cent refund. The remaining ten per cent I hope to recoup from the small boy, his mother or the large policeman at the time of the hearing.

Yours faithfully,

Herbert Pennywhistle
Cell 3
The Police Station
Froghampton Magna

Nastasya Parker

The Apocalypse Alphabet

Hannah opens the curtains to watch the horizon bleed. Against its crimson glow, the trees look dull brown, the hills grey and aged. The planes are small as insects from her house, their belches of destruction barely audible. It's over, she knows. Victorious cities don't burn.

"Tomorrow will be good for playing outside, won't it?" her son asks, clutching her hand. "Red sky at night…"

"Not this sort of red." She ushers Jack to sleep and sits half the night at his side.

Today, they have not played, not during the final stand. Today, she put on lipstick and wore the dress her husband called *hot*. She and Jack sat inside, blinds lowered, phones off. She didn't want to hear what happened to his father; she wanted to feel it. She wanted him to feel her while it happened, to see her somehow, to see beauty.

Hannah made Jack practise, tucking him behind the sofa to get accustomed to crouching small, staying silent. He managed two hours today, and she rewarded him with the last biscuit.

They practised numbers and letters, too, since the primary school shut last month when most teachers were drafted. As more places closed and more people were ushered to the defensive lines, Hannah's creativity has contracted to a frail sphere of survival, and the problems she gives Jack now resemble the riddles constantly plaguing her: "If there are three tins of soup, and five of fruit, how many do we have all together?"

And the alphabet chant she's taught him, rife with reality:

A is for ants, marching in a row.
B is for basement room, where we can go.

Jack was still singing the rhyme merrily that morning as he scribbled each letter. Once released from his studies, he puttered about the house, discovering objects of war everywhere. Saucepan army helmets, wooden spoon pistols. For one more day, she has let him think war is a game.

Now, as the eerily illuminated night falls, there isn't time to wonder if Hannah's husband was quickly shot, or tormented for hours. No time to imagine what wounds desecrate the body to which she was inextricably linked, or whether there is no body, merely bomb-blasted fragments. There's no time to wonder if he did, indeed, see her in his last thoughts, and derive comfort from it.

She has ignored the friends who banged on the door, wailing about the end. She doesn't need their battle news; she sensed the loss before the blaze.

A steady stream of traffic winds from the town, on the route passing the house. The ants are marching. They won't get far enough away, not all of them at once. At least Hannah has a Plan B.

She considers Plan C, though. Flirts with it, wonders if it notices her lipstick.

C is for capsule, washed down with a flask.

As she feeds her dog his last meal - scraps of meat, with a dash of cyanide - he whines in excitement spiked with doubt. It's been so long since she spared meat for him. She holds him in her lap and wonders if they should all partake of the same dish.

There's no time for this either. Under the ancient oak by the road, Hannah rests the dog's body, cupping her hands to plough leaves over it. The leaves are damp and cool, life on the brink of decay, and she filters them through her fingertips, wondering what will remain in the end.

She is crying, but barely has time to notice. Cars moan past. Far down one end of the road, flashes rend the night. The suburbs alight now. In the opposite direction, another gleaming - taillights, she thinks, traffic stopped where it's trying to join the highway from the city. Car horns sound reedy and helpless against the rumble of explosions.

"Uh-oh," says her son, rising early and trotting to the window. Jack wears his father's t-shirt, and it flaps around his skinny legs. "Red sky in the morning, better take warning!"

She already has. She tells him the dog fell in love and moved in with his dog-bride's family overnight. She tells Jack, "It's time for our plan. Pack one bag of your favourite toys."

They huddle underground in the cool damp, with the slumbering scent of decay. She and her husband dug the little room before he was drafted, and stocked it before the shops shut. Back when the TV still insisted defeat was impossible. Now, approaching shell-slams rattle the stacks of canned food and shake Hannah's meagre supply of faith in Plan B. The shelter might hold against ground fire, but what about bombs?

"Close your eyes and imagine fireworks," Hannah whispers, and Jack obeys, his fingers woven together in front of his shins, his eyelids almost translucent, spidered with delicate veins, in the limp white glow of an emergency LED strip.

Surely they won't search when they come. They'll expect everyone to have fled. They will be delirious with triumph, bloated with victory. Surely they'll just rampage through.

An explosion, ever closer. She switches off the light. Jack reaches for his teddy, and Hannah clutches her own bag. It holds wedding photos and what's left of the money. The poison, should it come to Plan C.

C is for capsule, washed down with a flask.

And should she be prevented even from that...With shaking hands, she reapplies the lipstick in the dark, in case they find her.

D is for deal; give whatever they ask.

100

Chloe Turner

While the Mynah Bird Watched

When their turn comes, the sun is dipping low, casting long shadows against the pockmarked walls of her consulting room. They've been here before – this man, this girl. Agnes recognises the slump of his shoulders, the sprouting hair at the base of his neck where a shave is overdue, the dusty outline of an old stain on his lapel, under a pin for the city's soccer team. When Agnes motions for them to sit, he slumps in his chair, as if the air has been stolen from his lungs.

The girl is different. From the outside, her condition manifests itself only through the bald patches across her scalp, and those beads of fever-sweat across her brow. Her hollow cheeks would not mark her out in that waiting room, where malnourishment and anaemia are merely background noise. The bulging masses of her liver and spleen are a secret that only Agnes's tests have revealed. But the girl sits tall in the man-sized chair, her beaded braids swinging even after she is still. Agnes is reminded of someone, long ago, as the girl fixes her across the table with that unbreaking stare. As she grips the desk at the meeting of cracked green leather and well-worn *kiaat* heartwood, knuckles whitening as she presses down on the heavy stitching.

"My wife will come. She must have been held up at the market. Please, wait." The man is upright now. He has realised that their turn could slip away.

"There is a line. Many to see before I can go home." Agnes traces the thin skin at her temples, feels the mesh of tendons and skull beneath.

"A minute, please. She will not be long."

He is right, because the door opens then, revealing a scene of confusion. Ndali is trying to keep a woman from entering, and

Agnes can hear the grumble of the queue. Another woman, a baby slung over her shoulder like a dishcloth, shouts something from the far side of the hall.

"I'm sorry Doctor, she…" Ndali is doing her best to keep the peace.

"It is fine, Ndali. Madam, please, come in."

The voices in the hall subside as Ndali ushers the door closed. Agnes sits back in her chair. A police car whines past the window.

"Claudia, where have you been?" the man demands of his wife. There is an angry twitch above his eye.

"A truck hit the water tower. They closed the road. I got off the bus to walk."

Claudia has not looked at Agnes yet, so she does not know who sits across the table. As she fusses with a scarlet jacket that struggles to contain a spreading waist, Claudia does not know that the woman opposite is recalling a time, long ago. A dusty classroom, at lunch recess, the window open wide to the parched air. A mynah bird chattering on a generator lid. A yellow lunch tin, splayed on the tiles, and three girls squawking louder than the mynah as they unwrap every one of the careful parcels Agnes's mother has packed.

How they mocked the country food she had grown up with; her headdress with its garish zebra design, and her skin, darker than theirs – almost blue-black – and paint spattered with the fairy-prints of vitiligo. Claudia was beautiful then. High cheekbones, where now there are sagging pouches. Fine, white teeth, where now there is yellow rot and holes. Slim, bony fingers, where now there are swollen joints, a blackened nail above the thin silver band on her ring finger.

Agnes spreads her own hands across the table. Presses down at the fingertips as the girl did before, so that the white patches where pigmentation has been lost stand out even more against the brown. She wonders what will come out when she speaks.

"These drugs that Maria needs. They are expensive."

"You can't expect us to pay. We have nothing."

"I know that. But you have seen the line. There are many in need. I must think of the rest."

"She is dying. She must have them. Claudia, you tell her."

The man's eyes are rolling, red threads across yellow, as he pleads for his daughter's life. But Claudia has seen Agnes now – really seen her – and her mouth sags open. Perhaps she too is thinking of the broken hinges of that lunch box, and the maize balls crushed underfoot. Of text books with fluttering pages as they bump against the brick sides of the well. Of bright spots of red through a sky blue polo shirt, where the compass point has found its mark.

Claudia stares at Agnes until the doctor meets her eyes at last. Then Claudia looks down. Runs a tongue over cracked lips.

There is a long pause. The man wipes a hand across a sticky brow. A bluebottle crawls across the windowpane, its legs thick-black and furred. The girl fidgets. Another police car passes, and the patrolman's whistle sounds from the railway stop. The fly buzzes against the glass – suddenly, frantically – its fine gauzy wings grazing the dusted pane. Claudia does not move. Her head is still hung.

When Agnes speaks again, she keeps her body very still. She says what she needs to, and no more. Then, as she writes, she feels her jaw unclench. Her biceps slacken. She feels the tension slide from her shoulders, like the *oshana* that streams through the valley after the rains. She rips the sheet from the pad and hands the prescription to the girl.

As they usher their daughter from the room, Claudia and the man are profuse in their thanks, but Agnes turns away as if she cannot hear them. She keeps her eyes on the photograph propped on the mantelpiece. On the blue sky and the green of the sweet potato vine, the dirt-grey thatch on the homestead where she was born. She lets them blur in front of her eyes, until she hears the weighted door pull closed. She does not want them to see her tears.

'While the Mynah Bird Watched' was first published in Halo Magazine, Issue One in 2016.

Natalie Lee

The Night

The boy the text the date the grin the heart the beat the wash the
shave the spray the smell the shirt the cuff the shoes the shine the
hair the smooth the gel the hair the hair the check the look the
blush the hair the step the glide the spin the moves the beat the
time the phone the keys the door the slam the shout the street the
night the moon the light the walk the step the skip the lamp the
street the wish the hope the heart the want the girl the date the date
the place the time the nerves the date the shake the hands the check
the sweat the check the mouth the breath the teeth the check the
hair the cool the wait the doubt the wait the hope the pray the girl
the walk the smile the skirt the sway the hair the smile the legs the
legs the fuck the legs the heart the pound the gulp the laugh the shy
the smile the nerves the shake the blush the speak the sweat the
smile the yes the yes the yes the talk the lips the eyes the stroke the
hand the cheek the mouth the touch the lips the kiss the kiss the
sky the night the stars the lift the heart the beat the pulse the girl
the shout the can the stone the chuck the lamp the stone the smash
the glass the shock the dark the scream the run the hand the hand
the hand the run the hand the hunt the chase the shout the heart
the pound the chase the trip the fall the kick the punch the chin the
nose the blood the stamp the beat the heat the burn the cool the
dark the beat the ask the mouth the beat the wall the kick the name
the tag the shame the kick the heel the shoe the bite the tears the
shame the tag the name the chill the dark the path the lost the girl
the loss the fall the shame the shame the drop the fall the girl the
hand the call the come the run the leap the chance the flight the
beat the heart the bruise the blood the gang the run the dark the
run the breath the run the drop the dark the hide the hole the dirt

the dark the walls the cut the rock the fall the crawl the soil the blood the wound the hand the stretch the rock the wall the dirt the floor the still the warm the breath the air the stale the dark the hide the weep the shame the quiet the rock the blood the cut the still the shame the dark the light the fade the fade the still the air the still the dust the still the calm the still the quiet the stand the crawl the ask the call the girl the love the want the urge the crawl the light the voice the call the dirt the earth the stone the crawl the dirt the kiss the kiss the crawl the light the hope the voice the ask the call the night the sky the moon the breeze the girl the hold the kiss the tongue the urge the want the shy the lash the curve the shy the lick the tooth the tongue the tongue the tooth the bite the lip the kiss the want the want the yes the shape the leg the pull the lean the chest the shirt the skirt the ask the yes the tight the tight the push the cry the fall the fall the rise the fall the laugh the slap the tease the eyes the want the pull the soft the touch the sigh the kiss the deep the deep the deep the drown the girl the night the night the fall the night the joy the dance the jump the shout the self the name the self the walk the hands the hold the kiss the speak the yes the promise the yes the home the key the door the hush the tip the toe the shut the click the latch the still the dark the stairs the shoe the hand the shoe the creep the dark the creak the freeze the dark the dark the hush the house the boy the hand the rail the stair the step the grin the door the bed the dark the shirt the moon the socks the stars the legs the gleam the moon the sigh the dream the girl the eyes the close the moon the stars the night the dream the dream the dream the girl the night the hope the night the wish the night the love the girl the kiss the heart the night the love the night the night.

Kate O'Grady

Porange

Ellen needed a wig, and she needed it fast. The party was that evening at 7 p.m. 'Wear A Wig' the big, black, bold Helvetica letters demanded from the bottom of a pink invitation that Ellen had found in her mailbox two weeks ago, wedged between a council tax bill and an appeal from Amnesty International. The invitation is covered with psychedelic swirls, and in between the swirls are photos of a beaming, soon-to-be forty Stephanie, sporting several assorted hairpieces: a huge red afro, a blonde beehive, a jet black pompadour.

Wendy's Wig Store is located between a pawn shop and a car wash.

"Yes, plenty wigs. Come see," a woman's voice tells Ellen when she calls. Rows of white, faceless, polystyrene heads topped with shiny wigs are lined up in the window. Inside, a woman stands behind a glass counter, a female customer wearing a black coat browses the merchandise, and a man at the far end of the store eats noodles from a carton. The jangle of the doorbell makes them all glance Ellen's way when she enters.

"I called earlier. I'm looking for a party wig," Ellen says.

The wig is hard to miss. Iridescent orange, it stands out from the mousy bobs and light brown page-boys that surround it like a single red poppy in a field of grass. A cross between a saucy Betty Paige and a sultry Cleopatra, the wig speaks volumes, but mostly it says, 'I'm the life and soul of any soiree.' 'I'm transformed,' Ellen thinks as she gazes at her bewigged reflection.

"Oh sweetie, joo look beautiful."

Behind Ellen, reflected in the glass and sitting at another mirror, is the woman in the black coat. She is smiling and holding one of the mousy bobs. Beside her lies another wig, that she has just

106

removed, a curly brown one. Her head is mostly bald, apart from some thin strands and a few flattened clumps of hair.

"Joo look beautiful," the woman says again. She speaks like Al Pacino in *Scarface*.

Ellen smiles back. "Thank you."

The woman behind the counter gives them both a free stocking cap before they leave.

"Easier to pull the wig on," she says.

The man, finished with his noodles, bursts into a rendition of 'Yellow Submarine', while Ellen and Sylvia, or as she says it "Seel-vee-yah", pay for their wigs. The three women grin at each other.

Later, at the party, everyone tries each other's wigs on and shrieks with laughter. Ellen goes out on the deck to smoke a cigarette. It is November and cold and she is shivering before she takes the lighter out of her bag, but she needs a moment alone.

'Porange'. That was the colour Stephanie called Ellen's wig. Not quite pink, and not quite orange, but some shade between the two. They'd both laughed and sipped champagne, and said that, yes, 'porange' really summed the colour up. On the deck Ellen drags deeply on her cigarette, and the only colour she can think of is the pale blue of the veins that ran beneath the skin on Sylvia's head.

Mark Graham

Wayland Smith: Warrior of the Milky Way

The milk float trundled out of the yard and into the street-light puddle night. The Boy Rob, hood up, stared vacantly into the darkness, dreaming of Abigail's red hair tossed across a white Primark pillow.

Fox-faced Wayland Smith, eyes lusting after adventure, accelerated to a reckless 13 miles an hour.

Earth my Body
Water my Blood
Air my Breath
And Fire my Spirit

The silent wings of a road-killed pheasant swung from the rear view mirror.

Tomorrow is the big day, Boy, your initiation, then you can call yourself a Man, a Warrior of the Milky Way."

"Um."

"Remember all I've taught you, give honour to the Goddess and you'll be fine."

"Whatever."

The milk float came to a halt outside Walkers the Bakers, where, behind the blinds and darkened door, a fluorescent sun had already risen. To the dawn chorus of Heart FM, the white robed priests of Demeter were performing the sacred rite of bread baking.

Wayland's thin arms, as strong and knotty as the heart-wood of oak, hauled a crate of double cream from amongst the milk bottles. He jogged the cream to the bakery door, blue overall flapping against skinny legs. The Boy Rob, dragging along behind, carried a crate of semi-skimmed.

Wayland knocked. The door opened. A vision in white overalls and hairnet shimmered before them. Gloria, the baker's wife, Miss Iced Buns 1988, statuesque and alluring.

"Cream horn?" she purred.

Wayland swallowed, hard.

"Vanilla slice." he replied.

Oh, Wayland, you are a one." A paper bag passed between them, discretely.

Back on the road the familiar routine began. Milk bottles lifted from crates, paths beaten to dark doors, empties collected. Birth, death, divorce, all of human experience reduced to a message in an empty bottle.

"An extra pint please."

"No milk today."

"Just one semi-skimmed please."

Orders amended and milk delivered, they moved silently on.

As The Boy Rob set down a pint of sterilised milk (makes the best rice pudding) on the step of 38, the letterbox flew open and a hand proffered a mini Mars bar, which he took with grunted thanks. Walking, head down, back to the milk float, The Boy Rob stopped and cringed. As the sun breached the horizon, Wayland, with due reverence, lifted a pint of full cream Guernsey milk from its crate. The world stood still. He turned towards the Eastern horizon. The first rays of the rising sun broke from behind the old mill, and Wayland, face lit with a golden light, lifted the milk bottle high above his head in salute.

I am a Warrior
I am a Druid
I am a Milkman
My soul will never die,

he proclaimed in a voice that rose from the earth and filled the sky.

Puncturing the golden foil, Wayland threw back his head and, with reckless disregard for the cholesterol content, drank until milk ran down his chin and the bottle was drained.

"Why do you do that?"

"Because if I didn't, the sun wouldn't rise."

109

"It would."

"How do you know?"

*

Much later, as they trundled back to the yard, empty bottles clinking, Wayland was in a reflective mood. "We are a dying tribe," he announced, the usual gleam in his eyes dimmed.

"Twenty years ago thirty floats rode out of this yard. We roamed the streets through rain, wind and snow. We were always there, servants of the Goddess. Kids' cereal, Mum's cuppa, Dad's flask, we brought the sacred milk of the Mother to their doors. Now we are no more than a dozen, and the floats are half-empty. I can remember floats with crates piled to the roof, to the roof! Now they barely cover the decks. We are old men, stooped like ancient hawthorn trees. We are a dying tribe." They joined the queue of milk floats rolling into the yard to be tethered to their power cables and fed electricity.

*

That night, beneath his Forest Green Rovers FC duvet cover, The Boy Rob carefully traced the route of the milk round in his head.

"Two semi-skimmed at 18, then on to Summer Street," he pictured each delivery, front door step, back door, barking dog, possible glimpse of the beautiful Ms Emery in her nightie at 43.

The alarm bleeped. 4.30am.

Clothes on, coffee, pushbike.

The Boy Rob freewheeled through the gate and into the uncharacteristically dark and silent yard, eerie with the absence of hustle and bustle. He lent his bike against a wall, and, hands in pockets, sauntered towards the office. The lights of twelve milk floats, drawn into a circle, split open the darkness.

Standing centre stage was a figure in white, back turned. Twelve milkmen stepped from their floats, and stood as erect as their age would allow.

"Enter the Temple and approach the Goddess," a voice commanded.

"Really?"

He stepped into the circle of light.

The figure turned to face him.

110

Gloria, draped in a white bed sheet, a bottle of gold top pressed to each breast.

"I am the Goddess," she proclaimed

Then the clouds parted and the naked full-moon revealed herself in all her splendour. The yard was bathed in silver light, and the world was enchanted and magical. Gloria's voice was transformed, becoming richer and more powerful. Gloria's lips continued to move, but her voice came from everywhere and nowhere -

> I am the Goddess, Maiden, Mother, Crone
> I am the Moon, full and new
> The Hind
> The Hare
> The Crow
> The Shrew
> I am Willow, Oak and Gorse
> I cause Fate to run its course

In the half-light the twelve ancient milkmen grew taller, the shadows tattooing swirls and spirals onto their faces. They were muscular warriors ready for the fray, strong as oak trees, fearless as stags.

> HAIL TO THE DARKNESS AND THE LIGHT
> HAIL TO THE GODS AND TO THE GODDESS
> HAIL TO THE MILKY WAY, they boomed.

"Step forward," commanded Gloria.

The Boy Rob shuffled forward, cheeks glowing red. "Take the Milk of the Breast of the Goddess, freely given as a gift to life and the living."

She thrust the two bottles forward towards him. The Boy Rob took them, assiduously avoiding eye contact.

"Do you swear to serve me, The Sacred Mother, and to carry my Blessed Milk safely to all who have need of it?"

"If you like."

"Do you swear to tread this path with pride, to bring honour to this hallowed task?"

"Suppose so."

"Then you shall be called a Warrior of the Milky Way, and your name will be remembered in the Sacred Stories of the Tribe."

"HAIL TO OUR BROTHER, WARRIOR OF THE MILKY WAY," boomed the twelve milkmen, beating the sides of their milk floats in unison.

"BROTHER WARRIOR, BROTHER WARRIOR," they roared.

Gloria leant forward and gently kissed Rob on his cheek, her breasts brushing lightly against him. She looked deeply into his eyes for a moment then turned her back and walked slowly away, disappearing into the shadows as the moon was once again swallowed by cloud. The mighty warriors shrunk, old and stooped again, they formed a line. The Boy Rob walked along the line, tucking a pint of gold top under his arm so he could shake the proffered hands. Milkmen slapped him on the back, congratulated him, smiled warmly, tears in their eyes. At the end of the line stood Wayland.

"The people are waiting for you, Rob. Go and take the bounty of the Goddess to them."

Rob climbed into the float, and, to the cheers of the assembled milkmen, drove through the gate and into the dark.

At Walkers the Bakers, Gloria winked and handed him a cream horn.

With a new spring in his step, Rob roamed the dark streets. A pint of semi-skimmed at 18; two pints of full cream at 27; a pint of sterilised for Mrs Jones (makes the best rice pudding); Ms Emery in her nightie at 43 (result!).

The light grew, and as the sun began to rise, Rob stopped. Shaking his head and smiling to himself, Rob lifted a bottle of full cream Guernsey milk from its crate, held it up to the sun and roared

I AM A WARRIOR
I AM A DRUID

I AM A MILKMAN
MY SOUL WILL NEVER DIE

And, puncturing the golden foil, he threw back his head and drank until milk ran down his chin and the bottle was drained.

Geoff Mead

The Acorn and the Oak

Frank was a successful writer. He knew he was successful. He'd published several books. Every morning Sharon told him so. Once he was dressed and sitting in his favourite high-backed chair in the bay window, she brought him a mug of tea, two ginger biscuits and his battered laptop. She plugged it in, because the battery didn't hold a charge anymore, placed it on the cantilever table in front of him, and opened the lid.

"Here we are, Frank," she'd say. "Time to write."

Sharon was young, much younger than him. She was tall, blonde and pretty. Pretty like? Pretty like someone else he knew.

"What shall I write?"

"Oh, I don't know. Write another book, like the other ones."

"Like the other ones?"

"Yes."

Then Sharon would disappear. One minute she was there beside him with tea and biscuits, and the next minute, gone. Frank wondered where she went.

"Just popping off," she'd say. "I'll be back soon."

Outside the bay window, Frank could see a large oak tree, slightly to the left of centre and halfway between the window and the hedge. This morning there were no leaves on the tree. Maybe he could write about that? Sometimes there were those little shiny oak-seed things among the leaves on the tree or on the ground underneath. Not today. No leaves and no oak-seeds today. He thought about the tree for a while. He was sad that it was bare. He drank his mug of tea, dunking the ginger biscuits to make them soft. Two biscuits. One wasn't enough and three would be greedy.

The pale blank screen of the laptop glared at him balefully. Baleful, that's a good word, thought Frank. I'll use that word. When

I write. The laptop was awkward, the keys too close together. If you weren't quick, it repeated the same letter over and over again. Or else it told you that you'd spelled something wrong. Frank didn't like the laptop. He couldn't remember buying it. Maybe it had been a present. Why would anyone give him something he didn't like? He was much better off with that other writing thing, he thought. Frank imagined his beautiful old Imperial and its two-tone black and red ribbon. He flexed his fingers as if playing over the keys. He could write on that. He'd written whole books on that. Sharon said so.

Maybe he wouldn't write just yet. He might rest a while first, to see if anything came. He put his head back against the wing of the chair and closed his eyes. Just for a while. Just for a little while.

"Frank. Frank. Wake up."

The voice was insistent. "Frank. Wake up. You've got a visitor."

Frank blinked his eyes open. It was Sharon speaking. "Margery's come to see you. That's nice isn't it?"

"Who?"

"Margery. Your wife."

Frank looked at Sharon, fresh-faced and smooth-skinned. He stared at the swell of her breasts under the white apron that covered her pale-blue striped dress.

"Come on, cheeky. It's Margery. She's come to see you."

"See me?"

"Yes, Frank."

Frank looked beyond Sharon to the woman standing behind her. Her hair was thin and white. She wore glasses and the skin on her face and neck was wrinkled and scrawny. Gold and diamond rings gleamed on her left hand. The backs of her hands were mottled with dark blotches. She was old. Margery wasn't old.

"She's not Margery," said Frank. "I don't know who she is."

"Well, she's come to see you anyway. Now don't make a fuss."

Frank felt panic rising in his body. He wrapped his arms round his chest, hugged himself and started to rock back and forth. He stared out of the window, his gaze fixed on the oak tree. "I don't know this woman. I don't know who she is. I don't know. No. NO. **NO**."

Sharon put an arm round his shoulders. "It's alright, Frank. She won't hurt you. Look." She drew his face round in her hands to look at the old woman who was weeping. "She won't hurt you."

Frank's breathing slowed and he stopped rocking. The old woman sat down on a chair beside him, reached out her beringed left hand and stroked his cheek. Her touch was very gentle. Frank liked it. He unclasped his arms from his chest and took her hand in his.

"Hello, Frank," she said. She was smiling now. She seemed nice.

"I'm writing," he said.

"Are you dear? What are you writing?" she said.

"A book," he said. "Sharon said I should write another book."

"Well, that would be lovely. If you feel like it," she said.

"I do like writing," he said. "But the words. Sometimes the words aren't there. I want to write but the words aren't there. Margery would know. She'd be able to help me."

"Yes," said the old woman, "Margery would help you. She'd do anything for you. Do you remember her?"

"Of course I remember her. She's my wife. I wish I could see her."

"I'm glad you remember her," said the old woman. "What is she like?"

Frank closed his eyes. "She's very slim," he said. "Like a dancer, and she has long red hair. And bright, blue-grey eyes that are always smiling. And she wore white at our wedding, though maybe she shouldn't have, if you know what I mean?"

"I do," said the old woman, squeezing his hand. "Do you love her?"

"I've always loved her." said Frank. "From the moment I first set eyes on her in the hospital when I made it back from Dunkirk."

"I expect she couldn't resist you, Frank," said the old woman. "A brave, good-looking chap like you. Do you know where she is now?"

"No," said Frank. "We got married and had children. They grew up. But I don't know what happened to her."

He opened his eyes and looked at the old woman. "Do you know her? Do you know what happened to her?"

116

"I know her very well, Frank. I hear she's very well, she still loves you and she's very sorry that she doesn't see you anymore."

"Why? Why doesn't she see me?"

"I don't know, Frank. I think it must be very hard for both of you."

There was a long silence between them. The images on the television in the corner of the room flickered. The quiz show host beamed a toothy grin and burbled inanely, "Today's star prize is a holiday for two in Grand Canaria. All you have to do is say which of these statements received the highest vote amongst our studio audience."

"Let me turn that off," said the old woman. "I'd rather listen to you." She released her hand from Frank's grasp, stood up and went over to the television. Frank watched her as she walked away. She seemed to be shaking and when she returned, her eyes were glistening. He looked out of the window as she sat down.

"I'm a writer, you know. Sharon says so."

"Yes, dear. You are very good writer."

They sat together side by side for a long time without speaking, staring at the oak tree. Its hollowed trunk was gnarled with age and scarred by canker and lost limbs. A sparse scattering of twigs clung to its skeletal form. It seemed almost drained of life. A solitary rook cawed from a broken branch. Spring was a long way off. Perhaps it would never come. Frank didn't mind. He'd seen many springs. One more or less would make no difference.

He turned to the old woman by his side. "If you see Margery, please tell her that I miss her."

"I will," she said. "I promise."

"I'm very tired," said Frank. "I'd like to sleep soon. Would that be alright with you? To sleep?"

"Quite alright," said the old woman. "Thank you for staying - for letting me stay - so long. I'll go now and leave you in peace." She stood up, retrieved her hat, coat and gloves, picked up her handbag, bent over and kissed him lightly on the cheek. "Goodbye, Frank. Goodbye, my dear." Then she walked briskly to the door and let herself out into the corridor.

117

Frank turned back to the window, he wanted to fall asleep looking at the tree. As he settled himself, his eye caught the screen of the laptop, still open on the table in front of him. He saw some words in bold at the top of the page. He couldn't remember writing them. They looked like the title of whatever he had been going to write: 'The Acorn and the Oak'.

Acorns. Of course. That's what oak-seeds were called.

He raised his eyes to the tree and smiled.

Acorns. Bright shiny beginnings.

What a good way to end.

A Ship Called Crazy
&
Other Stories
May 2017

Pam Keevil

Platform Two

It had proved remarkably easy to find Graham. Or rather *Dad*, as he wanted Jenna to call him. She was not sure. He was unknown to her, except in her imagination. For years she'd made up stories to explain his absence. He was a spy and had left her mother because he might put their lives in danger. He was a member of the royal family and her presence would destabilise the succession. Or he was a famous actor, with an equally famous wife, whose perfect lives were showcased in *OK!* magazine with remarkable frequency. All scenarios had one basic feature; as soon as he realised he had a daughter, he would arrange to meet and when they did, he would beg her forgiveness, show her a lock of baby hair or a much-creased photo of her first birthday party, although he'd already done a runner by that time according to her mother.

She checked her watch. She was only thirty minutes away from finding the answers to all the questions that had plagued her life. Thirty minutes. One thousand eight hundred seconds. She could count them. Except her brain would be creating scenarios that had her snivelling back the tears before she got to ten. How else could she pass the time?

The station was crowded. Students bent over with vast rucksacks on their backs like human snails staggered towards the ticket office, clutching bottles of water and jabbering in unrecognisable languages. A handful of women dressed with t-shirts that announced they were *Emma - Mother of the Groom* or *Sandy - Chief Bridesmaid* followed a woman in a white lace veil and a tiara. Her buttocks protruded from microscopic pink shorts and wobbled as she walked, enveloped in a cloud of vape. Jenna felt her mouth twist downwards. She tried to smile. She couldn't. No doting father had paid for her wedding. She and Rob had managed

121

themselves on a shoe string and her Uncle Dave had walked her down the aisle. It wasn't the same.

A group of school children all in twos, with adults arranged at suitable intervals, crossed the concourse in a giggling stream of red sweat shirts. They all carried small backpacks with the name of the school printed on them and clip boards. She raised her eyebrows as the woman at the back passed by. "Rather you than me," she murmured.

The woman smiled. "As long as I don't lose one, I'll be all right."

It had only ever been Jenna's mum at school events. And the kids noticed. All this crap about single parent families being the norm was just that. Crap. She'd always felt judged by her peers. Ridiculed. Perhaps things were more lenient now. She doubted it. She checked her watch again. Coffee. That's what she needed. She crossed the concourse and climbed the steps to Costa. She'd select a seat that overlooked the platform where his train was due to arrive. Perhaps he was here already. Perhaps even now he was watching her, waiting for the appointed time before their rendezvous. God, it sounded like the script of a second-rate movie. She ordered an Espresso. But it was a second-rate movie. She hadn't even got a recent photo of him. Instead he insisted he'd wear a red carnation and she should carry one too so they could recognise each other. She had still sent him countless photos of her, Rob and the children, his grandchildren. She took her coffee and perched on one of the high stools overlooking the concourse. The clatter of the information screens as trains departed and arrived fought with the rumble of wheeled suitcases, and over and above everything else was the endless hum of voices, the essence of human interaction. Why had he never contacted her? Why hadn't he tried to find her? Surely, he couldn't have hated her mother so much? Or was it easier to disappear, start again and pretend she had never existed?

When she spoke to him on the phone his voice had a Geordie twang. Her mother had said he was from the north.

"Don't get your hopes up," her mother had warned her. "He's a waster. A useless lump." Was he? She'd soon find out. She drained her cup. The bitter hit of caffeine jolted her back to reality. She swallowed. It was time. She'd go and stand by the side of platform two, half obscured by a concrete pillar. She would watch as everyone spilt off the train. She'd spot him and that would give her time to gather her wits, to walk forward, stretch out her hand. "Graham…Dad?" she'd say. After that she had no idea what would happen. She'd trust to luck, fate or whatever was watching over her that day.

She walked down the steps, holding onto the railings for support. Her legs had never felt this weird before. As if she was drunk. Each footfall threatened to catapult her forwards. She grasped the cold metal and stood still for a few seconds, drawing in great draughts of fetid air. What had her mother said? "Don't get your hopes up. Unreliable, that's what he was and always will be."

What if she was right? Jenna walked, dreamlike through the swathes of people each intent on a journey. Going somewhere. Anywhere. Most of them were heading home. And that's where she wanted to be. Home. Safe and with her all dreams still intact. She wanted Rob to hug her. She wanted to see the twins as they came rushing out of school with their book bags, their spelling lists and a soggy piece of paper that they said was a painting of mummy or the dog. If she left now she could sink back into her life.

The metal gates at the end of platform two swung open. A train snaked its way along the track and under the metal and glass tracery of the Victorian roof. There was still time. If she left now he'd never know. She'd say she'd been ill or delayed. He'd understand. He had to. He owed her that. People were getting off the train. They were hurrying to the exit. She threw the carnation into the nearest waste bin and ran.

The carnation lay there. Undisturbed. It landed next to a second red carnation and the stub of a train ticket from Newcastle.

Jan Petrie

Keeping Time

An ordinary door – same as all the others in this flat, same as a countless others in the city – yet it takes all your strength to turn this particular handle and let its full weight fall away from your grasp.

The room gapes at you, wide open now. Slow down every movement before you step across the threshold. Don't look down, not even for a second. Concentrate on just breathing: long inhale, longer exhale. Do it twice.

Okay, now you're inside. You scan the tops of the walls like a surveillance camera that's stuck on one axis, following the line where the wallpaper has been overlaid by a floral freeze, the slanting sunlight's exposing all its careful little joins.

Are you imagining that sound like a dull, persistent handclap?

Back against the wall, your feet perform a kind of awkward shuffle around the edge of the room until you reach the far corner. Only then do you let your gaze fall a fraction; just enough to witness how the wind is trying to drag the heavy curtains outside, creating that slap-slapping sound as they flap against the frame.

You edge your way over to one side of the window, alert to every noise from outside. Listen. You hear only the traffic, the rumble of an overhead plane, the to and fro whine of someone mowing a lawn. A trace of cut grass comes to you on the breeze.

Blare of a car horn sends a shockwave fizzing through your veins. You can't see exactly where it came from, so, by increments, you move closer to the glass and listen again.

False alarm. Must have been from further along the street.

You wait for the trembling to subside; willing your arms to hang loose at your sides, for the shiny tops of every car and van to keep on passing by.

But, as you might have guessed, they don't. One of them pulls up right outside. A shrill whistle cuts the air and someone shouts out, "Oy! Dev man!"

You peer down to witness their leaning conversation followed by a high revving roar; the momentary clash of gears before the car shoots off again, spitting gravel.

Back in the room's shadows, you wait for that engine's long tone to fade until it's less than the buzzing of the fly that's trapped against the closed top window. You'd reach up to let the poor thing out into the air, but what if the sun winked off the windowpane and attracted someone's attention up here? To you; to this damned room.

And still you have no plan, no course of action to follow. Stuck here in the present, your thoughts refuse to go forward and not for one second do you want them rolling back over what's just happened.

Shut your eyes and look up into the sky's brightness and enjoy the rosy glow through your eyelids for one single, solitary moment before it's lost.

Now check your watch. Seventy-one minutes have already passed; every extra one is a luxury you can't afford. Get this over with for goodness sake (though there's not much goodness involved). Isn't it time to face your own, most particular music?

Cue orchestra, exhale and try to imagine a gentle, calming melody. Stare down at the carpet beneath your bare feet feeling its soft, green pile on your skin. Take one stride forward, only about a metre, and focus on that sturdy leg.

There you go. Nothing out of the ordinary – softwood, mass-produced in thousands; maybe even tens of thousands.

Yet the pace is already quickening. Let your gaze travel onto the cover, to the spot where the fastenings aren't quite restraining the duvet's bulk. Hold it there. Let it rest on the repeating pattern; that precise motif.

Already something's not exactly right, is it? Impossible to ignore the small crimson stain not quite hiding itself amongst all those fat little tulips and telling its own tale.

Don't stop there. Go on; you're only looking.

125

Start with that naked foot, toes pointing upwards and already turned the colour of an approaching storm. Travel the length of his surprisingly thin leg with the handful of red scratches across the shin.

Speed up; that's it. Your not-so-innocent gaze reaches the shadowy junction between splayed legs; that shrunken back penis tucked up beneath the protruding ridge of his gut. You feel the pressure building in your skull; how the air inside your ears is pulsating; whooshing in and out to the beat.

But you're not yet ready for the climax, for the crescendo that's coming.

Skip across instead to one tanned, open hand, to that finger with its gold ring still catching the sun's rays. Flung in abandonment across the bed, see how the forearm tanned darker than the skin nearer the shoulder.

And so there you are, by a different route, at the back of the head; the short, greying hairs with clotted red roots; the darkening halo now covering most of the pillow.

You did this. This is *your* work, or what it's led to.

Did you really expect those eyes to open, like anybody might up and walk away from such a thing – such an act?

That low whine stops abruptly as that same busy and persistent fly settles itself on the very tip of his nose. Watch its oh-so-casual walk across that unresponsive cheek. You could brush it away, but won't there always be many more ready to land on this particular quarry?

You want to bolt again, but the steady tones of the second movement have already begun to stir your thoughts and you remembered why you're in here, what it is you have to do.

Go on, tear your stuck-fast eyes away from the gory tableau on the bed and begin your search.

Look, one of your shoes is over by the window. And there's the other not quite underneath the bed.

Pull them on. Feel how they've made you stand a fraction taller.

Concentrate now: it's time for the whole replay. You'll need to remember every last movement you made in here; to think of where fingertips strayed, handles were pulled or turned; lipstick slicked lips pressed themselves into scarlet crescents on the rim of a wine glass; hair fell back onto that bed.

Don't forget the grip you had on the neck of the bottle now come to rest on the bedside rug; lying there as jagged as a mantrap.

So many small details crowd your mind; it's hard to decide exactly what *did* happen here only eighty-one minutes ago and it's quite some task to erase both your past presence along with your present presence.

Those spiked heels (stilettos maybe) get on with the job of carrying you back and forth; beating out their matter-of-fact rhythm on the hard kitchen tiles. You hope those too-big rubber gloves will insulate you from all the things your hands are doing, impervious, as they are, to all bodily fluids.

You work meticulously despite the steely odour ever present in your mouth and doing its level best to choke you.

It's not long – just an age – before you're all done.

Or done for.

You pause for a last one final scan around the room, like a hostess expecting guests at any moment. What a performance. Hear those flapping curtains: how they continue their slow applause. Scurry on down the stairway now. Wouldn't you know it, your luck's in at last. No one's labouring up to pass you with a nod. No one greets you in the entrance lobby.

You're out through the front door. Close it with care. Make sure no one witnesses how you slip off those day-glow gloves to snap them up inside your handbag.

You even manage to resist a giveaway backward glance to that open window, to the room where I'm still, lying naked on the bed.

No need to, is there? Won't you always be entering this room? Even on bright, sunlit days like today you'll feel its cold shadow creep over you. Rest assured – I'll always be here, lying in wait for you.

You've plunged straight out into all the heat and bustle, into the welcoming cacophony of just another regular day in the city. Of course, you'll need to make up those lost ninety minutes despite the weakness in your legs as they carry you on your way.

Don't worry; no matter how often you glance at that wristwatch, I'll still be keeping the time.

Jason Jackson

#truebeauty

My name's Jay, and I'm a photographer. Or that's what I've always wanted to be. What I really am is unemployed, thirty-six years old, single, and skint. There's not much I can do about the thirty-six or the single, but the rest is about to change.

Because six weeks ago I had an idea. Like all great ideas, it's simple: I take Polaroids of people in the street, and then I give them the photo.

I also do one more thing, but perhaps I need to go back to the beginning to explain.

My girlfriend - sorry, ex-girlfriend - gave me the idea. Actually, considering the whole law-suit thing, I'll re-phrase that. She did three things which somehow coincided to give *me* an idea. You see how I'm framing it? That's how my lawyer puts it. *It's all about how we frame it,* he says. I laughed at first. I thought it was a photography joke. Frame? Geddit?

Turns out lawyers don't joke.

Anyway, for my birthday, Marie got me an original Polaroid camera. I had one when I was younger, and I loved that thing, but I threw it in the sea one night in my mid-twenties, when the impossibility of making it as a photographer was hitting home. I had other cameras by then, but letting the waves take it was symbolic. The next day I enrolled on a teacher-training course, and I didn't take another photograph for ten years.

So this new Polaroid was such a cool present because Marie had been there when the original hit the water. Childhood sweethearts, you see. *Ahhh.* What made it an even better present was the note attached – '*Back in the game*'.

You see, I'd resigned from teaching. I was going back to photography. And this time, no one was throwing anything into the sea. I'd been telling myself that I wasn't thirty-six, I was *only* thirty-six (see how I framed that?) and I had the rest of my life in front of me. I'd already chatted to Marie's brother, a web designer, about some ideas for the site I was going to need. Wedding photography, okay?

Now, it's not exactly William Eggleston. But I'll tell you what else it isn't. It isn't Year 11 on a wet Wednesday in February. It isn't break duty. It isn't marking essays 'til midnight.

Anyway, it was all about keeping the money coming in. What I was really going to do was street photography. I'd blagged some gallery space through a contact from uni days, and I was going to have an exhibition. I was going to sell prints. And of course, I was going to get a contract to shoot for a magazine – *Vice* maybe, or something bigger.

All I needed to do was take some pictures. I'd got myself a camera - credit card, of course - but the Polaroid was a cool present. I really was back in the game.

The night I had my big idea, Marie was getting dressed to go out. She was telling me something she'd heard at work about a bloke going round drawing pictures surreptitiously of people on the tube. He only let the person know they'd been sketched when he handed them the drawing as he jumped off the train. By all accounts they were brilliant. No one knew who the bloke was, and it'd caused quite a stir. You can see where this going. Substitute Polaroid for sketch, and there's your idea. But no. It was what happened next that made the whole thing click.

Marie was in front of the mirror, about to put on her makeup, and I was holding the camera. She turned her head towards me and I instinctively pressed the button. When the image popped out of the slot, I shook it a little and held it at arm's length. It was a shot in a million. Marie's a good-looking girl, but there was something about her face - no make-up, totally natural, her smile sudden and real - that made the image absolutely captivating.

"Christ," she said, "that's good."

"Did you buy me a magic camera?" I said.

"We both know I'm hot, but *that*...?"

"Let me have it a second."

She passed me the photograph, and I took a pen from the bedside cabinet. In the white strip underneath the image I wrote #*truebeauty,* and I handed it back.

She laughed. "Well, it's a damn sight better than a #*selfie,*" she said.

And that was it. Simple.

The next day was Saturday, and I went into town with the camera. I took over seventy-five shots. Each one was someone caught unawares, smiling, natural, beautiful. Under each image I wrote #*truebeauty,* and I smiled when I handed it over. When I got back home, I switched on the computer. Over half of the people had uploaded photographs of their Polaroids onto the thread.

Over the next week, I took three hundred more. I went out in the morning. In the evening. I checked online every night. By the end of the week, #*truebeauty* was trending all over social media. It was the anonymity that did it. Yes, the photographs were good - I really do think that Polaroid is magic - but it's the handing-it-over-and-running-away that really gets people interested. Marie thought it was great. She kept looking at the thread as more and more people uploaded their photos of the shots I'd taken. By the third week I noticed the images selling online. Someone asked a hundred pounds for one. And got it.

So, I started playing around a little. It's amazing what a different colour pen can do. Images with #*truebeauty* written in blue instead of black suddenly became collectors' items. And the ten I did one morning in red? Someone put one on eBay. Four figure sum.

One evening, Marie was opening a bottle of wine, and she said. "How come all of these people are making money out of our photographs and you just keep giving them away?"

There were two things which concerned me about what she said. Mainly it was her poor business sense: she didn't realise that the photographs were only worth that amount of money precisely because I *was* giving them away, and that as long as I kept giving them away - feeding, but not saturating, the market - then the price would only keep going up. When I did choose to reveal myself, I'd be in the optimum position to cash in.

So, yes, her bad business sense upset me. But what was much worse was her pronoun usage.

"They're not *our* photos," I said. "I take them, not you."

"But I bought you the camera. I gave you the hashtag idea."

"Yes to the camera. No, no, no to giving me the idea," I said.

I'm going to draw a veil over the rest of that conversation. Suffice to say we didn't get to drink the wine.

In the week following the argument, three different magazines - including *Vice* - ran the story of the #truebeauty photographs. There was a half-hour local news special - mainly interviews with the subjects of the photos - with some talking heads banging on about this new development in what they called 'street-portraiture'. Suddenly, it looked like there might actually be some money in *#truebeauty*.

It's strange how in relationships you always think time spent together is like a flood defence for when the rains come. Those hours you put in, watching each other's favourite television programmes, biting your lip when you have to go out as a couple with people only one of you likes. It's insurance to get you through the bad times. Well, not when there's money at stake.

I told her I didn't care about the money; I cared about my intellectual property. She said I was a liar. And if I wasn't a liar, I was pretentious. And an idiot as well. Those flood defences got breached pretty swiftly.

And now there's a lawsuit. Lawyers. Claims and counter-claims. Because last week, I announced on the thread - my first and last post - that I would be staging an exhibition of thirty new *#truebeauty* photographs, the last ones ever to be taken. And if you wanted to be one of those faces in the frame, then you had to turn up at the gallery - with its blank walls ready and waiting for the pictures to be hung - and bid for the opportunity to have your picture taken. I'll make a killing just on that. Then I'm going to exhibit them for a week.

And then I'm going to auction them off. Like I said: a simple idea. *My* idea. I don't feel guilty, because I've got nothing to feel guilty about.

And that first *#truebeauty* shot I took of Marie? She ripped it into tiny pieces and threw them at me.

Shame. Would've been worth a small fortune.

Michael Hurst

Stolen Orange

The air is tight with cigarette smoke. Sunlight from a crack in the curtains illuminates the haze as it rises to the ceiling. Lee is alone for the first time this afternoon. He can hear Nathan in the kitchen, making a racket as usual. Anthea is upstairs. There isn't much furniture in the room. Apart from Lee's sofa, there are some hippy paintings, a glass coffee table and a tall cactus with a cowboy hat balanced on top. The cigarette smoke drifts through the beams of sunlight and forms fantastic columns, phantom totem poles.

Two large Guinness ashtrays are on the coffee table. One is brimming with ash and cigarette butts. The other is clean and contains an orange and two apples. Lee sneers at the sight of the fruit. Nathan doesn't eat fruit or vegetables. The first time they met at the university canteen, Nathan ordered a burger without chips.

"Chips are potatoes. Potatoes are vegetables," he said.

Then he opened the burger and scraped off the sauce and salad.

"Why do you scrape off the sauce?"

"Ketchup is tomatoes. Tomatoes are fruit."

After a term of scraped burgers, it was fried chicken for three months. That was Nathan. One thing after another. And the latest thing was juggling.

Nathan's transformation into Juggling Man surprised his friends. His usual style was nonchalant and cool, but showing off his new skill revealed a talent for showmanship. He rarely used the traditional balls, preferring to take whatever objects were available. Cups, girls' purses, fruit. The constant performances soon irritated Lee. It was egotistical. Why should everything stop for him? Anthea felt the same, although she was too polite to say so.

The orange and apples on the coffee table are not for eating. They are there for juggling demonstrations.

Lee perches on the sofa. He's wearing a t-shirt, and warm air falls on his right arm from his shallow breaths. His throat feels twice its usual size. He looks at the cactus with the cowboy hat as though asking for permission.

The flush sounds upstairs. Nathan noisily stirs cups of tea in the kitchen.

Now or never.

Lee springs forward and grabs the orange from the ashtray. He scuttles round the sofa, drops the orange and stands on it. There is resistance, then a satisfying release as the peel splits and the flesh spews out onto the carpet.

"You need three things to juggle," he thinks. "Let's see you do it with two."

He only just manages to wipe his shoe and get back to his seat when Anthea enters the room. She doesn't see the space he's made for her, and sits cross-legged on the floor by the table. Her dark hair falls over her face. She lights a cigarette with fingers still wet from the bathroom.

Lee has the uncomfortable feeling that she is waiting for Nathan.

Nathan comes in, his thin coarsely-knitted jumper extending to the top of his legs. He carries three mismatched mugs in one hand, and swings his free arm as he walks. Anthea smiles when he places the mugs next to her on the table. She reaches up and offers him her cigarette. Nathan frowns at the ashtray with the apples and the missing orange. He looks at Lee and raises his eyebrows.

Lee says nothing.

Nathan plucks up the two apples in a deft movement. He juggles them one-handed, using his left hand to smoke Anthea's cigarette. The apples almost touch the ceiling.

Anthea clasps her knees and stares.

When he's sure both his guests are paying attention, Nathan catches the apples in his right hand. He puts the cigarette in his mouth and smokes without removing it between drags.

"I learned a cool thing," he says. "You can rip an apple in half with your hands." He places his fingers theatrically at the top of one of the apples and cleaves it down the middle with a single

135

tearing action. Then he does the same with the second apple and tosses a piece to Lee.

"On the house," he says, and juggles the three remaining halves. They tumble through the smoke like the jet of a fountain.

Lee clenches his toes. The acid scent of the crushed orange bleeds into the room from behind the sofa.

Joanna Campbell

Paper Sails

Some mornings, on the way to school, I dropped my satchel on a rock, stripped off and walked into the sea. When the school bell chimed in the distance, I waded back to the shore, but often couldn't bear to leave. Instead, I stood in the shallows while the tide sucked my bare feet blue. If the sun warmed my back, I let the current gather me up again with the foam-washed grit and broken shells. On rough days, the water buffeted my legs, forcing me to sit, and bellowed in my ears, but it couldn't uproot me if I burrowed my hands and feet deep into the compliant shift of the sand.

*

Today, the sea is outside, a matter of metres away. I am in a stifling village hall, attending a birthday party. My wife, Mary, tells me to hand my nephew his present, a sailing-ship I carved in the clinic. He is bombarded with presents in cellophane, in boxes, plastic figures pinioned by wires. They mount up beside him, but he hugs the ship for a moment. In his hands, it seems to weigh less than it did in mine.

On my last day, I made the sails from my papery clinic gown. It crackled when it was first handed to me, eventually softening to a leafy rustle. Then the whispering began, night and day. It was a relief to cut into it, snip it to pieces, some to keep, some to discard.

Beside the thirty paper cups of squash my sister-in-law has squeezed out of one bottle, stands a litre of fizzy wine. I spot it as you would notice a fly has settled on your slice of cake, yet still consider eating it.

"Is that to test me?" I ask.

"There are six glasses, Colin."

137

A swift head count reveals seven adults, twenty nine children. They have prepared well for this party, for the delicate issue of my attendance.

I am enlisted to organise Musical Bumps because, according to my sister-in-law, children relate to me. In reality, the adults are desperate to keep me occupied while they take their celebratory sip. This is the real hardship - not the dryness of the do, but the soft-shoe shuffle around my decade of broken promises.

When a scowling teenage elder pauses the music, I point at the unfortunate child who sits down last.

"I'm afraid you're out," I tell her, a girl in a flouncy frock with tight arm-holes.

Coaxing her to the chairs at the side of the room is akin to dragging a small, recalcitrant elephant. By the time the music blasts again, her face has turned turkey-cock red.

After I have ousted a bawling boy with a fringe like Hitler's moustache, a glaring girl with a pony-tail that sprouts so tight and high on her head I can think only of coconuts, and a monster who kicks me viciously in the shins, it is clear I have stepped wildly out of line.

The teenager deigns to mutter, "You don't *tell* them they're out."

Hitler and Coconut are sniffling. Thug is sucking his thumb.

"But they *are* out," I say.

"Yeah, I know," says the teenager. "But they're still in."

"Still in?"

"Yeah. You have to let them all keep on dancing. You're supposed to *remember* who's actually out. When you work out who the winner is, slip it a tube of Smarties quietly or they'll all want one. If any of them start moaning, give them a fun-size."

She restarts the music. *Everyone's a Winner.*

The nightmare is recalling who is out and who is still in the game. My head spins from wine fumes and ear-splitting noise, from being set adrift. When did the rules change? When I was a child, out meant out. No way back in. You sat at the side and stayed quiet so the eventual, lucky winner could claim the undiluted spotlight.

My nephew's ship has run aground in a corner. Someone's dancing feet crush the sails.

"Look at your boat," Mary says, coming up to me, pointing, as if the damage is my fault.

"I'll go out and buy some better paper," I tell her. "Give me ten minutes."

She gives me a sharp look. Rather than make a scene, she turns away.

I follow her into the sweltering kitchen.

"You made promises, remember," she says, wrapping slices of cake in squares of kitchen-roll, the jam bleeding through.

"It's hard, Mary. I'm still treading water."

"I wish to God they hadn't served wine."

"The rest of you deserve it. It's only me who has no control."

"I thought they taught you that in the clinic."

"But I didn't have to put it into practice there."

I step outside, the sail-less boat under my arm. The evening lights from the town nod and dip in the sea. The noise from the party recedes.

Musical Chairs is the next game, the worst nightmare of them all with its stampede to be first to sit down. And always one chair too few.

There's an off-licence eight hundred yards away. They wrap bottles in sheets and sheets of tough, white paper. I have made promises. Yes, I am ready to dive back in. No, not just put a toe in the water. Actually immerse myself. But I've never learned to swim.

Roaring breaks out from the hall as the dreaded game reaches the most terrifying part. Not the frenzy when the music stops, but the unbearable tension of the final pair circling the one remaining chair.

My nephew is at my elbow. Someone must have sent him. "Can we sail the boat?" he asks.

"The sails need replacing."

"Can't we put it in the water anyway? See if it floats?"

Cheers erupt inside. Someone has won. The others will be protected from the sting of their failure and rewarded for taking part, however early they left the game.

"Please can we? To see how far it will go?"

We walk down the slope to the rumpled sand and wade into the shallows, kicking off our shoes on the shore. I pass the sail-less boat to my nephew and he places it on the water with the utmost care. It stays upright for a minute before it begins to keel over. Before we can set it straight, a mutant wave smothers it in foam and sucks it out of sight.

My nephew gasps, panic-stricken.

"Never mind, "I tell him. "Years from now someone will dive below and discover it encrusted with barnacles."

His young forehead wrinkles, as if he is hearing a foreign language. "But it could be right here, by our feet," he says. "You never know." He crouches down and plunges his hands in the water. A new wave takes him out further, drawing him a little deeper. I grip the sodden sleeve of his party shirt.

"Let's give up now."

"Not yet."

I offer to gather driftwood and make another. "It's not as if it was much," I insist.

He shakes his head. "It's my best present."

We don't have to go far, only up to my knees and his waist, before we find the ship. We can't decide who touches it first and call it a dead-heat. We haul ourselves out, trousers clinging, salty and fishy. For the rest of the evening we'll breathe the tang trapped in our skin.

We slap and drip across the sand, our shoes tied round our necks.

I ask him, "Will the children who are out ever realise they lost the game?"

"The winners make sure they know."

Of course they do. Only adults pussy-foot around the truth.

"The next one's Pass the Parcel. There's a prize in every layer."

"So what's the point of it?"

"Don't know really. Mum likes it because it's quieter when everyone sits down."

"And what do you like best about your party?"

He shrugged, pretending to ponder, then said, "When they all go home. Then I can get at my presents. But Mum'll say it's too late tonight and I'll have to wait 'til tomorrow."

"That's too bad."

"But I got to sail my boat. That was good."

"It was."

"And we rescued it, don't forget. We got it back from the brink."

"Yes, we did. We saved the day, didn't we?"

"Can we try it again tomorrow?"

Early in the morning, the sea will be flat and silent, on fire from the sun. "Yes, I'll be here. We'll do it all again, if we can."

His mother won't let him. She's calling our names now, frantic. In a minute, the panic will change to fury at the state of his clothes.

"You'd better take the boat then," he says. "Then you can make some new sails for tomorrow." He runs to his mother, leaving me alone with the battered little vessel.

"I'll try," I call after him. "I can't promise though."

David Jay

Dream Noir

An actor paces up and down, clutching a cigarette and a page of script. The stage is formless and dark, except where a cone of light beams down on him. Smoke from his cigarette swirls silver-grey.

The actor wears a striped suit with sharp lapels, and a fedora slouches on his head. He paces up and down in sudden bursts, then stops, screws up the page and chucks it on the floor.

"It can't be done. Who am I? What the heck's my motivation? Somebody tell me."   From the darkness, a gun slides quickly towards him across the floor. He stops and picks it up. "A gun? So I'm here to kill someone, I guess. But who? Surely not myself? Suicide was a no-no in the old Hollywood."

A low divan glides onto the stage. On it reclines a platinum blonde clad in a low-cut sheath of black silk. Her shoulder-length hair falls forward, masking one side of her face. Only one green eye, set off with mascara, looks out. Her voice sounds like smoke and honey. "Need some company, mister?"

"Take care, doll. As you see, I've got a gun and I know how to use it."

"A rod? Well, a rod is a dandy kind of weapon, but it's hardly a motive, is it? You'll need to find a motive if you want to kill. That's the way it goes, buster. And finding a motive won't be easy. You don't even know me yet."

The man weighs up her words, scratching his bristled chin with the gun barrel. "Maybe my means is my motive. I could shoot the gun 'cause it's here in my hand."

The blonde swings her silk-stockinged feet from the settee to the floor and pats the space beside her with slender fingers, tipped by long red nails. "Come and sit close to me, handsome, and relax. Whiskey?"

She picks a decanter and two glasses from a tray attached to the arm of the settee. "And why don't you put that gun away?"

"I ain't sure why. Heck, I may need it."

"Are you the kind of guy that would shoot a dame?"

"No, ma'am. Leastways not a lady." He puts the gun into his side pocket where it bulges against the clean outline of his suit. "And if the dame is not a lady?"

She slides the sheath above her knees and tucks her feet up beside her. She places a cigarette between her scarlet lips and hands the man the lighter from the tray. "Give me flame, mister."

He leans towards her to light her cigarette, but before he knows it, she has slipped her hand into his side pocket and taken his gun.

She points it at him coolly. "How are you feeling now, big boy? Scared?"

She holds the gun against his temple, but then he presses his lips to hers. There is a slow, smouldering kiss. The gun in her hand is lowered, pointing safely away. They pull apart.

She puts down the gun beside her and matter-of-factly begins to apply her lipstick. He tries to pull her towards him but she points the lipstick at his eye.

"This is as far as we ride on this train, handsome. Ever heard of censorship? Of the Hays Code of 1930? No sex outside wedlock."

"But you and I could drive to Vegas. Get a licence."

"Great idea, but I'm already married."

"To whom?"

"Rocky Scarpone."

"The mobster? I might have guessed it."

She pouts bitterly. "He's a no-good. He beats me, too."

"Beats you bad, huh?"

"Uh huh. Look."

She pulls aside the curtain of blond hair to reveal a black eye. He bridles.

"The dirty rat."

"I don't suppose you have a name, big boy?"

"Powers. Tom Powers. And you?"

"Gloria. Full name Gloria Inez Chelsea. Pleased to know you, Tom."

She lifts her face for him to kiss but he places one hand on her jaw and pushes her face away. "What's the matter, Tom? Did I suddenly lose my allure?"

"You're Rocky's girl."

"And I wish I wasn't. He beats me up. Then he feels sorry and buys me diamonds. I don't know which he likes best, beating me up and giving me diamonds."

Gloria adds in a low voice, "Now you and me, Tom, we could be very close. It kind of depends on you, your motivation."

Tom remains seated, a little apart. "I don't know. I don't know if I can trust you, Gloria."

"It would be a big mistake giving me the kiss-off."

"Okay, I won't pretend. You got me, you got me dangling like a fish on a hook. So what do you want from me? What's next for us?"

"We could get rid of Rocky, take his money and go to Cuba."

"You want that?"

"Uh huh. But Rocky's gonna be here real soon, and I'm nervous, babe."

She gives him the gun, lights a cigarette and blows a smoke ring. She speaks huskily. "You've got means *and* motivation now, Tom. If you want them, that is. But you gotta be careful. Rocky's been out on a job tonight and, when he's been out on a job, Rocky tends to come back crazy mad."

"Don't fret. I know what I have to do, babe."

They kiss a long kiss, like it's a last kiss. Then a key is heard turning in the lock. Tom grabs her wrist and pulls her behind the settee where they both duck down. A figure appears in silhouette on the edge of the pool of light.

Tom fires his gun and the man crumples to the ground. "That takes care of Rocky." Chelsea stands and walks quickly over to the body. "Oh, my God!"

"So he's dead. He had it coming to him!"

"Oh no, Tom. This isn't Rocky the character. It's not even the actor playing Rocky. It's...the director of the play."

"It's what? Hold it, everybody! Can we stop here, please? If the director's gonna play tricks, like pretending to be dead, I shoulda been told. Tell him to get up."

144

"No, Tom. He's really dead. Those were real bullets in your gun."

"Real bullets? I've killed him? You can't pin this on me. Nobody told me. Blame the props department!"

"Don't get so angry, Tom."

Tom walks over to the victim. There is a long pause. "He was a lousy director, anyway."

The voice of a powerful middle-aged woman calls from the shadows. "And…cut!" Gloria turns towards the voice. "Cut? I thought this was a play, not a film.""It's a play about a dream, a dream I keep having. But at the same time we're filming the play. Tom has shot the director of the play, but I'm the director of the film and I'm very much alive. Are you following me so far?"

The actor begins to weep. "But is he dead? Tell me he's not really dead. I killed him! He was my mentor, my brother and I killed him!"

The corpse of the theatre director stirs. He sits up and speaks. "Of course I'm not dead."

The actor, distressed, throws himself into Gloria's arms. "What is going on? What are they doing to me? Who am I?"

The lady director speaks. "You're a speck of flotsam in an ocean of nothingness. Get it?"

"Okay. I can work with that. But do I still kill Rocky and get the girl?"

"Well, right now we don't know if Rocky exists. We only have Gloria's word for it.""So what's the point of me?"

"A good question for which I don't yet have an answer. Okay, everybody. It's a rap. Same time tomorrow."

"But I still don't know my motivation!"

"You get a paycheck, don't you? That's your motivation."

The actress playing Gloria removes a handkerchief from her sleeve and wipes the actor's face. "You've got my lipstick on you still. And there's a tear rolling down your cheek." "It's been a horrible day."

"Maybe you should think of doing those cigarette ads on television."

She leaves the stage, followed by the two directors arm-in-arm. The actor is alone. The crumpled page of script still lies on the floor. He takes a kick at it, slips and falls backwards onto the floor. He remains there on his back, quite still.

He pulls out a pack of cigarettes and a book of matches and lights one. Silver-grey smoke rises. The cone of light above him fades away. The red glow of his cigarette brightens for a second or two, and is gone.

Philip Douch

Journeys

Martin sat in the waiting room. He picked up a dishevelled copy of *The Metro*. Various points scattered across the national rail network were the only places that he'd ever read it. Or, more accurately, looked at it.

He soon came across those little snippets of frustrated pseudo-romance that were *The Metro's* stock in trade:

Girl with the turquoise ear-rings at Temple Meads last Tuesday morning. I was the man in the blue suit who caught your eye. Coffee?

Guy with the Dr Who scarf on the stopping train to Salisbury. I was the bubbly blonde beside you. Could I be your attractive female assistant?

Martin sighed. Why not just head that section 'Looking for a shag' and be done with it? And then there was the 'Entertainment News'. The conjoining of those two words seemed somehow inherently inappropriate to Martin. As if to prove his point, a largely unknown and largely undressed woman was describing a largely unspectacular rise up the popular music charts as 'a marvellous journey'. He sighed again, more heavily.

Thank you for the opportunity, Lord Sugar. It's been an amazing journey.

Strictly has been the best experience of my life – it's been a fantastic journey.

Thank you, Mary. Bake-off has been the most incredible journey.

How about Goodbye, Lord Sugar, I've been on a television programme with you for quite a little while, but I guess I won't be on it any longer now?

Or, Well, that was a shitload of dancing for not much benefit.

Or, There goes another Victoria sponge in the sodding bin.

It's just, thought Martin, they aren't actually journeys, are they? They are mildly interesting things that have happened to people, taking place sequentially over a short period of time. And that's how everything happens, isn't it? One thing, then another, then another. For a journey, thought Martin, there really needed to be some sort of vehicle involved – like a rollercoaster for instance. Ideally, an emotional one of course.

Martin wondered just what an 'emotional rollercoaster' would be like. He imagined stepping into the little metal carriage, clicking himself into his safety belt and giving the weather-beaten youth his two pound coin, only to hear the machinery whispering, "Bloody hell, Martin, I'm scared. I've done this hundreds of times and, honestly, it doesn't get any better. Those tight corners – I hate it, Martin, I hate it."

Martin could see in his mind's eye the panicky little train shuddering, with tears leaking from its sprockets.

Anyway, whilst he was thinking about all these things that weren't really journeys, Martin was sitting at Cheltenham Spa railway station awaiting the delayed 18.34 to Swindon, which, ironically enough, was starting to look like it wouldn't be providing much in the way of a journey either

The first clicking of the Tannoy had come at 18.31. "We regret to announce that the (tiny pause whilst a button is pressed in a little office somewhere) 18.34 to…Swindon is delayed by…sixteen…one-six…minutes. Great Western Railway apologises for the late running of this service."

Martin stood. Relinquishing his slightly sticky seat, he meandered across to what passed as 'refreshments' in a railway station. He pondered the array of items laid out before him. It struck him that the UK's railway system held maybe 95% of the nation's supply of Giant Muffins. There was a similarly high percentage of plastic-wrapped slabs of solidified slurry going under the generic name of 'flapjack', improbably differentiated by the prefixes fruit, cherry, chocolate, and - presumably misguidedly courting the health food market - yoghurt.

Then Martin noticed a concession to the five-a-day brigade. A chipped plate on the counter featured one over-ripe banana. Small. 50p. He was almost tempted. But good sense mercifully got the better of him. However, sparked into a virtuous reflex by the sight of something that had clearly once resembled fruit, before he could stop himself he went for a blueberry muffin.

Martin sat back down again. The room was slowly getting fuller. Not just with people but with food detritus. The table surfaces offered up a mixture of ingrained tea-stain rings and stagnant pools of spilt coca cola, the occasional ripped plastic sweet wrapper going for a desultory little sail at the edge of the dark brown ponds. Martin recalled reading that if you leave a tooth in a glass of Coca Cola it will gradually disappear. He wondered if Coca Cola could also eat away a whole table if allowed simply to lie there overnight. Then he wondered why anyone would leave their tooth in a glass of the stuff.

The disembodied pre-programmed station announcer made another appearance. "We regret to announce that the...18.34 to...Swindon has been cancelled. Great Western Railway apologises for any inconvenience caused. Passengers for... Swindon will now be served by a...replacement bus service. We have no idea at all where it might choose to go on its way to...Swindon. Though probably not by a route any of you are...likely to recognise. But while you wait, why not try one of our...delicious muffins?"

Martin wasn't sure if he had started to hallucinate.

He absent-mindedly picked up the copy of *The Metro* again. He returned to the pseudo-romance section:

Arthritic old blind man with the salivating guide dog on the 8.06 from Stroud. I was the voluptuous nun with the nipple tassels. Fancy getting into the habit?

Woman with the luscious lips I lunge at lasciviously each morning on the 7.44 from Castle Cary. How about it? Sorry not to have asked before. But better fellate than never?

Martin knew he was tired, knew he was hungry, but was becoming increasingly uncertain about the blurring of what might or might not be real. Even more so when, only minutes after the announcement about the replacement bus service, a bus actually turned up. The driver was Lord Sugar. Counting the passengers and laughing uncontrollably as they did so, were Prince Philip and the Chelsea centre-back David Luiz. Martin was again unsure about his grip on reality, principally because Prince Philip appeared to be both jovial and polite.

"All aboard what's going aboard," shouted Lord Sugar genially, and he rang a little bell before ramming the gear stick into reverse and backing violently into a straggling line of pensioners transferring from platform one to a second bus.

"Twenty-five points, Alan," shouted Prince Philip gleefully. "And a bonus point for the one in a wheelchair."

Lord Sugar whooped with laughter as Prince Philip clapped his hands and asked to see everyone's ticket. There was a brief judder as Lord Sugar hammered into first and sped forward, evidently driving back over a prostrate body before squealing out onto the open road.

Martin reached inside his jacket for his mobile phone, thinking he'd give his wife a call to tell her he was at least now on his way. Interestingly, however, his fingers alighted not on his phone but on an effigy of a human figure, skilfully moulded from marzipan. It bore an uncanny likeness to Jose Mourinho.

He beckoned David Luiz over. "What do you reckon, David?" said Martin (for he knew that the classy Brazilian defender had been signed by Mr Mourinho in his triumphant first spell at Stamford Bridge).

"Absolutely," said David Luiz. "Spitting image of him."

Martin felt unreasonably proud of his powers of recognition before biting off Mourinho's left leg and offering the remaining limbs to Prince Philip. Who, as it happened, wasn't really into marzipan.

The rest of Martin's ride was relatively quiet. Unusually, though, the bus did stop once to pick up a hitch hiker. It was a hugely pregnant Bruce Forsyth. For some reason, nobody seemed to find this remotely strange. Martin was merely a little apprehensive that Mr Forsyth might go into labour before they reached Swindon. He wasn't confident that the celebrity bus crew necessarily possessed the skills to facilitate childbirth. He shuddered to think what might happen if Bruce were to require a Caesarean.

However, in due course, and apparently undistracted by a choir of singing armadillos that had emerged out of thin air to populate the back seat somewhere between the turns for the B4696 and Cricklade, Lord Sugar pulled the bus safely into Swindon station car park. Before Martin got off, David Luiz asked him for his autograph and he duly obliged, personalising the signature with 'To David. Shame about the World Cup Final but thanks for the ride.'

Martin's wife was there waiting for him as he came down the steps. "Hi love," she said, pecking him routinely on the cheek. "Sorry you were delayed."

Martin looked at her. He shook his head vigorously as if trying to clear it. "Hi," he said, before adding a phrase he had never thought himself remotely likely to utter. "It's been an amazing journey."

Sian Breeze

Spring Clean

I listened to the broom, enjoying the quiet hush of the bristles kissing the floorboards. I liked watching the pile of dirt growing and merging into a new form. Building slowly like a castle on a sandy beach. I watched the dust and the hair clumping together into a mound, boasting the grime and the guts of the past week, and I knelt down, sweeping it out of sight into the pan, surveying the crisp lines of wood.

I pulled my collar from my neck, separating the skin from sweat, cursing the polyester company uniform. I stood still for a moment, catching my breath, surveying the scene. Feeling dizzy at the size of the rooms.

Then the polish. I studied the row of silver bottles. They stood in a proud rainbow of coloured potions. I held my finger in front of me like a wand, waving it around choosing at random, my lucky pick. I settled on the yellow one and I pulled it out, shaking it to check its weight. I always sniffed before I sprayed, inhaling the soft lemon and chemical hues.

The four windows were lined up in front of me and I started on the left, writing my name in the thick layer of dust on the inside of the ledge. But remembering myself, I wiped it quickly away with a cloth. The smells of the polish melted into the heat, going straight to my head. I bent over trying to feel the breeze that was sneaking through the cracks in the locked glass. I held the cloth upright in my left hand. I was careful not to knock any spores of dead skin and lint onto the freshly swept floor. I wiped the ledge in clockwise circles, pressing firmly on the microfibres, checking after for left over smears. I wiped ledges and mantles and light shades and ornaments. I wiped and I sprayed, admiring the gleam and going over my movements again and again until I was happy, and I knew he would be.

Then the heat came over me. It was thick and stifling. The dizziness and the sweat stuck my polyester green uniform to my skin. I watched the room swaying in front of me and pinched the skin on my hand to stop myself from fainting. I looked at my watch and at the locked door in front of me, feeling my chest shrinking around my heart.

Careful not to catch my name badge in my hair, I raised my dress and apron upwards over my head watching it melt into a pile in front of me. I unlaced my shoes, and pulled off my cotton socks. I felt behind my back at the tight clasp of my bra; I sucked in and unlatched, throwing the black lace over to a chair. Feeling the freedom in my breasts, I then slipped my knickers off, tentatively looking back at the door. I screwed them up in a ball and placed them on top of the black bra.

I stretched everything upwards towards the ceiling, feeling my skin breathing again. I felt the soft heat on my nipples and cheeks, and wiggled my hands. Then I stood naked in the light. My skin was free again, the lines of sweat evaporated into the air.

I only stopped to reach for my bottle of water when I saw his face in the reflection of the polished mirror.

He was sitting in the next room, staring straight towards me from the table. I knew his brown beard and dark hair from the photos I had polished. The ones with him and a woman in a red dress. We had never met in the flesh; he paid the company by standing order. And here he was now, facing my naked back in silence, watching me.

My clothes were in there with him. Still piled on each other on the chair directly in front of him. I would have to walk towards him, meeting his eyes if went to collect them. I looked up to the mirror, placing my water glass down in front of me. He hadn't moved. He was still sitting there, expressionless, watching me.

I looked at the vacuum resting by my feet, and slowly, I bent over and I switched it on, never looking back up at his face. I started to hoover the room I was in, pointing the nozzle under chairs and into corners, all the while facing the ground. I tried to focus my mind on the job, forgetting the eyes that I knew were watching the shapes of my body.

I waited for him to speak. For a cough or a sneeze of acknowledgement. But there was nothing. Just the sound of the vacuum cleaner.

Claire Morris

Bodgers

In 1916, after the cherry harvest was in, Reg Dean and his son Alexander walked from the Weald of Kent to Buckinghamshire in time for the timber auction in Great Hampden. The countryside they passed through, usually thronging in late summer with labourers bringing in the last of the crops, was half empty this year. In the villages it was the elderly, the women and children who were out in the streets, and they gave the travellers hostile looks as they passed. The two slept in barns and under hedges, and arrived in Hampden on the last day of August. They went first to the office of the Duke of Buckingham's land agent and collected a catalogue showing the sites in the beech woods where the stands of timber were for sale; then spent the day visiting each location to assess the quality of the trees. There was plenty to consider because the woods would be their livelihood for the winter, and their home.

The auction was held in the Hampden Arms, and the beer flowed freely from nine in the morning, paid for by the Duke's Hampden estate. Reg and his son, who had lived locally in Lacy Green when Alexander's mother was alive, were greeted cautiously by the other bodgers as they came in.

"He's getting to be a man now, your Alexander."

"Fifteen, July past."

"Looks older."

There was a pause and Reg saw an uneasy flicker in the other man's eyes. Then the auction began and they got the stand they wanted, in a sheltered part of the beech woods where the trees were straight and not rimey from exposure, and looked to be good splitters.

At a sale they bought equipment, and walked up into the woods to stake out and prepare their patch. They owed the Duke of

Buckingham £28/2s/4d and would have to turn out thousands of chair legs to pay him in the spring. Alexander walked ahead of his father, and Reg saw what the bystanders had seen. The slender child's body had become muscled and powerful; he was as tall as Reg himself, and would be a lot taller if the size of his hands and feet was anything to go by. The man should have rejoiced in this vigorous growth of his son, but instead remembered the sour looks of the people they had passed, and only felt anxiety.

In the wood, among their trees, they set about immediately to build a hovel, cutting and binding saplings for the walls, and weaving brushwood and straw together to make the roof, the man watching his son critically as he worked. Alexander wanted to be off after rabbits and was rushing things.

"Cut the struts at an angle so the rain runs off, like I showed you."

There was activity all around them now; the bodgers were pleased to be back in the woods and whistled and shouted jokes to each other. Most of them lived in the village and would go back at night, but they worked on through the dusk and lit candles, so it was an eerie thing to see the glow of flickering light among the trees. Reg and Alexander made a fire and boiled up a kettle of tea, sitting in the shelter of the hovel and gulping the smoky brew with pleasure. The cottagers packed their tools away and went home, and father and son lit their pipes and sat quietly listening to the small night noises of the wood.

Reg looked again at the boy - his only family and his working partner. Reg's wife had died when Alexander was seven, and Reg had gone out of his mind for a while. He stopped working and lost his cottage in Lacy Green, and the two of them became vagrants. This in itself wasn't a hardship, and in time, as he came to his senses, Reg developed the routine of summer fruit picking in Kent, and wood turning in Hampden in the winter. There were records of their existence in government archives, but as itinerants they weren't registered in any parish, and Alexander had barely been to school. Reg went about training him as a craftsman and taught him how to live on the bounty of the countryside, believing this to be the best education any boy could have. But he was aware that change was everywhere, brought about by the war on the continent, and evident in the dissolution of country life that they'd witnessed on their walk from Kent. He hunted around for reassurance.

"King has Windsor chairs in his castles, orders them special," he said.

"But there isn't that many bodgers now," said Alexander. "Just half the usual at the auction today."

"But everyone still needs chairs."

Over the next few days the woods were full of the noise of saw and spade as the bodgers prepared their stands. They worked in pairs, and the first job was to dig a seven foot pit to lay the tree trunks across for sawing. Reg and Alexander had their pit ready by the end of the morning; then after a pause for bread and beer they set about assembling the lathe. The uprights needed replacing but the wheel and the treadle were still good. They cut a whippy sapling and attached one end of it to the treadle of the lathe and the other to a corner of the hovel roof then adjusted the metal centres for angle and balance.

The carts would be coming from Wycombe to collect the first loads of chair legs in two weeks, and Reg could already hear the razzle of gouges against revolving green beech as the bodgers hurried into production. He and Alexander were usually slower to get going because the boy was still learning, but this year Alexander surprised him at his first attempt on the lathe, turning out a chair leg of curved and tapered perfection.

After tea, when they'd lit up and were resting their aching bodies by the fire, Reg said, "You'll be a better turner than me. That was beginner's luck, but you have the rhythm, and the eye."

"Mechanical lathes do it better and quicker now."

"Maybe, but there'll always be call for handmade furniture."

"I don't know, Dad. Things are changing."

They smoked on thoughtfully and a pair of little owls started up calling in the distance. Then the peace was broken by scattered shouts on the edge of the woods, men hallooing instructions to each other - not in the familiar accents of the local people but in harsh commanding tones. Reg and Alexander covered the fire and ducked into the hovel. The crashing and cursing came near, then receded, and the two moved back into the open to watch the lights disappearing down the track towards Hampden.

"What was they after?"

"It's my belief they were looking for you, son. A conscription gang. I was talking to Sol Butler and he says they're taking them younger and younger. He says, looking at you, you could be sixteen or more, and I got no papers to prove anything else."

"I don't mind fighting."

"Cannon fodder...meat, that's what you'd be. There's hardly any boys survived local. And you heard the stories what it's like."

"Dad, I want to go. You know, walking from Kent, I didn't like the way people was looking at me. We can't stop it, you and me - it's the war. I got to go. And those people looking, they're right. I'm a man now. I ought to be in France fighting."

Alexander turned away from his father and looked in the direction the conscription gang had taken. Reg said, "And me? What do I do?"

"You'll be all right, Dad. You'll get another partner. Or get a job in one of the chair factories in Wycombe. It's good wages."

The woods had settled down again. Reg walked away from the fire and leaned his back against one of the beeches. It seemed to him he sensed the life in the tree - the flow of its sap, its straight fibres and sound heart. The resentment Alexander's words had called up in him calmed a little, and he made himself remember how it was the same lust for action that had taken him to the South African war sixteen years before. With his woodsman's training he'd known how to survive, and Alexander would survive too.

"All right, boy. You go into Aylesbury tomorrow. But if you tell them you're fifteen, they'll maybe not take you."

That night father and son sat up late by the fire. They didn't speak or think much about what lay ahead: they were absorbed in the sounds around them, marking the whereabouts of badger and weasel. This precious way of life was coming to an end - perhaps not in this generation, but within their lifetime. They knew it and there was no need to talk about it.

All You Need Is Love. Or Is It?
November 2017

Kate O'Grady

A Hint of Blue

Her exact words were, "Don't come back without it." *It* being the ugly blue vase her mother gave her as a birthday present last year. Yesterday afternoon I donated the vase to a local charity, along with a coffee table, a floor lamp and an armchair. I was having a spring clean. Never underestimate the power of a spring clean. Even though I am a thirty-five year old man, I am a sucker for a book with a title like 'The Life Changing Magic of Tidying Up'. Of course, I always go too far.

After the enchantment of a tidy apartment wore off, I decided to de-clutter by removing pieces of furniture and stacking them in the hallway. Ten minutes later the coffee table, the lamp, the armchair and the vase were in the back of my Honda Civic and on their way to The Salvation Army. Holly wasn't too upset about the missing furniture. The pieces were old, but she drew the line at that awful vase.

"Find it, or don't bother coming home," was the last thing she said to me when I left the flat this morning.

The thing is I have too much time on my hands. Too much time, and a developing crystal meth habit. I'm a writer slash freelance journalist. Or, I should say, I am a blocked writer. I write, but I struggle with it. I certainly don't make much money from it. I haven't sold a story in six months.

Mostly, Holly supports us both. She's a primary school teacher. We met in college thirteen years ago. I was a creative writing major and she was studying early childhood education. It was love at first sight for me when I spotted her on that bench outside the Students' Union. She had a Louise Brooks bob at the time and wore bright red lipstick. I was coming back from my run around the lake and heading over to the dorms. She was reading a book. It was May and warm, and she was bare legged. As I got closer to the bench I noticed that she had an ankle bracelet on her left ankle. It was a delicate single strand with a tiny silver heart attached to it. I made a beeline straight over to her. As she turned to look at me approaching, she shielded her face from the sun with the side of her palm so that she could see me better, and I got my first glimpse of those traffic-light green eyes.

Holly is the love of my life.

I have always taken things to their limit. As a child, I built Lego towns on the kitchen floor of the tiny apartment that my mother and I shared. I didn't stop until every piece in the box had been used. As a thirteen year old, I played the video game Mortal Kombat for six hour stretches after getting home from school, and then I played it for twelve hours at the weekend. When I started to run I progressed from track to long distance to marathons to ultramarathons. I am not satisfied until I have taken something to its limits. This worries me. Right now I have been snorting meth for a couple of months, just once a week, every Thursday. It's not a problem at the moment, and using it has certainly increased my writing output, not to mention the fact that our apartment is the cleanest it's ever been. Yesterday evening, after the trip to the Salvation Army and a couple of top-up lines, I was down on my hands and knees in the bathroom with an old toothbrush and a bottle of Flash scrubbing the floor behind the toilet. I've seen the photos though. I've read the news articles. I know that it starts out with euphoria and increased self-confidence, and ends up with open sores, tooth loss and paranoid hallucinations.

I told Holly I loved her for the first time at the annual fancy dress party. We'd been dating three months. The party theme that year was 'Beatle Song Characters'. Best fancy dress party I've ever been to. Ten guys came along in bare feet with knotted hankies on their heads, rolled up trousers and white vests.

"Day Trippers," Holly and I said simultaneously, and we both laughed and clinked glasses at the bar. Tom Rafferty, my best friend at the time, spent the entire evening dancing while wearing a giant tin-foiled cardboard hammer on his head. "Maxwell did it," was his opening line to girls, as he pointed to the hammer.

162

One student, who's name I can't remember, had tree branches attached to his arms and torso, and the branches were festooned with red and green lights that flashed on an off.

I'm "Norwegian Wood," he told me later, outside, when we shared a joint.

"Oh, right, Norwegian Wood," I said. "Very creative."

Holly was 'Lovely Rita, Meter Maid'. Her outfit consisted of a very short grey pleated skirt, a white shirt and a black peaked cap. I, in a nod to my literary aspirations, came as 'Paperback Writer'. The costume was cumbersome. I was sandwiched between two pieces of thin plasterboard that were painted to look like the cover of 'Catcher in the Rye'

That night was one of the happiest nights of my life. I think the DJ played every Beatles song ever written. Holly and I kept requesting the love songs. I still cannot hear 'Love Me Do' without my heart turning somersaults.

"I love you Holly," I said, around midnight.

"I love you too," she said, and I knew she meant it.

The party didn't break up until after 4 o'clock in the morning.

"OK," the DJ said, "this next song is definitely the last one." There was a couple of second's silence, and then that famous intro, from the French national anthem, all those trumpets and horns, and then the singing, those immortal words, 'All You Need is Love', blasting through the hall. As I said, one of the happiest nights of my life.

The Salvation Army store is huge. The big items: the faux leather couches, the teak entertainment centres, the double beds, are in the front, close to the windows. I was outside before the store opened this morning, waiting, smoking a cigarette, peering in, thinking about what Holly had said about not bothering to come home unless I found the vase.

"If it's still here, it will be in the glass and housewares section," the big guy with the keys said when he let me in, and he nodded to the back of the room. That's where I am now, staring at endless rows of glass items on wobbly black shelving systems. I've been scanning this labyrinth of discarded goods, searching for a hint of blue, for the last fifteen minutes.

163

Everything here looks fragile, damaged, easy to break. Everything looks like it could topple over at any second. One wrong move and it could all come crashing down on top of me.

Tais Brias Avila

Ashes and Knee Pins

"Just take it away, please," I say to them. "It was my boyfriend's and I can't look at it anymore, I'm sick of it."

"It's all right, love. Don't be upset now, my sister got divorced last year, I know what it's like," says the big one. He glances to the other one, a sharp rise of the eyebrow.

I know what they are thinking, I would think the same. I do look like a batty cat lady. Standing in the doorway, still in my pyjamas at lunchtime, my eyes all puffy from crying, demanding that they take the blasted sofa as fast as they can.

What's happened is plain for everyone to see. At least, I hope it is: poor girl, poor ugly fat girl being cheated on by Phil, who was always way above my league. This fucking sofa is the only thing left of him. Now it's just me. I don't even have a bloody cat.

*

We slept together for the first time on this very sofa. Of course, it was in his flat then. We had met in the pub earlier in the evening. He spilled my drink and offered to buy me a new one. I liked the way he towered over me, solid muscles all over. He was a winker.

"I'm sorry princess! I'll get you a refill." *Wink.*

"You wanna come to mine for a nightcap?" *Wink.*

"I'll text you soon." *Wink.*

I was taken in. Of course, I was. He played football, knew people everywhere, he even had a steady job. I felt so lucky, my friends at work said so.

"You are so lucky, he doesn't even have a family!" Lorna said, walking back from the pub one night, right at the beginning. Back then, the fact that he had no family didn't seem to me to be lucky. Of course, in the end, Lorna was right. She always is.

165

The day he asked me to move in together we were sitting on the sofa, watching telly in his living room.

He moved into mine. It was far too soon, but I assumed he was in a rush because he had no family; he wanted his own home. I just couldn't believe he wanted me to be his family. Of all the girls he could've had, he chose me. I felt like the luckiest girl alive. I smiled all the time. I had to hide it at work though. I work in a crematorium, you see? It is not really a place where you can go around smiling like the cat that got the cream.

Yeah, that's what I was: the batty cat lady that got the yummy cream.

The sofa was the only thing he brought with him. It had been his in his nanna's house. The only thing he had left of her. Her smell had sunk deep into the cushions, no amount of spray could mask it.

He sold all his other furniture. "I don't need anything else, princess. You are all I need." *Wink*.

So, I put up with the sofa, but goodness, it was an ugly thing. I took pictures on my phone and showed the girls at work. We laughed so much; you don't get many chances to laugh when you work on the funerals all day.

The second time he hit me I fell straight onto the sofa. I could've been lucky and fallen into the cushions, but I wasn't. I knocked my head on the wooden arm-rests. Five stiches. The nurse took me to the side.

"I need to ask you, lovely. Are you sure this was an accident?"

I laughed, "Oh yes. Sure it was. I'm just so clumsy!"

Because that's what Phil said, that I was a clumsy fat cow. Useless fat cow. Idiot. Good job I worked with the dead, 'cause I would've killed them on sight if they saw my fucking face. *Smack*.

And later, much later: "I'm sorry, princess. I didn't mean to hurt you. I just lost control this once. Don't leave me, I'll die. You and me, princess." *Wink*.

Things only got worse, because that's the direction bad things generally take. He promised he would change. Perhaps I believed it, for a short while.

166

"Get out," said Lorna. "Anything you need, I'll help." She meant it too, she would help me. Lorna always helps, that's the thing with best friends.

The twelfth time he hit me he tried to suffocate me. I remember thinking I would die with the flowered pattern etched onto my cheek. Silly, the things you think sometimes. This time it was different from all the others. This time I knew what had provoked him. He had found out I was planning to leave him.

"Where do you think you are going, you disgusting fat cow?" *Wink. Smack.*

Shortly after, I started working night shifts and things finally began to change. Lorna got a job in the crematorium, in the office. It was nice having her there, but I barely saw her. I started working in the processing room, operating the cremation ovens. It was hard work, but I enjoyed the calmness of it. I worked alone all through the night, but it never got lonely. Everything was controlled by a computer. A spaceship: the dead, their ashes, my computer and me, at the command centre. It was good.

I would normally get back to my flat at 8.00 in the morning, just as Phil was leaving for work. I slept all day and spent my evenings in the gym. I knew that things would only work out if I got fitter. Phil was happy. I was if not happy, at least determined to make things better. I had a mission - a plan - and it was working. Of course, he was still a mean bastard, but I didn't mind so much now. At least the shame was gone. The shame is the worst, you see? Much worse than the blood and the bruises, although those hurt too. Sticks and stones, will hurt a lot. But the shame? That stuff will burn you from the inside out.

In the end, Phil died on his precious sofa. It was a Friday evening and Lorna had just called to tell me about her day at the office, which had been awful. The CCTV cameras were down, and this being a bank holiday weekend they wouldn't fix them until Tuesday morning. I had five caskets to process through the ovens over the weekend and the computer wasn't working properly. As soon as I hung up I went in to cook Phil's tea and I added some crushed painkillers. I'm not sure what they were, pink and yellow capsules.

167

Courtesy of Phil, I had accumulated a whole rainbow of them over the last year.

Lorna was there shortly after his heart stopped. We worked fast and distributed Phil into five rubbish bags.

I took the bags to work in the boot of my car. They were very heavy, but it was nothing compared to what I'd been lifting at the gym. Over the next three nights I added a bag to each casket. Inside of the first one, Mrs Robinson's, I put the bag with Phil's legs. I knew the metal pins wouldn't melt, so I picked them up carefully from Mrs Robinson's ashes. With the last one, Mr Jones, I put in Phil's head and his wallet. After it was cremated I couldn't resist scooping up some of the ashes. I put them in a Tupperware container and took them home in my handbag. I know, I know, it was a silly and sentimental thing to do. But I felt I ought to, I didn't want poor Mr Jones to have to share all eternity with Phil's head.

*

The two men are still looking at me. I guess I've been quiet for a while. They must be waiting for an explanation of sorts. I really must look crazy.

"My boyfriend left me," I say with teary eyes. "Went up north with some woman."

I hope I'm convincing; I have been repeating this line to everyone since last Saturday. Everyone has been very nice.

"It's all right, love, we'll take it away. Going straight into the incinerator, you won't have to think about it no more."

And off they go, taking Phil's sofa, where deep inside the cushions I've put Phil's ashes and his knee pins. I sewed it shut last Tuesday, when I gave him a little private funeral. I know, I know, silly and sentimental.

Lorna calls just after they leave. "Is it gone?"

"Yup, gone."

"How are you feeling?" Lorna, my lovely Lorna. She knows what I am capable of, but she still worries about me. Best friends are really all we need, don't you think?

"I'm quite relieved actually. It really was a bloody ugly sofa."

Martin Spice

The One

Dear Aunt Trimble,

I write to you in a high state of excitement as I think it entirely possible that I may finally have met THE ONE. I remember asking you, when I was a teenager and boarding with you whilst Mama and Papa were in India during the late '50s, how I would know when I met THE ONE. You replied that I would know immediately, although you also added that it was not an experience you had yourself enjoyed. At which point, if I remember correctly, Uncle Cyril had looked more than a little askance. So sorry - how insensitive of me to mention dear Uncle Cyril when he is so recently demised. Anyway, what I am writing to tell you is, and yes, I am going to repeat myself, that I have finally met THE ONE, and, of course, I knew immediately, just as you said I would. It is absolutely thrilling. I am plucking up all my courage to speak to her soon.
Your loving nephew,
Arthur

Dear Arthur,

How marvellous to receive your letter so full of news about your studies and your fascination with the world of medicine. Or perhaps I missed that part. Anyway, I was, of course, delighted to hear more about THE ONE, and when you next write perhaps you might include such superfluous information as her name, how you met her, what attracted you to her and so on. Trifling details, I know, but they will help me better to visualise the object of your new found affections.
All my love, dear Arthur,
Trim

Dear Aunt Trimble (or may I now call you Trim as most of your other friends and family do?),

Silly me, I realise now that I should have told you more about Aggy in my last mail, but the truth is that I knew very little about her when I last wrote. We met when we were asked to share an electron microscope to study some slides of human excrement and identify which showed evidence of amoebic dysentery. It was quite fascinating as you can imagine.

I remember dear Mama and Papa saying, before they died in the cholera outbreak, that everyone in India had amoebic dysentery all the time, but I think they meant bacterial dysentery which is entirely different, as the slides show - despite being horribly incapacitating. Mama said that the children there have the seats of their pants cut out so that they can defecate spontaneously, as it happens frequently without warning.

Anyway, Aggy and I were partnered together and picked up a bit of a conversation at the end of which I was able to ask her a personal question. "Agatha," she replied. "But you may call me Aggy." So there you have it. THE ONE is Aggy. She is perfect in every way and was quite entranced by my anecdotes about the children in India. I suppose it was all quite out of her experience.

Love,

Arthur

Dear Arthur,

What a delightfully romantic way to meet your future spouse. I am so pleased to know her name. Perhaps when you can spare a moment you can add a few more details such as her appearance, background, upbringing and so forth to help an old lady understand what it is you have found so appealing.

Much love, darling Art,

Trim

Dear Trim (I am taking the plunge and calling you Trim although you did not expressly give permission),

I thought I would delay writing to you until I had my next class with Aggy, and then I could tell you a bit more about her. Today was the day! It was the tapeworm and other parasites of the digestive tract class, and I have to say it was completely fascinating. I am beginning to think that I might switch my future specialism and work in this area in memory of Mama and Papa.

Anyway, Aggy and I fell to talking, and, you will scarcely credit this, she also comes from Surrey where her parents have 'a house and a bit of land'. Turns out the house is Charleton House and the bit of land is several hundred acres. She was so modest about it. "Just a few old fields," she said, "where we keep the horses." Turns out the horses are racehorses and they have a filly called Aggy's Delight running in the Oaks this year. How exciting is that?

But, dear Trim, I am concerned now that she may be out of my class. What do you think?
Your ever loving Arthur

Dear Art,
The only class you need to worry about is the intestinal diseases class. Only vulgar people worry about social class - in matters of the heart, love is all that matters. I should have saved myself a lot of trouble if I had known that before I married Cyril.
My love,
Trim

Dear Trim (how easily I have lapsed into calling you that!),
Twice now you have asked me to describe Aggy to you, and twice I have neglected to do so. She is tall, but not too tall. She has hair like gold and a little pointy nose that is endearingly sweet (and does not, incidentally, unlike mine, get in the way when using the electron microscope). Her neck is like a swan's, her legs like a gazelle's and her lips are like plump cherries which hide teeth-like pearls. Now you see why she is perfect. I am quite intoxicated.

How are you, by the way?
Much love,
Arthur

Dear Art,

I am well, thank you, although suffering a little from the indigestion caused by the clichéd menagerie employed in your last letter. Could you not have managed a little plain objective description? I have no idea what Aggy looks like and have instead an image of a zoo after a carpet bombing raid with legs and bits of animal corpses everywhere. Perhaps it would be better if you didn't try again to describe her, and I will wait until we meet, which we undoubtedly shall if indeed she is THE ONE.

Dare I ask, have you asked her out yet?

Love etc,

Trim

Dear Trim,

I have asked Aggy out for dinner on Monday and I am going to ask her to marry me. I am all in a dither about what to wear, but I think my flares, a flowery tie and my corduroy jacket should set the mood nicely. And a bottle of champagne, of course. Do you think I should buy a ring and propose on one knee?

Please advise.

Art

Dear Art,

Monday is a bad day to go to any restaurant as it is always the proper chef's day off. If Aggy has horses and some acres in Surrey she will know this and be unimpressed.

You will find it difficult to buy a ring on one knee, as it is unlikely you will be able to see over the counter. You may propose on one knee if you do not consider it melodramatic, and if your torn ligaments allow you to stand up afterwards. It is essential you appear fit for purpose.

I have to say, I fear your actions may be precipitous, so you must prepare yourself for disappointment in the event that everlasting bliss is denied you.

You are a brave man indeed.

Good luck,

Trim

Dear Trim,

I have been engaged these three days. I am in a daze. I was so doolally in the gastroenterology class that I could not even focus the microscope. Fortunately, Aggy was there and had a steadier hand than me. I have discovered that a firm hand is a wonderful thing.

Aggy says that it does not matter that I am not handsome, have no title, own no horses and choose to go to restaurants on the wrong night - I am a breath of fresh air after all the aristocratic twits her parents have lined up for her. Oodles of love from your ecstatic nephew,

Art

PS Aggy says that all you need is love - and a solid upper middle class background. I think she is right, Trim, don't you?

Dear Art,

No, I don't. But good luck anyway.

Much love,

Trim

Melanie Golding

When the Night Comes

Knock knock knock.

"They're asleep," says Jonno.

Father Kay says, "That's the point, I told you."

"But Father, if we wake them up, don't you think they will be less likely to listen to the Word?"

"More fool them."

KNOCK KNOCK KNOCK.

Father Kay shouts into the letterbox, "Hello? Anyone home?"

"They're not going to answer," says Jonno. "Let's try next door."

At the house next door the shutters are closed tight. Every house is fitted with shutters now - without them there is no way to eliminate the deadly, relentless glare from the suns.

In old time, it would be mid-afternoon. Now the twenty-four-hour clock is used less and less, as people decide their own rhythm. Most people have fallen into a pattern of waking for eight hours and then sleeping for four. Father Kay hates those people.

"The greatest sin is to ignore the old timings. People must be made to realise that the preservation of God's intended night in the face of this endless day is the root of the challenge. They need to wake up."

Jonno tips his head back and scans the sky, tinged green through his protective goggles. It is empty apart from the old yellow sun and the new, white one, hunched low down and enormous, a massive glaring eye. He sees no birds, and no clouds. Both are rare over the land now. It has been almost a whole year since night fell for the last time.

They go inside the unlocked porch, where the sunlight is diffused by screens fixed to the glass. With the door shut, they can

174

both remove their goggles, lower their hoods. Father Kay bangs aggressively on the door. After a few seconds, Jonno can hear footsteps from inside the house. The door opens a crack, and from within the dark interior a young woman squints out at them. Short blonde hair, messed up from being asleep, the girl's eyes are etched with worry.

"Yes?"

Father Kay has a slight overbite that makes his craggy features rather charming. Jonno has seen the way women react to him, preening and fussing, when he turns his smile on them. He turns it on this girl now, and she recoils.

"We bring Good News."

"Oh, really?" The girl's worried frown travels through relief to annoyance as she steps back to shut the door. Father Kay puts his boot in the gap. It's too hot for boots — it always is, but without them their feet would fry.

"Night will come," says Father Kay. "Exactly one year to the day it went away. The Lord has spoken to me. He will come and with him he will bring the night. A gift, for our faith."

"Get your fucking foot out of my door," says the girl, kicking at Father Kay with her small, bare toes. He doesn't seem to feel it.

"Come to the Church at the appointed hour," says Father Kay, thrusting a leaflet into the gap between the door and the frame. "And you shall be saved."

The girl disappears for a second, and the door swings open, revealing the neat hallway within. On the hall table there is a framed photo of a happy family, two parents and an older brother, the ocean at their backs. This girl is at the centre of the scene, smiling. The photo predates the second sun's appearance. The people in it are uncovered, and none of them are wearing protective goggles. They look happy to be in the light. And there in the sky, there are several large clouds. He is wistful at the sight of them. They might be full of rain.

She comes out of the dark of the kitchen, holding a large knife.

"Out of my house," she says, pointing the knife. "Now."

Father Kay doesn't need telling twice. He pulls his goggles and hood on, turns and walks his boots right out of the porch and

175

across the front garden, that pale brown collection of dust and stumps of rosebushes. He stands on the pavement and looks around him, expecting Jonno to be right there. He calls, "Come on, Jonno, we'll try the next one. This girl has no faith. She doesn't want to be saved."

Jonno is standing just inside the door of the girl's house.

"Where are you parents?" he asks.

She shakes her head. "They couldn't do it," she says. "They tried, but they couldn't sleep. It killed them."

"I'm sorry," said Jonno. "Your brother too?"

"Yes. But he didn't choose it. He died before we knew how dangerous the new sun was. He went out on his bike and got a puncture, tried to walk home without his cape. My mother found him. She never recovered."

Jonno pushed the door almost shut against the light.

"You're still here, though," he says, smiling experimentally. She lays the knife next to the photo frame and crosses her arms as if she's cold. Jonno is sweating in his layers and heavy boots.

"I thought about going with them," she says. "I've heard it's peaceful. Like floating away in a warm bath. And then, darkness. Proper darkness."

Father Kay is calling his name.

"You should go," she says. "Your papa's calling."

"He's not my papa."

'So why do you do this? Knocking on people's doors, frightening them? Peddling your poisonous hope?" She spits *hope* at him as if it tastes rancid in her mouth. Jonno tilts his head in sympathy.

*

On the screen at the front of the hall, a countdown clock marks time.

"My people," says Father Kay. "In only a few more minutes, the night will come. Have faith."

Jonno gets on the stage and adjusts the microphone stand, which is slipping. As he retreats he scans the crowd again for signs of Avril.

"Tonight,' says Father Kay, "when the night comes, the Lord will know that we are the true and we are the faithful. We, his faithful followers here in this room have been chosen, we will be saved, and we will be welcomed into the Kingdom of Heaven where angels will fluff up our feather pillows and sing us to the most restful, peaceful, joyful night of sleep in one whole year of this contemptible sunlight."

The crowd cheers in agreement, sending up Amens and Hallelujahs into the semi-darkness. The hall is fitted with blackout blinds but they are cracked and need replacing, and those stuck in seats where the piercing rays fall through are obliged to keep their capes on or risk blistering wounds where the white light would cut through the fabric of their normal clothes.

The door opens and a figure enters, dressed in a government-issue black, floor-length hooded cape. Many of the followers shield themselves with their own capes as the light assaults them, only letting their guard down when the door is safely shut.

The figure pushes her hood back. Jonno moves through the crowd towards her.

"You came," he says.

"Yes," says Avril, "I didn't want to be alone anymore."

He smiles at her, takes her in his arms. "You're not. You don't need to be, not anymore. There's only a minute to wait. Look."

The clock on the whiteboard shows fifty-five seconds and counting. Father Kay is directing people towards the stage, where they are filing past the chest dropping their capes, goggles and boots inside.

"The faithful will be rewarded," Father Kay is saying. "And we must prove that we believe. Come, discard your protective garments. We shall not need them, when the Lord brings the night."

"Let's do it," says Jonno, taking Avril's cape from her shoulders and leading her to the front of the room. But she is unsure. She pulls at his arm.

"What happens if?"

"Avril," says Jonno, "you must have faith."

Twenty-three seconds. Twenty-two. Jonno drops his gear into the chest. He looks at Avril. She places hers on top of the growing pile.

"Amen," says Jonno, and kisses her.

The countdown from ten is full of raw excitement, and when the clock shows zero seconds the room erupts in joyful celebration. Someone starts singing *Amazing Grace*, and a few others join in.

"Now is the time," says Father Kay, his voice wavering with emotion, his cheeks flushed. The crowd parts to let him by, and he takes hold of the handles on the door. He pushes them open. Jonno feels the pain of the alien light in his uncovered eyes.

Avril says, "It hasn't worked." But the crowd is already surging out of the doors and into the street. They turn their faces to the sky.

"Look," says one, "I see a cloud."

"The light is fading, it's fading, praise the Lord," says another.

Exclamations all around, and cries of pain that could be ecstasy. "The night is coming. Soon it will be dark again."

Jonno holds Avril tightly and kisses her gently. They walk together, through the open doors and into the light.

Mary Flood

Baby Love

It was only a little village in the heart of County Roscommon, but for two glorious weeks every year Crook Hill rocked to Buddy Holly, Elvis Presley, Sam Cooke and more. Across the length and breadth of Ireland, big bands belted out great music in town halls and marquees. During the festival our tiny hamlet of one street, two groceries and three bars came to life; sounds echoing far beyond the hills and valleys, as far as the mighty River Shannon itself. Talented bandsmen produced dreamy melodies and thunderous rock'n'roll on clarinets, trumpets, guitars and pianos, drawing the crowds in droves. They came on bicycles, in cars, in hired buses.

My dad started it all, to fund the football club. Roscommon had won the All-Ireland Football Championship and its captain, Jimmy Murray, lived in the village, spurring new interest in the game. But money was scarce.

Dad called a meeting, "Let's run a carnival and raise money for kit, decent changing rooms and a playing pitch."

No one demurred. Dad was chief organiser, MC and detective. He spied everything; those who slunk into the darkness when the music stopped; who went with whom. One night I heard him tell Mammy he'd caught two lovers 'at it' up against the Church wall near the tent. He'd shone the car lights on them, shaming the pair until the girl pulled the dress down from her shoulders.

"Straddling her, he was." Dad thumped the table. "They come out here from Athlone to commit sin. I blew the horn, woke the priest."

Mammy said, "You didn't know them, Tom. Could be from anywhere. What did you expect, holding dances?"

"There she was, legs spread wide, not ten yards from the Church, with the Blessed Sacrament in the tabernacle. Whoever she

179

is, in nine months she'll rue her sins! Our daughters will never behave like it."

That was last year.

It was June 1959. Nan Hall, my best friend, and I wanted only one thing: to fall in love. I was fifteen, Nan fourteen, our lives governed by romantic music; our mantra, Jim Reeves -

> *Put your sweet lips a little closer to the phone*
> *Let's pretend that we're together - all alone.*

"Nan, we *have to* get boyfriends during the carnival."

"Alma, your dad is always on the prowl, your mother on the Ladies Committee."

"They'll be busy. Won't see us."

"I don't know how to go with a boy, and I've never kissed one."

"You will."

I was determined to fall in love. The older ones had boyfriends; we were ready. That I'd reach my sixteenth birthday in a few months, and hadn't yet kissed a boy or gone around the back of a hall with one, was, well, nothing less than shameful. And the carnival was the best time to do it.

The Church ruled our lives, our daily behaviour; everything. Missioners shouted from the pulpit during Lent - sin, hell and damnation. We didn't want to go to hell. In school the nuns gave us the Prayer Book for Girls, which laid down rules - kissing for three minutes was a mortal sin, immodest touching another.

"So, Nan, we'll get off with two boys, go out of the marquee when no one is looking, and only kiss for two minutes."

"How will you know when it's two minutes, Alma?"

I didn't.

Our parents made us attend all the Easter Week ceremonies, stand for long hours during the Passion, go to confession every month.

"I have nothing to tell the priest, except silly things. Time we found something."

"I couldn't tell Father Kelly I kissed a boy. He knows me."

"But he can't tell, can he?"

We planned ahead. Hall's house - at the bottom of the village - was far enough from the marquee to keep Nan's parents from seeing anything. Mine would be busy in the tent. We gathered at seven o'clock, put on layers of caked make-up 'borrowed' from her mother's dressing-table, and red lipstick. Nora, Nan's older sister, said it came off when kissing.

Nan giggled, "Sure, why would we do that, Nora?"

Nora, a willowy tanned long-legged girl was my idol, and popular on the dance-floor. I was jealous, had shorter legs, a freckled face and reddish hair. Hardly a boy's dream. But I wanted love.

Marie Harmon floated down the stairs along with Sunniva Hoare, both in wide floral dresses puffed out over net underskirts. Mine was blue, Nan's pink - better with her dark curly hair. Our mothers had worked hard, inserting plastic clothes line wire into the hems to make the skirts stand out.

"Mammy, you can't rock'n'roll without a wide skirt," I'd pleaded.

As one, we paraded up the street to the tent; blues, pinks, yellows in empire line dresses, all straining for excitement - and love. Along the side, I saw Christy Healy eyeing me. I liked his titian hair and brown eyes. He liked me too. Nan lived beside him - but he liked me.

There you go and baby, here am I
Now you've left me here so I can sit and cry
Well, golly gee, what have you done to me?
But I guess it doesn't matter anymore

Buddy Holly's words filled my being to bursting point as we entered the marquee. As one, we sat along the bench inside the door. I saw Dad and waved at him.

"Enjoy the dance, Alma, I'll come and dance with you later."

"Yes, Daddy."

The band started up again - Sam Cooke -

Cupid, draw back your bow and let your arrow go-o
Straight through my lover's heart - for me

A surge of dark suits swept across the floor to select the girl of their choice.

"Nan, no one'll ask us. We're too young."

"Will you dance, Alma?" Christy came from nowhere, and for fifteen minutes, we swayed, waltzed and quick-stepped along with

181

all the other sweaty bodies gyrating around us. I could feel Christy's breath on my face. He was gorgeous. The Clipper Carlton played Elvis' 'Love me Tender' and he drew me closer. Romantic. All I'd wanted. Was it love? I saw Nan dancing with a fair-haired boy, and when a break came we joined them, just as my dad came along, and glowered at me.

Christy said, "Girls, would ye like to go somewhere quieter?"

I flushed, a thrill coursing through my body.

I looked at Nell, "Yes, let's."

Nan's boy was Bill Lohan from Glinsk, fifteen miles away. He seemed nice.

"I have a plan," I said.

We had to find a place, not far from the marquee, from which to return quickly. I had it. The Ladies' Committee made sandwiches in the Owens's empty house before the dances each night. Perfect.

"Let's go to the Owens's," I said. "It's open."

"One more twirl around the floor to let Dad see me again."

"We can't walk out the door with them, Alma."

I said, "Christy, Bill, wait on the street." And pulled Nan into the ladies, beside a smelly Nissan hut.

"Lie down, crawl on your belly, out under the canvas."

She spluttered in disgust, obeyed, and in minutes we were on the grass in the field. Free. Together, we slunk away into the darkness, to freedom - and love.

A single light shone in the house, in the front room where trays of food sat on tables.

"Upstairs, fast," I said, where two bedrooms beckoned.

"See you later," Nan whispered, giggling.

I felt hot, ashamed, didn't know what to do.

Christy pulled me onto the bed. "Come on."

We kissed, again and again until my lips were sore. Once his hand slid along my chest and I pushed it away, though it felt nice. He fumbled with his clothes a bit. A burning sensation boiled inside my chest.

"Is this love?" I asked him.

"Dunno, but it's OK."

182

From the marquee, an Everly Brothers tune wafted in the balmy air -

Walk right back to me this minute
Bring your love to me, don't send it
I'm so lonesome everyday

I wondered how Nan was getting on, and if my father had missed us from the dance. I saw the clock on the mantelpiece; twenty past eleven, thirty minutes had passed. We had to go.

I shouted to Nan, "Come on, or we'll be caught."

Christy said, "Next night?"

"Fine," I mumbled, fear clinching my heart. We scampered back to the marquee and rolled under the canvas as before.

John Foley said, "Aagh, Alma where were you? Your father was looking for you."

"Dance this one with me, John, please, please," I pleaded.

He complied with a wink of understanding, was a good dancer, and soon the rhythm caught us in its beat. I saw Dad and waved. He looked odd, didn't smile.

Rock, rock, rock until the broad daylight
We're gonna rock around the clock tonight

A month later, Nan came to our house, crying. "I'm late, Alma. So much for finding love."

"Nan, you didn't...?"

Simon Piney

Goodnight Irene

There are some stories of my friend and mentor, Sherlock Holmes, that I have hesitated to tell. The view that the public has formed of the first and greatest consulting detective is of a man of superb observation but generally cold and emotionless. On at least one occasion, his powers were eclipsed for a time, however, by softer feelings.

It was a fine and sunny day in July 1890 and we had just finished Mrs Hudson's excellent kippers. Holmes was standing at the open window in our apartments at 221b Baker Street, smoking a post-prandial pipe of particularly foul-smelling navy shag.

"Aha, Watson," he suddenly exclaimed. "We are about to receive a visit from our little Welsh friend."

"Athelney Jones, you mean?" I enquired.

"Precisely and hot from Paddington Station in a hansom. The matter must be urgent," Holmes replied.

"And how do you guess Paddington?" I enquired

With a snort, Holmes replied, "Guess, my dear Watson? You should know by now that I never guess. The cabbie is one Ernest Smith who only works out of Paddington because his doxy lodges in Praed Street."

In short order we did indeed hear the rap of the knocker followed by swift footsteps on the stair. The door burst open and in strode the red-faced and sweating figure of our old acquaintance clad in tweed coat and bowler hat.

"Bore da, Athelney bach" Sherlock called out, as ever teasing Jones about his Welsh ancestry.

"And good morning to you, Mr Holmes, Dr Watson," the detective replied.

Before he could continue, he was forestalled by Holmes.

"You come, I notice, hot foot, from Gloucestershire. The murder of a woman, I see, and recent."

"As ever, Mr Holmes," Athelney exclaimed. "You have the better of me. Have the local police wired you already?"

"In no way," said Holmes. "The details shout aloud: you have a Great Western Railway ticket in the band of your hat and a bee orchid stuck to the sole of your shoe. You have come from one of the commons above the small mill town of Stroud. Permit me to present you with a copy of my monograph entitled *Orchids: sex in the soil.*"

"Right as ever," said Jones. "But how do you know of the murder?"

"There are three clues which even Watson here could distinguish, if he were to take the trouble to observe."

"Really, Holmes, that is too much," I expostulated.

"You see, Watson, but you do not observe: on the back of his left hand there is a trace of blood but no sign of any injury. He would not come to me with a simple case of affray so it must be murder."

"But a woman? How on earth...?"

"Again simplicity itself. On the cuff of his right sleeve is a smear of red lipstick, and do you not detect a faint aroma of perfume? French, I think. I have written on this too in my monograph with samples: *What's that Smell? A Sensorium of European and American Perfumes.*"

"As ever, Mr Holmes, you make it seem so straightforward and you are right," Jones averred. "Now, I fear, you must prepare yourself for a shock. I suggest you sit down."

"What is it, man?" Holmes ejaculated.

"The victim, sir. I believe she was known to you. Miss Irene Adler."

For a moment Holmes stood as if turned to stone and then slumped into a chair.

Irene Adler, to Holmes always *the* woman, had bested my friend in the matter of blackmailing the king of Bohemia.

"I thought she had left these shores for Paris," I said.

"So did we," Jones replied. "But there can be no doubt. Miss Adler it is – or, rather, was. She was killed by a single bullet to the brain. The pathologist suggests that she was killed elsewhere and her body moved onto somewhere called Minchinhampton Common where it was discovered by a local man walking his dog."

Holmes, head in hands, groaned. "Whatever possessed her to return? Her very presence so troubles my mental faculties that I admit to being unable to think clearly. Watson, is this some medical brain storm?"

"No, old friend," I said, trying to comfort him. "I believe that, unbeknownst even to you, your feelings for the lady were strong and abiding. The news of her death had given a shock to your nervous system. You will recover but it may take a little time."

As I was speaking, we heard heavy footsteps on the stairs to our rooms and the door was flung open once more, this time with some force. There stood the imposing figure of Holmes' brother, Mycroft. His very presence, away from his habitual place at the Diogenes Club, stunned us into astonished silence.

"Sherlock, my boy," Mycroft boomed. "Jones, Watson. This is a bad business."

Holmes gave no sign that he had heard. His breathing was laboured and sweat stood out on his high forehead. Taking his pulse, I found that it was racing and I worried that he was at risk of syncope or heart attack.

"What do you mean, Mycroft?" I asked.

"The fact is that Miss Adler was working for us. There was to be a meeting between senior South African Boers and Imperial German agents at Lypiatt Park on the other side of the valleys where she was found. She had managed to seduce one of the rebels and was due to report back yesterday. We fear the outbreak of further hostilities in the Cape Colony."

"So, what happened?" I exclaimed. "How could you ask a woman to go into such danger?"

"She had suggested it herself. Her price was a royal pardon and I understand that she was recently widowed and was hoping to renew her acquaintance with my poor brother," Mycroft said with a sigh. "I had hopes that Sherlock and Miss Adler could find some

186

comfort from each other. As far as we can determine, she must have been discovered and shot to silence her. We have a couple of suspects in custody already but there are diplomatic problems. There is nothing for you to do, Jones, or you, Sherlock: the matter is now in the hands of my department. Our Home Secretary, Henry Matthews, is very worried: Lypiatt Park was the seat of the Gunpowder Plot and he fears the worst."

With that, Mycroft Holmes swept from the room and we heard no more about the matter until later.

*

For the next seven days, Holmes ate little or nothing, despite my urging and Mrs Hudson's best efforts. He consented to drink weak tea. He even eschewed the needle and the ten percent solution of cocaine. His pipe lay untouched. I feared for his sanity, even for his life.

Mycroft visited daily and reported that the perpetrator of the murder had been hanged in secret in the Tower. The Boers were in custody back in South Africa and the Germans had been politely, but firmly, returned to the Hohenzollern master in Berlin. Prospective clients were turned away from our door. A request from the Court at Windsor to investigate the threat of abduction of Prince George was refused, although I phrased the refusal as courteously as I was able.

At the end of seven days, Holmes appeared to return to his senses and never spoke of the matter again. Neither did I, fearing a relapse.

*

There is only one thing to add to this account: one which I shall never publish. At the very end of his life, on his farm in Sussex, I sat with Holmes as he sank towards death. The last word that he uttered before that great and noble soul departed this world was 'Irene'. I believe my own last word will be 'Sherlock'.

Lania Knight

I've Lost My Child

It isn't in a supermarket or the overcrowded racks of a department store. We are in a pickup truck. New Year's Day. Kansas City. The tags are expired. The polar blast predicted on the evening news hasn't yet arrived.

Lights flash blue, a siren squawks. We pull over. Roll down the window one hand crank. An inch. No more.

"Licence and registration," she says.

A lady cop. Shit.

The licence is at home, forgotten. The registration, after a frantic search, is found tucked under the visor. Due to expire at midnight.

"What's your address?"

This is when it happens. At this moment, my child and I become separated.

I, in the passenger seat, watch as my son refuses to tell the woman his address. His name he gives her, as they say, as if she were a dentist pulling teeth. And his birthday.

"You realise, if this ticket doesn't find its way to you, we'll summons you to court?"

My child, in the driver's seat, nods.

"And if you don't come to court, we'll issue a warrant for your arrest?"

Nod. Yes. He cranks the window, the slit disappearing as she tells him to wait in the vehicle.

During the exchange, I've texted my child's father. I have the address on my screen. "I'm going to tell her your address," I say.

My child, now a twenty-five-year-old man, long hair knotted, brown, his blue eyes bright over dark circles, neck thin, cheeks hollow, turns to me and says, "No, you're not."

188

Months later, the letter arrives. They came to arrest him. Somehow, he talked them out of it, or in his version of the story, he did. His message closes with the line 'You can sort this with my attorney, or you can fuck off.'

It is my fault, all of it, the list so long it stretches back to the eggs nestled in my ovaries when I was born, surely carrying defective DNA, ending with the zero I left off the end of my brother's street address that New Year's Day when I texted directions to my son. Because I read it wrong. Or I forgot. Or I just made a mistake.

I lost him that cold day on a side road in Kansas. Or, rather, I lost the will to find a way to love him one more time. I don't blame him. I still haven't forgiven my own mother. She fed me raw onions when I was a child. Put a lemon in my mouth and laughed at me. Told me, as an adult, to apologise to my big brother for biting his you-know-what when I was a toddler. Told me her heart hurt every time I said anything vaguely smelling of the truth. Asked why I was wearing that dress why was I stuffing my bra why was I talking on the phone why did I need pantyliners what did my dad say about her during last weekend's visit?

But I'm trying. I'm trying to forgive her, that is. In his own way, my son is trying to forgive me. I think.

Perhaps the gene sequence for his brown hair that looks so like mine keeps him chewing, chewing at the pain, like I have. And when he's ready, as I nearly am - I feel it coming! I swear. I swear I've cranked the window all the way down to let in the cold January freeze.

Chloe Turner

Show Me What You're Made Of

It was one of his things, saying "Show me what you're made of." Jutting his chin. It'd always be said in jest – to the stranger at the bar as he pressed a flaming Sambuca into their palm, to the kid he challenged to a race to the end of the beach. But there was always an edge to it, right from the start. He'd said it to her on their first date, challenging her to an arm wrestle on the corner table of Crown's snug bar. Di could see Ella in the background, doing those 'are you okay?' waggles with her eyebrows, but she'd had been drinking tequila since the news came out about her ex's baby that afternoon. She didn't feel the twist in her arm until the morning, and even then she'd blamed it on the way the spilt spirit made the beer-mat slide under her elbow.

Looking back, it had always been there, that edge. When they fought, sometimes Di would catch Michael sitting on his hands, or prising open a fist under the table like he was trying to work his fingernails into a clamped shell. But there was a gentleness about him too, or a controlled stillness, at any rate. You could see it in the way he used to play the guitar with his eyes on the horizon, his fingers drifting over the strings, barely grazing them. And watching him with a leaf beetle crawling across the callouses of his palm was the same: he'd stop whatever he was doing to let that glittered bug take its time. Of course, when you knew he would later tweeze off each of those six fine, articulated legs and lay them alongside the severed carapace of its lime-burnished wings, it tarnished the picture somewhat. Because that was the other thing about Michael: he had to get to the heart of everything.

In the early days of the relationship, there didn't seem anything sinister to it. Odd, sure, but back then it had been as much about the rebuilding as the taking apart. An old Triumph came first – a

190

'78 Bonneville – just a blackened shell when he bought it from the car-boot sale at the power station. A violin next, then an old hand-loom they found in the barn behind the cottage, and after that, it was his father's watch. Each had their innards splayed across the workshop floor, faithfully recorded on paper as such, like the exploded schematic in a how-to manual. And then, with varying degrees of success, came the reconstruction.

The motorbike seemed to come easily. They'd ridden it together all the way up to Applecross, where he proposed at the top of the slipway with a ring his mother had lent him. And he repaired the loom so well, they were able to sell it on eBay. But the fragile veneer of the violin did not take so well to the indignity of deconstruction. He wore his father's watch on their wedding day, though the mechanism had not turned since the day he'd released the spring and tipped the brass cogs across the kitchen table. When she joked about it while they waited to greet their guests at the door to the marquee, he gripped her wrist so tightly, she was left with a pink welt like a watch strap of her own.

That first winter he spent a few weeks inside, after squaring up to a bigger man in the pub. But when he came home, he touched her with such exaggerated gentleness, she let him back into her bed. He'd lost his job because of the conviction, and afterwards he took to spending hours alone in the workshop, the doors locked behind him. He rarely went anywhere for long, but while he visited his mother in the hospice one morning, Di opened the side door with the key he kept under the log basket. She saw then that his interest had shifted, from the mechanics of repair to something more like an inventory of parts. There were no more of the diagrams like engineer's blueprints. Instead, the constituent parts of whatever had taken his fancy were lined up sentry-like, graded by size and shape, everything with its place. She could acknowledge that there was strange beauty in the order of the thing.

She asked him once, what drove him to break apart so much. What he sought to find in all this deconstruction. She'd chosen her moment carefully: he was back from the hospice with a drink in his hand, and his mother had had one of her better days, not mistaking him for his dead brother, nor screaming for a nurse when he

191

arrived. It was before the miscarriage, so he was gentle around her, often stroking her belly, fanning his wide hands across the taut skin. He started to tell her: how he regretted the deconstruction – the essential violence in it – but that it was a necessary evil. Only by breaking it utterly could he get to the heart of a thing. Then the doorbell rang, with a delivery for next door, and by the time she got back, she knew from the white knuckles around his glass that she'd regret asking more.

He didn't take the loss of the baby well, coming so soon after his mother's death. They buried them together, in the village graveyard that looked over and down towards the Severn Vale. He'd not wanted anyone there, just the two of them, and the unsmiling undertaker from Murray & Sons. Di had brought a bunch of sweet peas from his mother's wild garden, but Michael kicked over the jar as they were leaving, and she didn't dare stop to right it.

After that he went out even less than before, and a month went by before she knew he'd be away long enough to open up the workshop again. He'd been so quiet in there – none of the usual orchestra of creak and thud and clang of metal on metal. She was intrigued as to what he was working on. He'd been tender with her those past few weeks, and her thirtieth was a month off. Could it be that he was working on something for her? The first chance she got – it had taken an abscess on his jaw to get him out of the house – she lifted the basket for the key. She'd never been any good at restraint.

To a stranger, that picture in the worktop dust might have seemed like a cartoon. A skeleton drawn for a child to cut and pin for Hallowe'en. But on closer inspection, the viewer would have seen the care with which the bones had been sketched in pen and ink, ordered first by body part and then by height, so that the effect was of a ghastly fence, pitched across the width of the page. So many bones needed a huge sheet. He'd used an architect's drawing pad, pre-printed tracing paper with space for the scale and notes. He must have bought it specially. And as the bones declined in size, coming at last to *incus*, *malleus* and *stapes* – the anvil, hammer and stirrup of the inner ear – beyond them, rendered in the same black ink, was lined up a sad collection of small metal items: two medicinal gold studs and a single hair band. She recognised in the sketch of the band the narrowing in the elastic beside the steel fastening, where it had thinned from overuse. On the far side of the sheet, in the pre-printed box for Job Title, a name had been rubbed out. It began with D, but she didn't pause to decipher the rest of the grooves left on the greased page. She did snatch up the sheet as she ran for the workshop door. She rolled it clumsily, to shroud those careful, dreadful drawings of all the parts of her. Last to slip under the rough scroll - he had drawn it so finely, it could be only hers - was the bald circle of her wedding ring.

Emma Kernahan

Still for Sale

'For Sale: Penis costume (inflatable). Medium. £15. Never worn.'

The ad was tiny. At first I scrolled past it, my thumbs working faster than my brain, though an image like that catches the eye. I went back.

There it stood, among the baby clothing bundles and second-hand wedding dresses: a stock image of a man, dressed, undeniably, as a penis, attempting to look simultaneously ready to party and as though, somehow, he was better than this.

I thought of the parties I used to go to in my twenties.

'Impress your friends!' said the company tag line. I put down my phone and imagined impressing my friends. Nothing says 'strong, independent woman' like six feet of dick. I pictured people waving goodbye to me at the end of another fancy dress party. 'That woman,' they laugh to themselves as they climb the stairs to bed, 'is a fucking *hoot.*'

I looked back at the ad. The model had done pretty well. The outfit covered him entirely, except for a small hole near the top, from which his face peeped - rather despondently. He looked blankly into the middle distance as though it was something a few yards away that disappointed him, and not the direction his career had taken. I thought of the client meetings I'd been to in my thirties.

Underneath the picture was a flurry of emojis and comments tagging the people who, nudge, nudge, wink, wink, could do with a giant cock. 'SFS' it said at the bottom. Still For Sale.

In the end, I said it was for a hen do. And I'm sure, one day, it will be.

When it arrived, I felt rather foolish. Uncertainly, I placed the flat-packed organ on the bed, where it winked at me from among the piles of laundry. And yet, as I stepped into the costume and inflated myself, I felt firmer with every breath. I faced the mirror, my hands thrust into the pockets - and leaned insouciantly against the wall. Finally, I thought, an outfit with *pockets.*

I soon realised that there was no aspect of my life that was not improved by being a penis.

On the school run, five minutes late, but no longer caring - testicles from foot to knee, "Sorry!" I would call out cheerily, bundling into the cloakroom. "Bad morning. I haven't even brushed my *hair."*

I rubbed past mums in sportswear, our man-made fibres squeaking and sighing gently. "See you at pilates, Karen." I would wave.

Initially of course, I caused quite a stir at Mini Monkeys Music Mayhem. Nobody there had worn anything except Breton stripes since 2014, when Georgie had said, sotto voce over the polenta cake, that Fiona's acid brights were "a bit much". Consequently, the children's section of the library on Tuesday mornings had the resigned, exhausted look of the chain gang, especially when everybody lined up for the hokey cokey. But that day, I think we all realised that something about me had changed.

Vacuuming on a rainy morning, the top of my outfit brushed the light fittings - I was suddenly so tall. Statuesque, striking even - bending from the waist to handle my hose attachment. I swept around the house with punchy little swaggers. I took to standing at windows, looking masterfully out across the street. Passers-by, feeling somehow that they were being watched, would look up - only to see my erect silhouette, sipping an espresso.

I started flaunting my curves. I went on nights out, no longer hiding the chunky knit of all my extra inches. Now I stood in the toilets applying lipstick and admiring my face, hairless and encircled by a tight ring of soft pink material. "Too much?" I would ask the girls, puckering up over a glass of Prosecco. "No," we would agree. "Nothing is too much."

Patting the smooth expanse of my giant scrotum as I angled against the bar, I would catch an admiring glance or two. It's the same old story though. They only see the penis, not the person.

"Hey! I'm up here!" I laugh, waving a polyester clad arm, my smile not quite reaching my eyes. Still, I always take their number. And for several days afterwards I send them unsolicited pictures of myself: half inflated, eating salad and laughing.

In hindsight, I suppose my entry into the world of large scale international financial fraud was inevitable. When you work at an investment bank and someone is shifting money out of accounts, nobody suspects the prick who's just come back from maternity leave on flexible hours. And besides, I've finally nailed power dressing. Shuffling into the boardroom sideways, wobbling slightly and oozing charisma during quarterly reviews, Merrill Lynch are none the wiser. Confident in my anonymity, I give the money to the undeserving poor: addicts, sex offender support groups, third generation benefit cheats - all those unlikely to be the recipient of little green coins.

But I don't want to get too cocky. So next, I plan to have one million pounds shot from the top of my costume like a confetti cannon on the steps of the London Stock Exchange. Dressed as a dick among several hundred traders, it will be the perfect crime. I'll be a ghost; an urban myth; a master of disguise; a modern day Robin Hood, who sometimes has to be helped free from London Underground ticket barriers during a getaway.

Later, police officers will squint disbelievingly at the CCTV images. "Can you describe the man in question?" they will ask bewildered witnesses, pens poised over their notebooks.

'Massive penis' they write, over and over and over again.

On Pulling Newts from Ponds
&
Other Stories
May 2018

Nastasya Parker

From Newcastle with Love

"In my country, when a man and woman are together…you know, on their wedding night, the girls of the town stand outside the window and call like unhappy birds, wailing because they believe a woman loses her soul to her husband."

My fiancé pales over his steak and clutches the tablecloth.

"But that is an old belief, only in small villages." I pat his hairy knuckles. At least his nose hair is under control. My sister and I studied his photo before I chose him. Long nose hair would have been a total deal breaker.

He smiles with only his lips. He doesn't seem to like showing his teeth. At boys' school they must have taken the mick out of him before the pricey orthodontics worked. I smile and show off the gap where my ex-stepdad knocked a tooth out. Funny, what scars different people.

He's too nervous to smile with his eyes. I should be nervous, because this isn't a done deal. But since he picked me up at the airport I see I've got the upper hand, for the first time in my life. He thought I'd look at his weak chin and slouched shoulders and get back on the plane. But I'm not that shallow. I'm looking past those, toward his wallet.

Not that I'm making it obvious. I've ordered the cheapest item on the menu, a posh salad. It's got vegetables in I've never heard of. "Like the neighbours make on their farm at home," I sigh, wiping my mouth with a silky napkin.

He twitches, his wine glass tipping. I may be laying on the homesickness a bit thick. Never make a man feel too guilty. They can't take it; they'll turn it back on you.

"I can't wait to see where you are from," I rush on, tossing my hair. It feels crackly from the short flight, but he's already stammered that I'm more beautiful in person than in selfies. "In the charming village of Mill-ton Key-nezz."

"Well, as I've said, I live in Kensington now." He grows out of his slouch for a minute.

"Ah! I forget. Silly me, thinking of past homes. No more will I do this."

"It's fine." It's his turn to give my fingers a reassuring brush. Then he waves to the waiter. Thank God, he didn't snap his fingers. That would almost have been a deal breaker. Almost. But I sensed he'd be polite, from his emails.

"You must be exhausted," he says. Concern looks good on him, complements his soft jaw-line. "Especially after that stop in Newcastle. It's so out of the way, so…north. Their accents sound like they live underground or something. Probably sheltering from the rain!"

I grip my glass to stop my own twitch.

*

"This is the craziest thing you've ever done," my sister said when I joined the dating site. "Well worse than selling lemonade made from stolen Fairy Liquid."

That was my first money-making scheme, nearly getting me an ASBO at the age of six. I'd been fed up of summer holidays with no free school meals, with Mum out doing God knows what, and the stifling flat's windows rusted shut. I meant to buy a house, already thinking big. That was the last idea I acted on - until now.

Crazy or not, my sister threw me a party, in the flat we stayed in after cancer finished Mum off. The girls from my nursing home job came. They'd made a wedding veil out of old postage stamps

"For the mail-order bride," my sister smirked. I stroked the tiny copies of the queen's face overlapping at the fringes. "You must have spent a fortune." I'd posted a few things when I was getting my papers. Cost me about as much as flying.

My friends shrugged. "Old Mrs Henry's family didn't want her stamp collection when she passed."

*

I haven't brought the veil with me. Too risky. In my pocket I carry a pale green stamp off the corner. Apart from my clothes, it's all

I've got from my real home. I bought shampoo from the Polish corner store, so the packaging's in a weird alphabet. I emptied my wallet - destroyed my NI card, gave my sister my last quid. I even got a few Ukrainian bob - whatever you call them - from a girl at work.

So my handbag is deflated as I stand on this Kensington street letting a rich geezer sort things with the taxi driver, but the lightness makes me feel almost high. I'm about to enter my new house. There are trees here, right by the road, and no gum on the pavement. The townhouses gleam white, all joined up, but I reckon they've built the walls thick so you don't have to hear the neighbours. And even if I do, they won't be shouting at each other. No one needs to shout at each other when they've got money.

My groom gives me a tour, pride lifting his shoulders. I narrow my eyes so I don't betray excitement. Because letting a man get overconfident is as dangerous as making him feel guilty.

Luckily his shyness returns in the bedroom. "You can choose the side you want." He pauses. "It will be better tomorrow, after we're married."

He sends me to bed ahead of him. "Go on and rest, I'll just catch up on some work since I didn't go to the office today."

Maybe he can't get it up. Impotence wouldn't exactly be a deal breaker, I think as I reach behind the bedroom curtains to open the window a bit. The air is fresh and the traffic far enough away to sound like gentle ocean waves. Alone, I slide between the sheets. They're posh as the napkin I had at the restaurant.

*

"You know what they say," my sister warned me, when my Ukrainian papers arrived from the forger. "People who marry for money end up earning every penny."

"Better than working my ass off for a tosspot who's dirt-poor." I examined my new birth certificate and passport, my photo floating in a sea of foreign words.

*

Tonight, my husband-to-be comes upstairs and I let him pretend I'm asleep. Silent, he crosses the room an inch at a time, and eases himself onto the other side of the king-sized bed.

Finally, I drift off to sleep, warmed by the sensitive crackle of his nerves and lulled by the distant traffic. I dream of a wooden cottage with carvings round the door, like I saw on a website about traditional Ukraine while I did research. Inside, he and I approach each other, stiff and scared, until we're inches apart, then melting together. I melt.

But there's a scuffle against the door, and a screech. It's the girls, I think, my sister and my friends crying for my soul because I really am losing it, like in that tradition I made up off the top of my head at dinner.

My husband jumps away from me. "Bloody hell!"

I open my eyes. In our bedroom, he's scrambling up from the bed. His curse was real. The other noises were real too, along with little mortified coos.

I turn in their direction to see a frantic bulge behind the curtain.

My fiancé's pale face shines in the dark. "It's a sodding bird."

It squawks in annoyance at his statement of the obvious and bats its wings against the curtain. I've had experience getting pests out of the house. I cup the curtain around the hidden body, real gentle, but it thrashes wildly. If this is like a soul, they're not easy to keep hold of.

Once I shove the window further open, though, the bird stills before bursting into the night. Anything could happen to it out there, but it flies. The same is true in here. Anything could happen.

*

"You're really going through with this." My sister kept shaking her head as she waited with me for the airport bus. "I thought you'd give up like you did all the other insane ideas."

"No chance."

"It can't be worth it. I mean, it's just money. We've got by without it."

I patted my pockets down, checking again I had everything. Purged wallet on one side, locked phone on the other. My hands slowed, and clutched. It wasn't just the promise of filling the empty purse. It was the phone, already weighted with his emails and WhatsApp messages, his hopeful compliments and promises

202

almost as outrageous as my own schemes. It wasn't that I couldn't back out. I didn't actually want to.

*

I close the window. My partner and I look at each other with nervous, embarrassed smiles.

"It's gone where it belongs," I say, almost forgetting to use the accent. Reaching for his hairy knuckles, I lead him back to bed.

Steve Wheeler

Fashion in Men's Footwear: Late 20th Century

The 1960s. With a shilling I can buy a stripy paper bag of lemon and lime chews. I watch the fat lady tip the sugary-lipped jar over the pan on the scales. I scrutinise whilst she adds and subtracts sweets with her Liquorice Allsorts spade, until the big-hand points to four ounces-o-clock.

Outside, on her bicycle leant on the shop window, Pamela Blackwell has been holding my bike upright, her bare legs resting on her handlebars. I'd seen her red knickers as she pulled up her knees, so I squat down and re-tie the laces on my new black baseball boots.

On the path that leads to the woods I can't keep up with her. I breathe only the dust from her sherbet hair in the peppermint light that ripples through the leaves.

"If you give me all the red ones you can kiss me," she laughs out of sight.

I think for a shilling I could have bought a ton of strawberry hearts.

"There aren't any red ones," I yell through tears, and wish that she'd notice my new black baseball boots.

I should be in the lead. I should be the one who decides what colour kisses are.

*

The 1970s. If I slide the driver's seat back as far as it can go, I can depress the clutch in my brown and cream, six-inch stacked platform shoes, although I can't feel if my right foot is on the miniscule brake or accelerator pedal.

Linda Osborne will be finishing her shift in the hotel restaurant at two-o-clock, just enough time for a pint in the bar. In her staff accommodation attic bedroom I unzip her out of her black waitress's skirt and unbutton her ironed white shirt. Her underwear smells of Sunday lunches.

"You're quite a bit shorter out of your shoes," she says on her narrow bed.

Linda knows where there's a party. I double de-clutch the car through the lanes whilst I stroke the inside of her thigh. The right hand bend is thirty degrees too many. My stacked right foot presses on the accelerator rather than the brake. A ditch and a dry-stone wall come between us and the party.

"You fucking idiot, you nearly killed me," she says before pulling down her denim skirt and climbing up the ditch to the road.

"Well I've broken a heel," I tell her. "And they cost thirty quid."

The hotel chef arrives on his motorbike and helps Linda onto the pillion. I stand on my one good shoe so I'm as tall as he is.

*

The 1980s. In the gentlemen's outfitters in Oxford, where university students of philosophy purchase their English mustard corduroy trousers, I buy black Oxford shoes with loops of perforations around the shiny toe-caps. I've got a diploma in business studies from the polytechnic, but in London's square mile we're all high flyers.

In the gentlemen's club in Soho we're measured up for girls and taxis hailed back to the company flat off Marble Arch. The fridge is stocked only with champagne. The boys take glasses and a bottle, each then peel off to the bedrooms where the girls peel off for their share of the bonuses.

But I can't go to the bedroom. I've fallen in love with Mandy who kisses me on the ear so softly, her hair as sheer and as black as her stockings. She tells me she's from Jamaica, and only does this work because her banker husband left her with two young kids, and there's the mortgage and the private school fees to pay, and the nanny when they're not boarding away. I start to make plans for when she and her children move in with me, and I help her find a proper job, and we have two sweet, light brown kids of our own.

"Lover, are we going to do it or not?" she asks in the kitchen, after the champagne and the talk has dried up.

"No," I say. "I respect you too much for that, and can we meet outside of work any time soon, somewhere non-business related, as it were?"

"After work next Monday," she says. "But I need something to make up for lost income tonight."

I give her a hundred and open the cab door for her in the sober London dawn.

"You're a proper gentleman," she says and kisses me.

I look down at my black Oxfords. "Yes," I think, "I am."

"We haven't got any Jamaican Mandys here. Never had," says the doorman of the gentlemen's club on the Monday night.

I tip the shoeshine boy a fiver and buy new laces I don't need.

*

The 1990s. The sun boils into the beach buggy my fiancée Alison and I have hired for the day. I drive in bare feet even though the foot pedals are too hot to touch.

We drive through villages where children's faces watch our passing from glassless windows and baking stoops. Down a track that leads through breadfruit and banyan trees, the children run after us, shoeless over the sharp road-stone. White sand arcs round the green water and black shadows of coral. We leave the buggy in the shade of eucalyptus and take beach bags.

We lay our hotel towels under coconut trees and walk the length of the beach, hand in hand. I stop and throw fallen coconuts into the waves. We watch them bobbing like swimmers' heads and wait for them to roll back up the sand. We've brought a picnic of wine and pink melons. I cut the melons with a knife borrowed from the hotel's buffet. I try to stab drinking holes in a coconut but miss and stab a hole in her towel.

"I hope I don't get stranded on a desert island with you," Alison says.

"We should go for a swim now we're here," I say. "Skinny dipping. We're the only ones on the beach."

"No way," she says, and asks me to hold her towel whilst she pulls on a one-piece.

"Reminds me of family holidays in Newquay," I say.

She won't go into the sea.

"It's too coral-ly and I didn't bring shoes."

Alison goes back into the shade and rubs in more high-factor. I do breaststroke over the warm swell. Two local girls come onto the beach and strip off at the water's edge. Under dirty dresses they're wearing bikinis but they toss the tops aside then high step over the waves. In the deeper water they arch their bodies then disappear under, their bottoms floating momentarily on the surface. I go back to the towels and stretch out. She's pretending to be asleep behind sunglasses. I close my eyes and listen to the two girls chattering like the frantic little birds in the papaya trees.

Then there's a heavy wet slap on my stomach. I don't look up.

"Ouch, what the hell was that for?"

"What was what for?" Alison says.

I look up. There's a lizard on me, rat-sized, but with a longer tail. It's fallen, or jumped, from the coconut tree leaning over us. It turns its head to one side and winks at me.

"Fucking Hell!" I jump to my feet, flaying at my stomach. The back of my hand touches the lizard's mouth.

"Arrgh, I felt its flicky tongue."

Alison starts to laugh. I haven't seen her laugh since we arrived. I'm not sure I have ever seen Alison laugh like she is now.

"Serves you right. Those girls felt your 'flicky tongue' when you swam up close."

The lizard slinks into the undergrowth. I watch the girls skip out of the water and dress. They don't have towels but the water evaporates from their brown skin. When they walk past us, they're dry as pebbles.

"We should make love now we're here," I say to Alison. "Deserted tropical beach, coconut trees..."

"And have a reptile crawl over me? No thanks."

We don't speak on the walk back to the buggy. Alison strides in front of me with her towel wrapped from her chest down. The top of the dashboard, behind the steering wheel, has been adorned with red and pink seashells and blooms of wild hibiscus.

"Gifts from the children," I say, and pull my camera from the beach bag.

"Put a flower behind your ear. Take the towel off. Let me take a photo."

She picks a compact mirror from her bag and smears sun block on her nose.

"Save it for the local fauna," she says.

One by one, my fiancée drops the seashells and hibiscus flowers into our slipstream. I stop at a roadside shack that has beach things for sale on a wooden trestle.

"I'm going to buy a pair of jelly shoes," I say. "I'm getting cold feet."

She raises her sunglasses. "Jelly shoes?"

"Jelly shoes," she says, "are for wankers."

Val Ormrod

The iFairy

Alex checked his pocket again to make sure it was still there. Every time he wrapped his fingers around the small box, he felt a renewed frisson of excitement.

The new device had been a closely guarded secret and nobody knew how it worked. Social media had been buzzing with speculation from those who professed to have inside information, but Alex knew the creators were too clever to give anything away.

Nearly fifty million of the latest 'must-have' accessory had been sold, just in pre-orders. And no one, other than the technical team who'd produced it, had seen it in action. There was no facility to try it out first, no YouTube clip, not even a demonstration at the Apple store, where Alex had queued outside half the night just to be one of the first to own it. The promise that this device would make the user's dreams come true was impossible to resist.

At last he was inside his flat. Impatient to try his purchase, he didn't even stop to grab his customary latte or plate of breakfast muffins, but made straight for the sofa. He took the new toy from his pocket and reverently unpacked it from the extravagantly padded box. Tiny filigree fairy wings, etched on the white and silver case, winked as the light caught them. He turned it over and over in his hands and kissed the seductive surface. It was perfect.

Your iFairy comes fully charged. Just lift the outer cover. Alex marvelled as the wonderful iridescent screen was revealed. *Rub gently and your fairy will appear.* He started to rub in a gentle circular motion.

And then, abracadabra, she was there. No bigger than a credit card, she unfolded from the device as if she had been entombed in the casing. She twirled once, just above the screen. It was the strangest sensation. Although he knew she was just a hologram, she seemed to occupy real space.

"Hi," she said, in a voice so lifelike it was unnerving. "I'm Myfanwy." Alex thought his aunt Blodwyn had come into the room. Surely the device was invented in California. He hadn't expected a fairy with a Welsh accent. Nor one with auburn pigtails and green leggings. They didn't look quite right with the wings. What had he expected? Just a regular fairy, he supposed - tumbling golden hair, a white tutu perhaps and silver dancing shoes. But if she was going to make his dreams come true, did it really matter?

"What is your wish?" the fairy asked. A rather grandiose tone, Alex thought. But this was more like it. He had a whole list of wishes and dreams.

"I want to win the lottery," he said quickly. "Top spot, jackpot, please, no other winners to have to share it with."

Did he imagine it, or did she look disillusioned? Stop it, he thought. This is just a piece of technology. It doesn't have feelings.

Then Myfanwy yawned. "Not that old chestnut," she said. "I hoped you'd be more original."

"What do you mean?" he said. "You're supposed to grant all my wishes."

She pushed her bottom lip out. A most unattractive gesture, he thought. Don't think that one's in the job description," she said. Then as he started to look annoyed, she went on. "Look, we had an iFairy Convenors' meeting last night. In all the trials, winning the lottery was the number one request. We can't have fifty million of you all winning."

"I'd have thought you'd be able to overcome those practical issues with your fairy dust," he complained.

"Just *how* old are you?" the fairy asked scornfully.

"You're a very contrary fairy," he said, hoping to lighten her up. Advances in Artificial Intelligence had been awesome in the last few years. Perhaps they'd managed to develop humour. "OK, if I can't win the lottery, I still want to be rich. You can make that happen, can't you? You are meant to be making my dreams come true."

"Be careful what you wish for," Myfanwy warned darkly. "Are your dreams always good ones? Or are some bad?"

"I only want the good ones," he said hurriedly. "And being rich is what I dream about most." He tried his most charming smile.

"That and being an Adonis with a lean, toned body like Aidan Turner in Poldark."

Alex could have sworn she looked him up and down with an *Oh yeah* expression but he decided to ignore it. "We don't make dreams come true," she said. "We can only help *you* make them come true. I can help you become rich but only with considerable effort from you. Then if you work hard and keep at it, I promise you'll be rich."

"How soon?"

"Depends on you," she said. "A year, maybe, if you're prepared to work extra hard." Alex's heart sank. He didn't like work. This wasn't what he'd expected when he bought his iFairy. It was a con. "As for that toned body," she continued, "I've started on that one already. Look!"

Alex followed her gaze, just in time to see his fridge being emptied. All the food was disappearing out through the door. He shook his head. What the hell was this device? He must be having hallucinations. He needed a drink. He strode over to get a beer but it had gone, along with all the food.

He looked for his ciggies but couldn't find them anywhere. Instead he discovered a gym membership card lying on the worktop. Then, to his horror, he found his car had disappeared from the garage. In its place was a bicycle. *A bicycle!* He hadn't ridden a bike since he was ten.

*

Over the next few weeks, it seemed more like nightmares coming true than dreams. Every time he switched on his PC he was overwhelmed by business propositions, contracts to read, an avalanche of paperwork. It was hideous. He was working from early morning until late at night. Not only that, he was also being starved. If he reached for a drink, it was immediately snatched from him. And however busy, he was forced out three times a day to run or ride his bike or work out in the gym.

Myfanwy was always on his case. She sat on his desk, hopped onto his knee, perched on his shoulder. Even when he closed the iFairy down, she still seemed to hover – in the pub, *no beer for you, boyo*, following him around the supermarket, *put those doughnuts back, fat boy,* even in the shower, *you've still got love handles, look,* and next to him on the pillow, *time to get up for your morning run, ha ha.*

After three weeks he'd had enough. It was like having a nagging wife. No, worse. Surely a wife wouldn't put you on a lettuce diet and expect you to keep to it for a whole week. He'd wanted a fairy with a magic wand for instant gratification. Not one that was forever whispering, "Naughty, naughty," and treating him like a schoolboy. He didn't want all this gruelling effort and running five miles before work. If it came to it, he'd rather have colonic irrigation and liposuction. You didn't have to diet these days. Which century was she living in?

He refused to let that green-legged Welsh tyrant bully him any longer. Blood up, he fetched a hammer and placed the device on the wooden board. The first blow splintered the casing and he thought he heard a tiny shriek. "Shut up! Shut up!" he yelled and brought the hammer down again and again.

*

The first people who viewed the YouTube video of Alex's hammer attack (for even in his frenzy he'd had the presence of mind to capture the assassination on his mobile) were in awe. How had he had the temerity to destroy one of the iFamily offspring? But then someone followed suit. 'My fairy was a bossy bitch-fairy too,' he tweeted. 'I could have strangled mine,' raged another. And suddenly the video went viral. Within three days he had twenty million hits. It started an epidemic of destruction. All over the world people were taking hammers to their iFairies.

It was not until he started to earn a share of the advertising revenue from his video that he realised the impact of his little act of demolition. He was going to be rich. His dreams were coming true after all. Could this have been Myfanwy's swansong? Had she decided to intervene one last time? No, that was nonsense. Who needed fairies?

With satisfaction he sat down to his meal of double cheeseburger and fries with a generous lashing of mayonnaise. He reached for his beer and savoured the first frothy gulp. He didn't want to be lean and toned that much, did he? Not to have to forgo treats like this surely? It was true he'd started to lose weight when

Myfanwy was being so harsh with him. He might even have achieved a body like Aidan Turner's if he'd persisted.

For a moment, he missed her. But it was only the briefest of moments.

James Northern

In the Firing Line

It was when the car doors locked that Brian knew that something was wrong. He had just dropped Nicola and the girls off at their play date. Nicola had pressed the doorbell on the threshold of the semi-detached suburban house and then glanced around to flash him a grateful grin. Erica and Abigail had been dancing excitedly on the spot, each of them with a tiny hand in one of Nicola's. Brian had been thinking of his afternoon ahead, dealing with the garden and listening to the football. But then the car doors had locked, of their own accord, and immediately the vehicle was in motion.

A car driving itself was no new thing, but usually you had to tell it where to go. Brian tried the joystick beside his left hand - steering wheels were a thing of the past, present only in classic cars these days. Touching the joystick should have restored manual control, allowing him to stop, but the car continued to glide along the quiet residential roads, taking bends with care and waiting patiently at junctions. He tried each of the pale yellow buttons on the touchscreen display in front of him, but he might as well have been tapping on a plank of wood.

"What are you doing?" he asked, exasperated. "I didn't tell you to go anywhere."

The car was trained to listen to his voice, but this time, it gave no response. He tried the door handle, but it would neither open nor unlock. The release button on his seatbelt seemed to have been disabled and the strap, if anything, seemed to have tightened around his chest, pinning him into his chair. They were on the dual carriageway now, heading out of town.

One panel on the black interior of the vehicle was still operating and that was the Sat Nav. It showed a map in motion, with a 'Time to Destination' in the bottom right hand corner: fourteen minutes and fifty seconds. Then he realised where he was going. He felt a further tightening in his chest and, this time, it wasn't his seatbelt.

The dual carriageway was busy and they were managing only fifty miles per hour. Good. That would buy him a few more minutes. On the horizon, he could see thin wisps of smoke rising above the countryside. They rose at steady intervals, perhaps thirty seconds apart. He was just beginning to panic, when the speakers crackled into life and a voice began to speak. It was the soft feminine voice of the vehicle's computer that he usually found so soothing, but this time it was different, more impersonal and official sounding than normal.

"Brian Edward Connor, you have been impounded under the Productivity Act for the following reason: substandard workplace performance."

"What? Why? What was wrong with my performance?" protested Brian.

"Evidence gathered by your employer fails to demonstrate adequate leadership skills."

"But I'm not supposed to be a leader; I'm a researcher."

"All state employees are required to achieve the minimum level in all corporate attributes. Leadership is corporate attribute number four."

Almost everybody was an employee of the state these days. Hard times could do that to a place. Brian was thinking fast.

"Compare me to my colleagues," he tried. "Take Peter Brown, for instance. What's he ever led?"

There was a pause while the computer checked the records. "Peter Frederick Brown," it said, "led a brainstorming session to choose the team name on 28th May."

"But I came up with the team name. It was my idea that got chosen."

"You have exceeded the minimum level in innovation. All state employees must achieve the minimum level in all corporate attributes."

"Could I make a phone call please?"

"That is not possible at the current time. Your communications devices have been impounded under the Productivity Act."

Brian remembered voting for the Act, not considering for a moment that he would ever fall foul of it himself. All citizens now voted on all major issues, the inevitable result of improvements in internet technology and the widespread distrust of politicians. When the Act was proposed, there had been no other options on the table. Desperate times had called for desperate measures; the nation had become alienated from its trading partners and the economy had collapsed. Homelessness, famine and civil unrest had taken hold. The welfare bill had risen to crippling extremes. Only one solution had presented itself.

*

The car was in a queue on the exit lane of the motorway. Out of the passenger side window, across a field of grass, Brian could see the incinerators. They looked a little like car washes, but grey, metallic and about twice the size. There were five of them, side by side, with funnel chimneys rising several feet above them. Individual lines of cars led to the entrance of each one, all of which originated from one single-lane road winding its way from the motorway exit. Every thirty seconds or so, a new set of cars, each containing one driver, would roll into the entrances of the incinerators. Grey doors would slide shut and, seconds later, slim puffs of smoke would emanate from the chimneys. Then the cars would roll out again on the other side, but when they emerged, the drivers would be gone.

The incinerators had been built outside every town and city, and, for a while, they drew widespread attention and more than a few protests. Within a year, they were just another fact of life, another blot on the nation's conscience, to be passed with averted eyes like a bad part of town. Their method was instant and painless. The relatives of the deceased would receive the ashes in the post, along with a copy of the final appraisal from the person's employer. Nobody could afford a funeral anymore.

"Would you like to record a message for your family?" asked the car.

"How long have I got?" replied Brian.

"Six minutes and thirty-six seconds."

Just then, Brian heard two short peeps beside him. Looking around, he saw a face that he recognised in a silver car that was stopped in traffic in the leftmost lane of the motorway, next to the exit lane.

"Dave!" he exclaimed. He knew Dave from work; they had passed many a hurried lunch break together. Dave looked concerned. Brian began to gesture wildly. "Help!" he mouthed. "Help me!" He realised what Dave was about to do just in time to brace. The crunch of metal was followed by the sound of a car door opening and then footsteps. Brian had a headache, but his arm had protected him. His door opened and a man leaned across him to release his seatbelt.

"Get out!" shouted Dave, yanking Brian out of his seat.

"How did you do that?" asked Brian. "I tried the door earlier and I swear it wouldn't budge."

"Safety mechanism in case of accident. The government can kill you legally, but only in one way."

Dave pushed Brian into the front passenger seat of the silver car, behind the smashed headlight and the crumpled bumper. "Take us home," he said when he'd clambered into the driver's seat.

"Going home," said the vehicle, and the engine hummed into life.

"They'll catch us, won't they?" asked Brian.

"Not for a while," said Dave. "The police are pretty busy these days."

"But I can't hide forever."

"You won't have to. I'll get on my laptop when we get home. Brian, you're about to get the best performance feedback any employee has ever got. And they'll listen to me; I'm a senior, remember."

"Thank you."

"Just tell me: what does my feedback need to focus on?"

"Leadership."

"Leadership it is. Just make sure you leave the car before I do when we get home. If you're on your own in a vehicle before your appraisal gets changed, you'll be taken straight back here again."

"OK."

"And make sure this doesn't happen next year. I'll only be able to save you this once."

*

Brian thought of Nicola and the children. He would see them again. The incinerators were behind them now, the five grey rectangles with the five lines of cars. Looking closely, he noticed that each vehicle was rocking slightly from side to side. He might have thought it was a dance, if it weren't for the limbs he saw thrashing against the window panes.

Jason Jackson

Here are the New Men

Here are the new men. Bury us in fields alongside our fathers, the earth soaked in rain, not blood. Leave lots of room, for we are no different to those who came before, those who come after.

We are new, primeval.

We are raging inside, but quietened. The world has blanketed us, and we must smile, silent, only singing drunk, dancing drunk, fighting drunk, fucking drunk. In the morning, we find our prison again.

Our fathers are dying, and we hold their cold hands on top of stiff hospital sheets, shake our heads with our brothers at the yellowness, the grey of the skin. Silently, we see ourselves, our sons, and later we find someone warm to hold against us, not a wife, or at least not our own.

Our sons are playing, picking up stones, making collections in pockets to be forgotten, found in some future with a smile of nostalgia, the cold of the earth.

We will be dead, and they will not remember enough of us.

We are buying food, cars, houses, insurance. We are married, divorced, and we are bastards, every last one of us. We are texting lovers at midnight, smoking in suburban gardens so the curtains won't smell, the lights of the city green and red and orange and too distant to be anything other than memory. We are hard in the shower in the morning, frightened of our passions as they twist inside. We eat cereal. Ride bikes. Fall asleep on couches which have our shape and stain in them, in beds too big and too small.

We work for idiots, are idiots ourselves, and ambition is tiny and black, whispering to us in words which stick like honey.

We remember Mr Fletcher with his clipboard, Gregg with his glasses and his civil service pension. We remember waiting for that promotion phone-call, the celebration champagne, and the nights of heavy worry, the nights of slow regret.

Once, we woke up and thought our lives could change. Once, we thought we'd met the only one. Perhaps there was a band or a book with the answer. Perhaps someone told us we were good, or getting better. Sunlight through an open window in summer showed us the world, how it could be, and someone read poetry to us.

More than once we shed tears.

We still buy flowers - for lovers, for wives, for ourselves, because there must still be beauty, apology and routine. We wrap presents and unwrap our own, stockpiles of possessions to be bagged, and we remember the gifts of the past, how they are broken.

Once, there was God.

We climbed a tree when we were younger, saw initials carved into branches high above the ground, reached higher, carved our own. We ran a road, getting faster, thinking, *if we run this road every day, and every day we get faster, we will never slow down, never stop.* We sang a song, heard its words, danced with grace on drunken legs, fell laughing into the arms of women with names like Rebecca, Rachel, Mary, Elizabeth. They held us, held us up, laid us down, forgot us.

We tried, failed, tried again, because there's nothing else to do.

Now, we keep gardens, allotments, mistresses and secrets. We fall in love thirty times a day, and our plants die, red spider mites sucking the leaves. Our sons give us hats to wear, gloves, they buy us jackets and boots, and in our dreams we hide in the woods, naked, shivering.

We smell of aftershave and sex, sweat and remorse, and we shower every day, scrubbing at our skin, feeling the muscles beneath, still strong, still strong.

We look in the mirror, and sometimes we turn away.

We cook food for the table, and we eat. We lift weights, and we smile sometimes. We read, put the book down, lie staring at the ceiling, silent in the grip of a sudden certainty, and we ink the words into our arms, mistaking their permanence for truth.

We try for change, stop drinking, cut back on meat. There is our fathers' cancer, and our friends who are killed by their hearts. We are there, the men in the photographs next to the television, the people we do not recognise.

We are there in the films which we watched with our fathers when we were younger, the same films that we watch now with our sons, and we laugh in the same places, hide from the same scenes, dream about the same women.

Our futures are in the smell of new furniture and the weight of our hearts in the morning. We live in advertisements, votes, promotions and mortgages. Our days are full.

We can't sleep, and there is never enough time. We trip and fall, and things will never be the same. Early in the morning, late at night, the light shows us ourselves, and we cannot hide. There is a pain in our heads, in our backs, in our arms, shoulders, knees. We clean, because there is always dirt, and when we talk, it is as if we are shoring ourselves up against the silence, words about wallpaper, paint, clothes and birthdays. We go to funerals and talk to strangers who found other strangers dead on the floors of bedrooms with single beds and no pictures on the wall.

Our hamstrings tighten along with our smiles, and our eyes narrow with our hopes.

And we find someone new. They touch our cheek, wake on our chest in the middle of the night, crying, and we put our hand in theirs, imagine that we are finally alive, because we are the new men with a plot waiting for us somewhere, but we are still here, still unready.

Joanna Campbell

The Journey to Everywhere

Bob Vole knew his meat. Busy hanging a fresh side of pig in the window, the sun was flashing in his eyes and the hog swinging wild and free when Hilary Hannaford glided across the square.

Bob brushed flecks of paper parsley from his apron. His boater slid off, thudding into the lamb's liver. He looked up again and there she was at his window, peering at the mince.

She was a strait-laced librarian, yet secretly starving for love, was Hilary. Two women in one. He was proud of this thought, which had arrived yesterday, unbidden, while he boiled his aprons.

Like Hilary, he'd never married, but he knew about flesh and bone. He knew the ways of it. There were people whose hearts were bursting with savoury stuffing.

Hilary cloaked herself in grey, demure to her ankles. She wore a pale carnation. But her heart throbbed, scarlet and shiny beneath. Like a good ox heart. Tough. Full of flavour.

She saw Bob looking and veered in a diagonal to the haberdashery, gazing at ribbons and cards of elastic. Her skirt swished as she turned. Her cheek was tinted a delicate rose. He caught a glimpse of the tiny sun-brightened hairs on her skin, like the whiskers on a lightly roasted strip of crackling.

Mrs Amberforth bustled in for her kidneys and told him the news. She'd come from the library with her week's worth of novels, where she'd discovered this was Hilary's last day as deputy. After thirty years.

Bob handed over her kidneys in silence. Mrs Amberforth squashed the bloody parcel into her basket next to *Villains and Victims*.

"Early retirement, do you think, Mr Vole? I couldn't get anything out of Mr Fetching. Tight-lipped as always. As if I were a

222

bluebottle asking to swim in his coffee. She wants a quiet life, I suppose. Mind you, she's always been a mouse, hasn't she, Mr Vole?"

Bob was craning his neck to follow Hilary's progress. She was uncharacteristically late for the library. Mr Fetching would be pouting at the clock, sweeping past the returns trolleys and frowning as he stamped the books himself.

Yet Hilary made no attempt to hurry today. She stooped to speak to a small boy reluctant to hold his mother's hand. The child was turning purple with fury. Hilary knelt, her skirts spreading in a perfect circle on the ground, and pressed a coin into the boy's palm. Bob read her lips: 'Lollipop'.

Bob mouthed the word silently. Several times. He could taste the flavour of red fruit on his tongue.

He looped Mrs Amberforth's sausages into a fat stack and stood there with them in his hand, watching Hilary unfurl and walk in yet another different direction, this time towards Tindall's Travel.

She was intent on Tindall's window, her carnation touching the glass, her breath clouding it. Bob stared, transferring the sausages from one hand to the other.

"Can you pass over those chipolatas, Mr Vole?"

He'd forgotten Mrs Amberforth. Mr Tindall was poking out of his door like a curious tortoise. Cupping Hilary's elbow, leaning close, his shiny polyester lapels brushing against her velveteen. As he steered her into his mean little shop, the broken blind askance, the sun-bleached posters curling, the sun slipped away.

Bob was sweating, the sausages oozing in his grip. He straightened his boater. He rummaged behind him, ripping apart the ties of his apron. He flung it across the blood-stained chopping block. Jowls quivering, he struggled past his astonished customer and abandoned his shop for the first time in thirty years.

Mrs Amberforth bustled off to set Chinese whispers rippling through the square until her story had Bob vaulting across his meat display, brandishing a cleaver.

Bob strode to Tindall's Travel like a hunter with a gun. Except he held a pound of best pork, lightly seasoned with sage.

At the window, he stopped.

Years ago, Tindall's posters had shown sand the colour of egg-yolk and sea the indigo of a baby's eyes. But Tindall had let them fade to fawn and milky blue. He'd tried to dress things up with a paper flower garland and a wine glass bristling with cocktail umbrellas. But the display didn't compare with Bob's rack of lamb, stiff with cutlet frills.

Although he'd never fancied Abroad, never been far beyond the Square in all his life, Bob once dreamed the same dream for four consecutive nights. He was on a tropical island, a rum punch beside him. Always the same swathe of white sand, the same boundless ocean creeping up the beach in lace-work frills that kissed his bare toes.

Bob peered through the slats of the blind and saw Tindall's arm coiled around Hilary, fingers snaking over her shoulders.

He marched in. Slammed his sausages down as Tindall gave Hilary a wallet stuffed with papers and marked *Travel Documents*. The six-month itinerary, he assured her, had been arranged with the utmost care and attention.

Bob backed out. He stood in the centre of the square, hotter and pinker than Danish salami, loosening his collar.

Hilary on a voyage? Just as he was plucking up the courage to invite her to dinner at The Slanting Partridge? Tindall had actually called her Hilary. He couldn't bear to think of her soft voice saying 'Peregrine'. Surely her next stop would be the library? She was overdue. Mr Fetching would fine her.

At five past five, would she still come in for her rashers, Bob's best, already wrapped in greaseproof?

There she was! Gliding across to the post office. That meant traveller's cheques. Or foreign currency. A six month trip meant Abroad, Bob was sure.

Hilary wasn't walking along. She was shimmying. She might skip the bacon. Have Pasta, or some other exotic dish, for her tea. Put herself in the right mood for France, or wherever she was going.

Bob had thought their interests dovetailed. But her sights were clearly set differently from his. Maybe she was more than two women. And they were all slipping away from him. She might never come back. The colours of his dreams blazed again.

224

"Miss Hannaford!"

She looked round and smiled. He strode towards her and clasped both her hands. They felt like lilies.

This was Bob's moment. It felt like the first time he'd used his triple-riveted knives, drawing each one in size order from the block, as tenderly as a midwife delivering a baby.

His tropical vision flooded back into his head and this time he envisioned more than himself. This time Hilary sat beside him, holding a worthy book and a slice of pineapple. She reached across and fed him a bite of the fruit. The thought gave him the courage to ask about her travel plans, pointing at the documents in her hand.

Impressed with his interest, Hilary unfolded her map. She guided him to a bench bathed in the weak morning sunshine and extended the map across them both. On his meaty legs and her dainty ones, it sloped rather. But it felt as good as his spot in the Caribbean sun.

"Just picture it, Mr Vole, the sugar-birds of Guadeloupe, the silver minnows of Santa Fe, the Alaskan caribou, the Tallulah river of Georgia, the Marmolada mountain of Italy - Dolomites, I think..."

"I had a yellow one of those in my youth, Miss Hannaford. Twin headlamps."

"Then there's the red-necked ostrich of North Africa..."

"Good meat, that ostrich."

As Hilary traced the route with her finger, with Bob following every inch, shadows fell over them: Mrs Amberforth and Mr Fetching, one in a state of suspense and the other without the essentials for her Toad in the Hole.

With a shout of triumph, Mr Fetching squeezed between Bob and Hilary, then pored over the map, waxing lyrical about rafting in the Smokies.

Was he going *with* her? Him in his pinstripes and pocket watch, and her holding her long skirts out of the foaming water?

They started talking about broadening horizons, bursting through boundaries.

Broadening, bursting? On a ticket from Tindall's? His little mouse, Hilary? How many women *was* she, for heaven's sake?

"Your last day as deputy for a bit then, Hilary?" Mrs Amberforth asked.

"Indeed," replied Hilary.

"So you'll be in full charge while Mr Fetching goes on his voyage of discovery?"

Bob spun Hilary to face him. "Does this mean you're on a journey to nowhere then, my dear Miss Hannaford?"

"Oh, not really. I'm always travelling, my dear Mr Vole, always."

Bob gulped.

"Mr Vole, my journey is via the printed page. Books take me everywhere I want to go."

In answer to his next question, she agreed to stroll a little further than the square later on. Yes, possibly as far as The Slanting Partridge. Once she'd been home to put his most reliable lean bacon in her fridge. And they linked arms to begin their short trips back to work.

Sarah Chapman

On Pulling Newts from Ponds

Lucy and I had passed through the gulf of babyhood together, when friendship was a mere matter of proximity. From there we had evolved to become one little girl split between two bodies. We gabbled a single language of our own devising; each of us so profoundly aligned that pain to one (physical or otherwise) transmuted to both in a way that the grown-ups found very frustrating.

But by our thirteenth year, the bond had begun to stretch, and with increasing frequency there were glimpses that her thoughts and mine were no longer so combined and that solid shield between us and the outside world was starting to crumble.

The holes in the web between us let in a ghosting awareness that things which had once seemed silly or funny, the clowning of adults, now had some deeper, sinister meaning.

We carried this unborn understanding heavily around with us, like an egg in the gut, hoping that one day it would crack, and anxious of what would happen when it did. This is not to say we were aware of it in any organised way, it was just a new sort of worry to cart around, alongside dentists and the wolf in the woods.

And when the stress got too much, when the stretch felt too tight, our recourse was to double down; to rush to the pond and forget ourselves harassing the newts.

I say 'harass' because that what the adults always said we were doing, and in truth the newts never appreciated our zoological efforts very much. They would writhe in our fingers, jaws flapping, their stiff tails flicking back and forth like windscreen wipers. You'd think a newt is silent; it's not. They hiss, gently, and exude a rhubarb-like odour, which I found particularly lovely.

The pond contained upwards of sixty of the little beasts on a good year. The females were universally a ruddy brown, whilst the males were black, streaked with marigold, knobbled, dashing and unmistakably virile. Even the young ones who hadn't come into their colours yet could easily be picked out from the females by turning them over.

Bulldogs have nothing on the average male newt.

You can catch a newt two ways: by stealth or surprise. My favourite was to lie, nose at the surface with the full length of my arm greened by the water. Lifting my palm in increments under a newt, I could bear it up into the air without it even realising I had done so. Sometimes the newt would be relaxed and permit tickling.

The biggest males were wily, and could only be collected by persistent attempts at the dash and grab. The danger here was not being bitten (for all their dramatics, they never bite) but of dropping or squashing the newt.

Once caught, they were set to bask in a sandbox generously topped off with water. Here we constructed them an oasis of sandbanks, and would squat until our knees creaked, watching them raft about in it. A freshly caught newt would settle in quickly (we could only assume their memories were short), and stretch himself out to sunbathe and be admired.

They got no shortage of admiration from us. We enjoyed the conceit that they were in fact alligators, waiting simply for the right conditions to grow up in. If only we had a swamp, we thought, we would have alligators.

We introduced pond snails to the banks in herds, and gazelle-like beetles, for the pleasure of seeing the newts lunge to take them. In dealing with the snails, the newts would often clamp their jaws on the soft underbelly of the animal and shake it loose from the shell with surprising violence.

Alligators in the making, for sure.

I empathised with them deeply; the pathetic ones who would play dead, and the bullies alike. Lying on the edge of the pond waiting for a snout to surface and betray one, I would dream my own newthood, and my alligator potential tucked inside of my soft newt skin.

228

In that state, I would hang in the water, the murk cool against my eyes, holding my breath. How rude a shock it must be for that world to be disrupted by the plunging hand.

The gasping outrage you would surely feel, hauled into the air! Confused, the newt is a helpless thing. It hasn't the sense to fight back. Try that with an alligator, and see what happens to you. Pluck a baby from the water, and it will croak high and loud, and mammy will come. Not so the poor newt. All it can do is hope that it's in for the false comforts of a sandbox, and not the darkest part of a heron.

It was an important lesson in leaving things in their preferred element, but one that passed us by.

The friendship broke over a secret. On my part I imagined Lucy's keeping of it a deliberate move to exclude me and was hurt, but it wasn't that kind of secret. The web had stretched enough to let the adults in; that was all.

The day her father moved out for good, I was an intruder in the garden. No keeping me out, and it wasn't like the event was advertised on every loose board in the fence to warn me off. I arrived in time to see the car pulling off, Lucy on the driveway, arms waving left-right-left-right, pale to the gills. She came wheezing down onto the grass after, her mother grimacing back into the house. Neither of them could explain. It was simply the kind of disaster that lands you flat on your back, looking at the world from a different angle. I didn't have the same perspective.

My goggle-eyes were still in the water, watching a blur of light and shadow separate me from my friend in ways I could only guess at. And to her, what was I at that point? A vulnerable thing, still waiting for the hand that was coming; that would come down one day and either lift me up when I wasn't paying attention, or snatch me out of everything I knew.

But it was also a lesson: If you are a newt, then learn to hide deep in the weeds. The hand will come, but before it does, buy enough time to harden your skin. Grow your teeth. Know who to call for.

When it grabs you, maybe then you'll be ready.

Rick Vick

Surprise

My resolve to see in the new year alone and sober began to fray when I found a bottle of single malt at the back of a kitchen cupboard being kept, no doubt, for a special occasion. I didn't remember hiding it but reasoned that now was the occasion and had a shot. That was at about 11.00. How the hell had I managed the wait? I congratulated myself and had another.

Looking into the bathroom mirror, wondering if I needed a shave, I met the deep set eyes of a forty year-old man who'd given up on a five year marriage and was adrift without oars or a rudder. "Something's gotta change," I muttered.

By 11.30, after a third shot, I found myself coated and at the front door of the flat. My intention not yet shaped in my mind, I followed my feet down the stairs and out to Highgate village. On they wandered over the road to Parliament Hill fields, past the tennis courts up onto the heath. There was a sprinkling of snow on the grass. The air was tinglingly crisp, the sky clear. Uphill, towards the highest point, I walked feeling unusually purposeful. As I got close to the top I saw lone figures and couples, hand in hand, emerging from the trees, coming from all directions. There were children skipping ahead and a few excited dogs barking and scampering about. There was a carnival atmosphere that hushed as the hour approached and everyone grew still. I turned to the south looking out over the silhouette of the city, way below.

I could identify the outline of St Paul's, Big Ben, and I imagined the silvery, serpent coil of the Thames. A sliver of moon hung suspended, begging for a wish. I made one, stirring the coins in my pocket.

The moment arrived with a cataclysm of explosions and the chiming of church bells from all over the capital. We raised a ragged cheer and all joined hands, and, in a slowly shuffling circle, we sang the old Scottish song. My right hand was clasped by a tall woman wearing an orange beanie. A white bearded guy in a ragged overcoat hung onto my left hand stumbling and singing heartily. As the song ended we greeted one another and some embraced. I found myself in the arms of the woman in the beanie. Our clinch lasted longer and was tighter than expected. We kissed each other on our chilled cheeks. Our eyes met. A surprise, like a gull flying close. Hers were light brown flecked with amber. A bird of uncertainty fluttered in my belly. She was striking, beautiful even, I dared. My height, slender. I sensed a quizzical openness in her eyes. What does she see in me, I wondered. I recalled the mirrored image of earlier. Maybe she likes rough, I thought. Bells were still ringing and fireworks exploding, lighting up the sky. She tilted her head to one side.

"Shall we go for a drink?" she said in a deep, husky voice with a hint of a Scottish brogue. We walked back down the hill. She told me she was staying in a friend's flat not far from where I had my billet.

"I thought I'd try being alone," she said. "Well, I tried and here we are." Our hands tentatively met and clasped.

The pub was heaving and drunkenly enthusiastic. We both had large single malts she ordered and insisted on paying for. Standing behind her at the bar I was tempted to reach out to touch her arse, provocatively rounded beneath a tartan skirt falling over red leather boots. We managed to find a corner table where we sat facing each other. There was something vaguely familiar about her face. She had prominent cheekbones and her jaw was almost square. Not much make-up, but her lips were bright red and her eyebrows plucked to sharp black arches. The gaze of her eyes meeting and seeming to penetrate mine, was slightly disconcerting, yet I felt an ease with her. She told me she was an architect. I was entranced by the lilt and deep tone of her voice. A little shyly I told her I was a poet.

"I write verse too," she said. "It sometimes feels more potent than the houses I design, as if words build something more substantial and mysterious." She paused and drank. I noticed her fingers were long, the knuckles pronounced.

"What part do you feel surprise plays in life?" she leant forward to ask. I didn't have to think.

"It's all about surprise. Like us meeting like this. The unexpected is what makes it all sufferable." We clinked our glasses. My bird in the belly reappeared. She touched the back of my hand with the index finger of her left hand. Then she dipped the same finger in my glass, lifted it and flicked a spray of whisky at my face.

"Surprise!" she mouthed laughing at my jerk of alarm. I wiped my face, then, meeting her eyes, I took myself by surprise.

"Do you want to come back to my place?" I asked.

"Sure," she said.

She took off her woolly hat as soon as we were through the door, tossed it aside and shook free a torrent of auburn hair. We hugged, and in that embrace I felt an urgency surge between us, like riding a surf board on a tsunami. She pulled off her sweater in one swoop of her arms, and I, not so adroitly, my jersey. Her breasts, firm as melons tipped with tiny cherries, pressed against my chest. We kissed, a deep electric reconnoitring. Still kissing we shuffled into the bedroom where we tilted and toppled onto the bed. Freeing my hand, I reached down to the waistband of her skirt.

"Surprise is all," she whispered into my ear, as my hand slid over her belly through a thick bush of hair and encountered an erect penis. I grasped it firmly.

Nick Browne

The Stardust Girl

When we first met I was young and she was elegantly middle-aged. She was slender, cashmere clad - cool in a way I hadn't encountered before. I was beautiful, brainy and broke.

"Ah, the stardust girl," she said, handing me a champagne flute and clinking my glass with hers, "Enjoy!" The pear-shaped sapphire ring on her finger caught the light from the chandelier and with it my eye, hers were the grey of surgical-steel, sharp and penetrating.

"From Ceylon," she said, noticing my noticing. "They're the finest ones, but I think rubies might be more you - Burmese. You only want the best, don't you?"

She wasn't wrong: I wanted the best of everything, in education, love and life. Her smile was conspiratorial, though I didn't understand why. I didn't understand much then and my accomplishments were consistent with that ignorance. I could write an 'A' grade essay effortlessly, flirt as easily and walk competently in heels. It was enough, if only I'd known it.

I don't remember much else about that evening. I was the guest of some braying prick called Rufus I'd met at Oxford. Somehow we had ended up at a drinks party full of his parents' friends and a smattering of lovely, well-bred girls called Sophie or Emma. It was the first time I'd drunk champagne, or indeed mixed with people who drank champagne without first having won the football pools. The plush carpet was a subtle shade of not quite cream, the highly polished furniture was all antique and the air was scented with eau de mammon and tainted with smugness. It felt aspirational.

I didn't see Her again for a few years. It was at the wedding of a colleague from Goldman's. I'd swapped my plump-faced bloom and much of my gaucheness for cheek bones and expensive tastes. My accomplishments now included a working knowledge of corporate finance and fluency in the language of privilege. I'd taken up step aerobics, networking and Piers, the elder brother of an old friend, who treated me like a prize he couldn't believe he'd won.

She was beautifully dressed in a pink, vintage Chanel suit. "Well, if it isn't stardust girl!"

"Lovely to see you again!" I gushed because somehow it was. She had replaced the sapphire with a marquise-cut diamond, less than a carat but of amazing clarity. In all the vulgar excess of the wedding, she was still cool. She glanced at my ring finger and smiled when she saw the pigeon- blood ruby I was wearing.

"Good choice. I hope the man is too."

"He is," I said, a little defensively. "You look well." Once more we clinked glasses, though by then I knew my Krug from my Dom Perignon.

"I am well," she said. "You, however, need to get a move on, choose well, invest your gifts wisely - stardust migrates, you know. You think it's yours forever, but it is only ever on loan."

I was taken aback at the contrast between the patrician drawl of her delivery and the craziness of her remark. I'd taken her advice on the ruby, but her blather about investment made no sense. I was, after all, the expert on investments.

Piers and I broke up soon after over his ill-judged liaison with a call girl. I met and married Henry, a banker at Chase. We were in love and promised eternal fidelity, in sickness and in health, till death and the whole nine yards. Two kids and an extended career break later, I was accompanying Henry's mother to the funeral of a family friend when I saw Her again. Without the reminder of my ruby engagement ring, which I'd returned rather forcibly through the window of Piers' Porsche, I'd all but forgotten our earlier encounters.

She was much thinner and more lined, but as immaculately dressed as before. Her jewelry was more restrained: jet earrings and a black opal ring. We met at the buffet, as she helped herself to a plate of crustless sandwiches and a cream slice.

"Ah, the former stardust girl," her smile was sad. "And did you take my advice?"

"What do you mean?"

"You know what I mean," she said. "There's not much stardust left. Did you use it well?"

"I'm fine," I said and meant it.

I'd been relieved to swap power suits for Power Rangers. Henry and I agreed it was a privilege: we were a joint enterprise raising a family together. He made the money and I gave the time. Henry was doing well at work: my insights gave him an edge. Once the kids needed me a little less, I could go back to the career I'd always planned.

Her eyes, now a little hooded, were no less penetrating. "If you say so," she said, and we clinked tea cups. "It's not all gone yet, you know, but it's going." She sounded so matter of fact it was disconcerting. I piled a plate with easy to eat food for my mother-in-law, and wished Her well.

I didn't go back to work. Anthony, our eldest, had a few problems adjusting to school and Joe proved to be dyslexic. By the time they were settled, my skills were out of date. Besides, Henry had grown used to me running the home, supporting his career and looking after his mother who'd developed early onset Alzheimer's. It was a joint enterprise so that was fair enough. I volunteered and organised. I lost my cheekbones and my networks, as well as my career, but I built a good life for us all. Then, when the kids left for uni and my mother-in-law died, Henry, now a senior partner, decided that he was no longer happy. He'd fallen in love with his soul mate. No one was surprised that this precious soul was incarnated in the voluptuous physical form of a woman a little younger than our eldest son. We were no longer a joint enterprise. There was no whole nine yards.

I didn't go to their wedding, but when Anthony married Eliza, of course Henry and his new love were there. I didn't put ground-glass in his food, but only because of the children, whose loyalty he still retained: he'd promised to give them the deposit on a flat they could never otherwise afford.

It was a lovely wedding and we served only the best champagne. I was mingling with our guests, friends of my boys I'd known most of their lives, when I saw Her again. Perhaps she was a friend of Eliza's family. She had shrunk, as old women sometimes do, so that she seemed too small for her powder-blue, woollen suit. The fingers that held the stem of her champagne glass were knotted with arthritis, too deformed for diamonds and as bare as my own. She saw me and her grey eyes narrowed in their pink pouch of skin, like a steel clasp on an old leather purse.

"Stardust drifts," she said softly, as if our earlier conversation carried on uninterrupted. "It migrates from the young woman to the older man."

I helped myself to another glass of champagne from the nearby table and peered into the throng of guests. I let my varifocals, on their convenient gilt chain, fall onto the cantilevered shelf of my matriarchal breasts.

She wasn't wrong. As I looked, I could see something, a kind of a silver haze, a soft, shimmering aura around my ex-husband and a drift of it half-buried his young wife, a glimmering halo of argent surrounded the blonde hair of my beautiful daughter-in-law, Eliza, and her bevy of clean-limbed bridesmaids.

She touched my arm lightly, "I tried to warn you. You had so much of it - more than I've ever seen. It all but buried you. You just didn't know it."

I nodded. "I know now. Thank you for trying," I said. "You couldn't have done any more. Maybe we can only see it when we've lost it." I was crying as I spoke, silent tears that rolled down my cheeks and would play havoc with my foundation. I turned towards her but she was gone. I scanned the crowd, but could see no sign of an old woman in a powder-blue suit. She had disappeared so completely I began to wonder if I had imagined her: the ghost of my own future.

One of the bridesmaids teetered unsteadily my way. She scintillated with stardust. It covered her hair like a silver veil, draped her shoulders in a soft shawl of starlight. She was dazzling and she had no idea. She had the world at her feet and didn't know it.

Stardust migrates and so does the power to see it.

I handed her a glass of champagne. Her smile was bemused, but she clinked my glass enthusiastically, "Hi, stardust girl," I said. "Can we talk?"

Judith Gunn

#peace

It's been fifteen years, well, fifteen years and eleven days, six hours 32 minutes and 7...8...9 seconds to be exact; it took fifteen years and eleven days for world peace to happen. Mind you, when I say world peace, it's not what you think. It's not eternal. It's not the blissful harmony of the entire world in peaceful coexistence forever. I doubt this will last. It's just one day, one day, when no shots were fired. But you know what? I think it was worth it, I really do! Just for one day, we did it for just one day!

So how did all this start? Why no shots? Well, it was not just one thing, one event; don't think that this is about North Korea letting off a nuclear bomb, or that idiot president invading Mexico, or dictators, or revolutions, or Las Vegas, or that school shooting in America, or that other school shooting, or the one in Florida, or the other one...or...you get the picture. No, it wasn't like that, that's not how it happened. It was more the drip drip of water torture that did it, not a massive tsunami (so as not to mix my metaphors) event. It was event after event after event and then there was one last straw (now I have mixed my metaphors) and it began.

Well, like all good protest movements it started with immolation. First it was the mother of one of those many US shootings. I honestly can't remember which one, but she was clever this woman and desperate. She poured petrol in a shape on the ground. She went live on Facebook, Periscope, Twitter sent up a drone to stream it live, gathered a crowd and a pretty large audience online, most begging her not to, some being evil. She lit the match, went up like a torch and from above the cameras revealed the words written in flame 'No more'.

That was it, that started a spate, a virus, a pandemic, if you like, of women and men from across the world who flung themselves into the flames. They did it in battle-torn areas, rural areas where quiet murder persisted. They did it in slums, they did it in high rise towers and then it happened, one tweet and a hashtag; @someoneorother tweeted 'Women don't have babies to be murdered by men - how about #nomore #nomorebabies.'

And #nomorebabies went viral.

This wasn't about no more sex, oh no, sex was still definitely on the cards. It was just about no more babies, not some kind of fertility fail because of pollution, not even a punishment, just a rest, a rest from creating a population that murders itself. Why should women do that? They asked. Why should a woman, give over her body (and boy does a woman give over her body) to have a child, recover from having a child (or not), nurse that child, lose sleep, lose sex, lose sanity, lose her job, lose her career, all in order to raise a child for somebody else to shoot?

Of course, nobody thought it would take off, but you know social media, it got everywhere and suddenly Facebook, Twitter, Tumblr, Instagram, Reddit even Google+, you name it, all were sporting women denouncing pregnancy and saying #nomorebabies. Initially no one quite knew why, until one female prime minister of a West African country stepped forward and said, "No more babies, until not one shot is fired across the world."

And the violence got worse - of course. They, whoever 'they' are, thought intimidation would work. They were wrong.

After only one year it was clear that the birth-rate was falling. The pledge was working. It was patchy at first, China's birth-rate plummeted, Italy, Germany, Australia were quick to follow with a 75% drop in two years. UK was 62% and the US 40%. Needless to say another mass shooting, this time in a children's soccer championship, kicked their birth-rate into the hills, once the soccer mums made the pledge, the birth-rate in the US was doomed.

To some women it was a relief, a relief not have children, children who would be sent to war to die, or worse than that, children sent to war to kill. Mothers who raised soldiers, brought up not only victims but killers. They raised children not only to be killed themselves but to kill another child, and so some other mother suffered what no mother should. It was a relief then to some not to have to fear that - either way.

Then #nomore went political and won! Political leaders who became #nomore won elections, but still gangs, extremists, random idiots, border disputes and power struggles claimed victim after victim, although it was slowing down. In fact, it slowed down a lot, enough to give us hope. Hell, in America in one year the gun violence death toll dropped from 9,000 (and that was lower…for them) to 998, under a thousand, just. There was hope, real hope, but there was backlash too.

A militant wing of #nomore developed, which definitely defeated the purpose of the exercise, but they didn't see that. They argued that if they could stop all pregnancy by fair means or foul, then the impulse to world peace (for a day, remember) would be stronger, it would happen quicker, it would be worth it. The mainstream wing of #nomore disagreed and, after the murder of two pregnant women in the UK, the militant wing was disowned, the culprits handed over, and it was made quite clear that world peace meant world peace, and women and their supportive, their very, very supportive men, had to accept that.

But there were benefits (other than much quieter journeys on trains and planes). At first there was panic on the stock market. If there were no young people, who would pay the tax that would pay our pensions when we got old? Financial institutions started spouting doom and gloom. There would be catastrophe; we would all die in squalor, living in a Mad Max dystopia!

But then a strange thing happened. The economy improved. Well, I say the economy, it was productivity. It is a wonder what women can do when they have got the time! All of sudden there were millions of women in their twenties and thirties who didn't have to find childcare, who didn't have to dash back from work to relieve the nanny, who didn't have to spend all their money on that nanny. They could push for that promotion, because they were there doing the job. They were available and able. They could lean in and take the prize and then improve it. Women made huge scientific advances, now they could devote themselves to their academic work and make sure the supervisor didn't pinch it. There's an all-woman team preparing to go to set up a base on the moon. There has been significant progress in environmental care, you know how good we women are at cleaning! The upshot of all that is that our pensions are safe, our productivity, our stewardship, our environmental policies and the readjustment of wealth particularly with reference to guns, is better. We can afford the NHS, education and the emergency services and we lowered the pension age for everyone! Think on that!

Peace does mean prosperity and now we have done it, now we are there! Almost. I'm not counting any chickens yet. Nobody is, not after the last two times. Oh yes, three years ago we nearly did it. There was countdown in Time Square, fireworks were made ready across the world. We got as far as number four in the countdown, and some asshole in Texas let rip on the party goers in downtown Houston, go figure. The second time, nobody was counting, it was more mooted and at ten minutes to midnight, breaking news told us that a family dispute in somewhere, could have been anywhere, except it wasn't, it was America again, a family dispute had ended in a shooting. For a minute we all hoped for life changing injuries, but it wasn't, it was death, so here we are again. Third time lucky and...Yes! There it goes! Midnight! All we asked for was just one day, just one day with no shots fired, no killing. We didn't think it would last forever, we know it's not over yet, but we were making a point and I think it was a good one.

Anyway now it's done, I've no regrets. I never got to have children. I missed the boat, but there have been compensations, because now I'm off to oversee the final decommissioning of Trident, a big old party up in the north to finish nuclear weapons in the UK. Oh, did I not mention? I became Prime Minister. Well, I had all that time on my hands, what else was I going to do?

Author Biographies

Tais Brias Avila
Tais is originally from Barcelona. She moved to the UK after finishing her studies in political sciences in Spain, and now lives with her family in Stonehouse and teaches Spanish locally. Tais has always been an avid reader in her native languages and in English. She prefers to write in English. This is her first published work of fiction.

Ali Bacon
Ali, a native Scot living in South Gloucestershire, writes contemporary and historical fiction. Her first novel, *A Kettle of Fish*, was published in 2012, and she has been listed for a number of short story awards, winning the Evesham Festival of Words competition in 2017. She has appeared twice at Stroud Short Stories and in the 2016 Greatest Hits event at the Cheltenham Literature Festival. *Silver Harvest* now forms part of her historical novel, *In the Blink of an Eye* (Linen Press 2018).
Website: www.alibacon.wordpress.com
Twitter: @AliBacon

Sian Breeze
Sian Breeze is a poet and writer who grew up in California but now lives in Chalford. Sian attended the first ever Stroud Short Stories event in 2011 to watch her then boyfriend Alex read his story *Flickers*. It must have been good because they are now married with two kids. Sian has always wanted to spend her life writing and has been short listed or placed in several competitions.
Website: www.mrsbreezeblog.wordpress.com

Nick Browne
Dr Nick Browne (N M Browne) has published nine novels for teenagers with Bloomsbury in the UK, the US and in translation. She has been nominated for several prizes including the Carnegie medal, but is yet to win anything more than a bottle of wine at a raffle. She teaches creative writing at MMU, the Arvon Foundation, the British Council and for Oxford Continuing Education. Inspired by Stroud Short Stories, she is keen to write more short stories.
Website: www.nmbrowne.com

Graham Bruce-Fletcher
Graham has been writing, editing and telling stories all his life, and occasionally gets paid.

Joanna Campbell
Joanna, a full-time writer from Bisley, won the 2015 London Short Story Prize. In 2017, her flash-fiction came second in The Bridport Prize, and the Bath Flash Fiction Award published her novella-in-flash, *A Safer Way to Fall*. Her short story collection, *When Planets Slip Their Tracks,* published by InkTears, was shortlisted for the 2016 Rubery Book Award and long-listed for the 2017 Edge Hill Short Story Prize. In 2015, Brick Lane published her novel, *Tying Down the Lion.*
Website: www.Joanna-Campbell.com
Twitter: @PygmyProse

Sarah Chapman
Sarah has lived in the Stroud area for more than 20 years, and spent 4 years in Japan where she studied brush painting and began writing in earnest. As of March 2018, she has begun work on a series of illustrated projects for younger readers. Her short story works are available on her website.
Website: www.sechapman.wixsite.com/creativeportfolio

Alex Clark

Alex's short stories have appeared in *Prole*, *Litro Online*, *Shooter Literary Magazine*, *MIR Online* and several anthologies by The Fiction Desk. She lives with her husband and daughters in Cheltenham, where she runs the quarterly live flash fiction night Flashers' Club (www.flashersclub.wordpress.com). She is periodically mistaken for the other, more famous, Alex Clark.

Website: www.theotheralexclark.wordpress.com

Twitter: @otheralexclark

Ken Clements

Born in 1943 in a village near Gloucester, Ken joined the army as an Apprentice Tradesman. His subsequent nine years worldwide service fuelled his wanderlust and interest in exotic locations. Ken's first attempt at writing was a record of his cycle ride along the banks of the River Mekong from Northern Thailand to the Cambodian border. This stretch of the Mekong has beguiled him ever since and provides the backdrop for many of his stories for the Newent U3A Writing Group.

Rommy Collingwood

Rommy is a published author who enjoys diversity in writing and exploring different genres. She can trace her interest in writing to an early age, which eventually led to a degree in English literature from the Open University and a Masters in creative writing from Bath Spa University. Her written works include a play for radio, a screenplay, poetry, lyrics, songs and short stories. Her most recent challenge is essaying the completion of her first novel - working title *Dogs Don't Speak English*.

Twitter: @MyalWoman

Stephen Connolly

Cirencester's Stephen Connolly has published a number of short stories, and his plays have been performed in Bath, Brighton, Bristol, Gloucester, London, Salisbury and Stroud. He graduated with an MA in scriptwriting from Bath Spa University in 2015. His radio play *Sky Pilots* was joint winner of the BBC Solent Radio Playwrights competition and broadcast on BBC Solent in May 2018. Off The Rock Productions will record his radio play *The Destiny of Shoes* in 2018.
Twitter: @SteveConnolly3

Philip Douch

Philip is a writer and performer from Stroud. He has appeared regularly at Story Fridays in Bath and at the Stroud Theatre Festival, as well as reading his work twice at the Cheltenham Literature Festival. He has won the Gloucestershire Writers Network short story competition, and his plays have been performed professionally in the studio theatres at the Cheltenham Everyman and the Nuffield in Southampton, as well as on the London fringe.

Mary Flood

Mary is a semi-retired English teacher and examiner, currently preparing foreign students for University entry in St. Edwards, Cheltenham. Her favourite novelists include Margaret Mitchell, Daphne du Maurier, Marian Keyes and Colm Toibin. Mary's novels and short stories are set in the Ireland of the fifties, sixties and later. She is a member of Cheltenham Fiction Writers and ALLi, the Alliance of Independent Authors. A short story, *The Eviction,* won first prize in Festival of Literature in York some years ago. *Baby Love* is her first story at Stroud Short Stories.

Melanie Golding

Melanie writes short stories and novels. She has had some success with selective short story events, having been chosen to read at venues in Bristol as well as Stroud. At the Mid-Somerset Festival in 2017 she won the short story prize and the Evelyn Sanford trophy. In 2016 she graduated with an MA (distinction) in creative writing at Bath Spa University. At the time of writing she is editing her first novel *Little Darlings* for publication with HQ in May 2019.
Twitter: @mk_golding

Daniel Gooding

Daniel was born in 1984 and has been published in *Dog-Ear*, *Drabblez Magazine* and *101 Fiction*. He also features in two anthologies from the New York-based publisher New Lit Salon Press, *Startling Sci-Fi: New Tales of the Beyond* and the upcoming *Fear Comes First: New Tales of Horror*. He lives in Bath with his wife and two children, and is currently working on a novel while also studying for a Master's Degree in librarianship.

Jane Gordon-Cumming

Jane moved to Minchinhampton in 2013, after thirty-odd years as an 'Oxford' writer. She has had many short stories published, as well as her own collection set on the Oxford Canal. Both her novels, *A Proper Family Christmas* (Accent Press) and her recent *An Easter Conspiracy*, are set in her beloved Cotswolds. She is also writing the biography of her grandmother, Florence Garner, the American heiress who married the notorious Sir William Gordon-Cumming.
Website: www.janegordoncumming.wordpress.com
Twitter: @OxfordWriter

Mark Graham
Mark is a writer and storyteller who believes in the power of myth. The personal and collective mythologies that we weave, individually and as a society, fill our lives with meaning. Without myth the colour fades from our experience. It's our myths and stories that make us feel alive to possibility and to adventure. We live in a world of enchantment and wonder if we choose to open our eyes to it.

Judith Gunn
Judith is the writer of an eclectic mix of short stories, traditionally published books and self-published novels. Her publications include biographies, co-writes, education textbooks and a novelisation. Judith is based in Stroud, has travelled widely, dabbled in radio drama and taught teenagers. Her work ranges from travelogue to media moments, from dystopia to *Dostoyevsky: A Life of Contradiction* (published by Amberley).
Website: www.judithgunn.com
Twitter: @JudithGunn

Kirsty Hartsiotis
Kirsty is a Stroud-based storyteller and writer. She has performed widely in Britain and beyond, and, with story-telling company Fire Springs, has co-produced ecobardic epics such as *Arthur's Dream*, *Robin of the Wildwood* and *Return to Arcadia*. She is the author of *Wiltshire Folk Tales*, *Suffolk Folk Tales*, *Gloucestershire Ghost Tales* (co-author) and *Suffolk Ghost Tales* (co-author). Wearing her other hat, for the past twenty years she's worked around the region as a museum curator.
Website: www.kirstyhartsiotis.co.uk
Twitter: @StroudStory

Sarah Hitchcock

Sarah lives alone in Stroud, unless you count a pet shrimp that appears to be immortal. She has a fine art degree, writes and illustrates children's books that no-one gets to read, sometimes enters short story competitions, and sometimes gets her work published in anthologies. Her paid work is in the education department at WWT Slimbridge where she attempts to inspire the next generation to fall in love with nature, and hopefully do something about saving it.

Michael Hurst

Michael lives in Prestbury, Cheltenham. His writing has been performed by Show of Strength Theatre Company and in the Gloucestershire Writers Network prose competition at the 2016 Cheltenham Literature Festival. His stories have appeared in the second print publication of *Ellipsis Zine* and in the online journal *The Cabinet of Heed*.
Twitter: @CotswoldArts

Jason Jackson

Jason's prize-winning writing has been published extensively online and in print. In 2018 Jason has won the Writers Bureau Short Story Competition, came second (for the second year running) in the Exeter Short Story Competition, and had work short-listed at the Leicester Writes Competition. His work has also appeared at *New Flash Fiction Review*, *Craft* and *Fictive Dream*. In 2017 he was nominated for the Pushcart Prize.
Website: www.jjfiction.wordpress.com
Twitter: @jj_fiction

David Jay

David has been writing short stories for the past four years. He has an English degree from Oxford University and has worked with words and language in many ways - as a book reviewer, an English language teacher, a programmer and in marketing. He published pamphlets of his poetry in his youth and was once chairman of Writers in Oxford. He moved to Stroud two years ago. Why? It's friendlier, more creative and more relaxed, he says.

Pam Keevil

Former head teacher Pam assumed she would write for children. In 2012 at Swanwick Writer's Summer School, she began to experiment with different genres including short stories, erotica and romance. She completed an MA in creative and critical writing at the University of Gloucestershire in 2016. Her first full length novel *Virgin at Fifty* was published by Black Pear Press in 2018. She lives in Ruscombe and is a member of two writing groups.
Website: www.pamkeevil.com

Emma Kernahan

Emma lives in Stroud. She writes poetry, flash fiction and short stories, and has read at Stroud Short Stories and at Bristol's Talking Tales. Her work can be found in literary journals *Occulum* and *Ellipsis Zine*. Emma co-curates a library of images called *Where Women Write* (www.facebook.com/wherewomenwrite1/), which showcases women's writing and is always open for submissions.
Website: www.crappyliving.wordpress.com
Twitter: @crappyliving

Lania Knight

Lania's first book, *Three Cubic Feet*, was a finalist for the Lambda Literary Award in Debut Fiction. Her stories and essays have been published in *Short Fiction, Shooter Literary Magazine, Fourth Genre, Post Road, The Rumpus, PANK* and elsewhere. *Remnant*, a science fiction novel, was published in 2018 by Burlesque Press. She lives in England and lectures in creative writing at the University of Gloucestershire.
Website: www.laniaknight.com
Twitter: @laniaknight

Natalie Lee

Natalie is a writer who lives in Stroud. She writes stories, of varying lengths, about the darkness and redemption in life - the moments where the life we live crosses the liminal, the threshold, into the interstitial spaces between what is known and what is unfamiliar, other.

Geoff Mead

Geoff lives in a house in Kingscote appropriately named Folly Cottage. The first thing he can remember wanting to do was, at the age of eight, to write stories. It took him another fifty years to find his voice as a writer. In the past few years he has authored six published books of fiction, non-fiction, poetry and memoir.
Website: www.cominghometostory.com
Twitter: @NarrativeLeader

Claire Morris

Claire started her writing career as a journalist on *The Scotsman* newspaper. From this rigorous apprenticeship she evolved a spare stripped-down style. "Make every word count. No flannel," her editor told her. She has carried this no-frills discipline into her fiction, requiring her readers to fill out stark narratives with their own experience and imagination. This doesn't suit everyone, but engenders lively debate among Claire's fans.

Elizabeth Murphy

Elizabeth lives and works in North Nibley, and is a member of the Wotton Writers Group.

Twitter: @Stancomberules

James Northern

James is based in Cheltenham. He enjoyed writing as a child and was inspired to take it up again as an adult after attending the Stroud Short Stories Greatest Hits/Fifth Birthday event at the Cheltenham Literature Festival in 2016. *In the Firing Line* is his first published work.

Kate O'Grady

Kate lives in Stroud, having recently moved back to England after living in San Francisco for thirty years. She has written since she was small, but has only recently committed to it in a serious way. Short stories are her first literary love, and it's the form she returns to again and again both to write and to read. She is thrilled to have two of her stories printed in this anthology of Stroud Short Stories.

Val Ormrod

Val has an MA in Creative Writing from Bath Spa University. Her memoir, *In My Father's Memory*, completed on the course, was shortlisted for the Janklow & Nesbit Prize. A member of the Forest of Dean Writers, Dean Writers Circle and NaCOT Poets, she also leads a U3A creative writing group. She has won awards in a variety of competitions, and reads her work at venues including Cheltenham Literature Festival, Mitcheldean Festival and Novel Nights in Bristol.

Twitter: @Ladybear6

Nastasya Parker

Nastasya wrote her first story at the age of four, and somewhat later, won the 2017 Gloucestershire Writers' Network Prose Prize. As well as Stroud Short Stories, her work has appeared in two Bristol Short Story Prize anthologies. She gained her degree in writing and literature in the USA, before landing in Dursley, Gloucestershire, where hiking helps her focus.

Website: www.nastasyaparker.com
Twitter: @Nastasyaparker

Jan Petrie

Jan is a local artist and former English teacher who lives in Sheepscombe near Stroud. She graduated with an MA in creative writing from the University of Gloucestershire in 2011. Her debut novel, *Until the Ice Cracks,* is due to be published in 2018. Jan's short stories have been short-listed and long-listed in various national and local competitions. In 2016 she won the Evesham Festival of Words Short Story Prize.

Simon Piney

Simon has been writing stories, articles and poetry for nearly seventy years. He was twelve when his first letter appeared in a newspaper. His poetry has been published in various now-defunct magazines. Simon has read a few of his short stories at Stroud Short Stories and is a member of a local fiction-writing group. As well as fiction, he continues to write on spirituality, psychotherapy and politics. He also gives eulogies at funerals.

Ken Popple

Ken was born in Boston, Lincolnshire, now lives in Stroud, and is an English teacher at Chosen Hill School, Gloucestershire. He spends time writing and recording songs, some of which are on YouTube, and was previously a musician on Creation Records.

Mark Rutterford

Mark is well known for performing his stories across the South West - using props, humour and heartache to grab your emotions. Published a bit, he is currently putting together two collections of stories. Mark works in South Gloucestershire and is a proud member of Stokes Croft Writers in Bristol, sometimes judging and hosting their public event Talking Tales.

Website: www.markrutterford.com

Twitter: @writingsett

Martin Spice

Martin was the principal of an international school in Malaysian Borneo before returning to England to replace working with writing. His work has appeared in the *Times Educational Supplement*, *The Weekly Telegraph*, *The Guardian*, *The South China Morning Post*, *Kitchen Garden* and numerous other publications. He is the author of *Spade, Seed & Supper: An Allotment Year* and *Lynx: Back to the Wild*, about a lynx cub rescued in Tibet and raised in Kathmandu.

Website: www.martinspice.com

Twitter: @spice_martin

Andrew Stevenson

Andrew lives in Nailsworth and has written stories on subjects as diverse as invisibility achieved by the power of concentration, the creation of a new animal that is a hedgehog on the outside and a badger on the inside and the making of unicorn soup. He has read many of these, and others, featuring his recurring characters Barry Parry and Herbert Pennywhistle, on radio and at public events including the Cheltenham Literature Festival. He is currently writing a novel.

Tony Stowell

Tony was born in Surrey and, after being commissioned in the RAF, graduated from Cambridge with an MA in history, to which he later added an MSc from Oxford in educational administration. He has lived in Tetbury for the last 30 years. Tony is Chairman of the Cotswold Writers Circle, and has written three full length novels, two light thrillers and a more serious book about education. His poetry has been read on *Poetry Please* on Radio 4.
Website: www.tonystowell.co.uk

Chloe Turner

Chloe's stories have been published in print and online journals and in two single-story chapbooks. As well as being short-listed many times in competitions, in 2017 she won both the Local Prize in the Bath Short Story Award and the Fresher Prize. Chloe's story *Waiting for the Runners* has been published in the prestigious anthology *Best British Short Stories 2018*. She lives in Minchinhampton, just outside Stroud.
Website: www.turnerpen2paper.com
Twitter: @turnerpen2paper

Rick Vick

Rick has been writing most of his life. He has published two pamphlets with Yew Tree Press: Indian Eye, and another with Adam Horovitz and Maria Stadnicki. He has also published a couple of books of verse - *Ask the Ferryman He Passes all the Time* and *A Coat of no Particular Colour*. A third collection is on the way. Rick facilitates creative writing groups in Stroud where he lives.
Twitter: @rickvick96

Steve Wheeler

Steve lives in Sheepscombe near Stroud and writes flash fiction, short stories and poetry. He has had work published in chapbooks and literary websites including Riggwelter Press, Reflex Fiction, Fictive Dream, Former Cactus and Slad Brook Poetry. In December 2017 Steve won the inaugural Farnham Short Story Competition, and has won the Bath Ad Hoc flash fiction competition a record-breaking six times. Steve has read his work at the Cheltenham Poetry Festival, Stroud Short Stories (twice) and The Flashers' Club.
Twitter: @StevenJohnWrite

Julie Wiltshire

Julie is from Cam and is a member of the Stroud Writers Circle. She has written poetry all her life, and in the past few years has started writing short stories and flash fiction. Julie has taken a two year creative writing course with the Open University and is working towards a BA (Hons) arts and humanities degree. Last year Julie read her poetry at the Cheltenham Literature Festival, the Evesham Festival of the Words and on Corinium Radio in Cirencester. Julie has also published an autobiography entitled *A Carer's Chaos*.

Lightning Source UK Ltd.
Milton Keynes UK
UKHW04f0627191018
330822UK00001B/92/P

9 781916 411807